RIGHTFULLY WRONG, WRONGFULLY RIGHT

Varsha Dixit is the author of the bestselling novels, *Right Fit Wrong Shoe* (2009), *Xcess Baggage* (2010), *Wrong Means Right End* (2012), and *Only Wheat Not White* (2014). She worked in the Indian television industry before moving to the US with her family.

Varsha actively interacts with readers through her website www.varshadixit.com and Facebook author page. Her Twitter handle is @Varsha20.

I0561722

RIGHTFULLY WRONG,
WRONGFULLY RIGHT

Varsha Dixit

RUPA

Published by
Rupa Publications India Pvt. Ltd 2016
7/16, Ansari Road, Daryaganj
New Delhi 110002

Sales Centres:
Allahabad Bengaluru Chennai
Hyderabad Jaipur Kathmandu
Kolkata Mumbai

ISBN: 978-81-291-4197-2

First impression 2016

10 9 8 7 6 5 4 3 2 1

The moral right of the author has been asserted.

Dedicated to friends,
and
readers of romance...

Contents

Note from the Author

When I started writing Right Fit Wrong Shoe in 2006 it was more of a cathartic process. Grieving over the demise of my father who I was extremely close to, I needed something to bring equilibrium. Something that was far removed from the emotional turmoil I was undergoing. Thus, I started writing random thoughts and disjointed story ideas. The idea that appealed most to me was a story of best friends.

Friendship has always played a very important role in my life and continues to do so. Friends are the family we choose and I have to say I chose well. Just like my two pivotal characters—Sneha and Nandini.

Aditya Sarin was not supposed to feature so largely in the book. However, with Nandini and Aditya's first meeting, on paper, I realized that these two need a book of their own and so did Sneha. Thus, a series was born.

When I envisaged Gayatri I thought of her as a quintessential vamp but with a back story. Even my bad had to have some good, some logic. Thus came Gayatri's strong bond with Nikhil and why it existed in the first place.

Hence, 'Right and Wrong' series became about three

women in three different phases of their lives. The series is an ode to friendship, to love and to our struggles. Struggles make us who we are, and our loved ones and good friends make our struggle bearable.

So cherish your loved ones, keep your friends close and never forget that whenever you need them Nandini and Aditya, Sneha and Nikhil, Gayatri and Viraj are only a shelf away. And me, I'm just an email away from you (varsha@varshadixit.com)

I promise to keep writing as long as you promise to keep reading. Go with love wherever life takes you. Thank you for being a part of my journey and good luck to each of you. To many more adventures! Happy Reading!

The Crazy Mad Scientist

'Hmm! A move to Luxemborg in my fifties should work. Assisted suicide is legal there!' The tragic thought was voiced in the most casual manner by the thirty-year-old man with a scholarly face, squared jawline, long and narrow nose and arched eyebrows. His black hair fell below the collar of his T-shirt in a rakish style, making his dark eyes behind the narrow rectangular glasses appear even darker and mysterious. His face was a combination of high cheekbones and sharp eyes. No one would dare call him a 'chocolate boy' with a face like that.

He sipped hot tea from a cup in his hand. It was strong with a sweet aftertaste. Someone on the street below lit a match. A flash of light and then darkness! Balance restored.

'A life that plans for death is more intelligent than a life that denies the inevitable end!' the man said to his audience. He was Dr Viraj Dheer, a scientist and inventor, laureate of several national and international awards. And his audience was a trio of shifty sparrows on the balcony rail framed by the sun rising on the Mumbai horizon behind them. Viraj leaned over the rail and threw some of the lightly toasted bread on the ground. 'Here you go patsies!'

His audience responded with quick hops and soft chirps. Sitting back Viraj studied the ocean from the balcony of his 1 BHK, sea-facing apartment at Juhu.

Even at five thirty in the morning, traffic noises were loud and the smog hung heavy over the sea, making the city look like a large tent made of over-washed sheets. Human chatter surrounded Viraj—the milkman's sharp call to the watchman of his building, the clinking sound of tin as a woman carrying a bunch of tiffins hurried past on the street, strains of radio music and bhajans that escaped through open windows and doors of nearby houses, the low and laborious sound of a ship horn coming from a cruise boat anchored at some distance in the sea.

The sparrows chirped and hopped around him. 'You should be out looking for worms! Don't get used to this multigrain bread. I won't be around for long.' He tossed some more bread. 'Netherlands could work too. The flying time to get to any of those places is probably the same.' Viraj shook his sneaker-clad foot. The fatter of the sparrows pecked at the crumbs that had fallen around his feet.

Viraj wasn't depressed, nor was he terminally ill. He was a brilliant but practical man who had made a deathly decision a long time ago. *When I feel there is no more to achieve, no more to know, no more to give, I would rather switch the lights off. It might be interesting to find out if there is something beyond death.*

Viraj shifted to a more comfortable position in the cane chair; his eyes behind the narrow glasses were gleaming and alert. *The Crazy Mad Scientist!*—a moniker that was actually a curse used by his late abusive father when describing Viraj, his younger son. People built hills out of moles; Viraj had built a life around a moniker. Finishing his tea, he got to his feet. The sparrows flew away, except for the fat one. The fat one raised its beady eyes at Viraj and then looked down at the crumbs. Giving Viraj a final you'd-better-not look, the sparrow resumed eating.

'Your love for food will get you killed!'

The morning breeze chilled Viraj's body. He felt alive. Viraj yanked off his loose T-shirt. His torso was buffed and he had washboard abs. With muscular arms and a taut stomach, Viraj's body looked more like a marine's than a scientist's. Weak and frail bodies came with their own tagline, 'You shall be kicked, trampled and beaten.'

Tossing his T-shirt on the floor, Viraj got down to do his push-ups. Twenty minutes later he rested breathless, with sweat dripping down his chest. He saw a few faces in the windows of apartments across from his balcony. A middle-aged woman smiled at him flirtatiously even as she watered her plants in a pink nightgown with a white chunni around her neck like a hangman's noose. Viraj swung his gaze few feet away from the flirty aunty, to the balcony where a girl in her early twenties did her stretches. She was none other than the flirty aunty's flirty daughter! Her tight black capris and hot pink tank top clung tightly around her curves. Stretching her arms up, she bent forward and touched the tips of her shoes revealing much of her cleavage. While in that position she looked up and gave Viraj an eerily familiar and flirty smile. The apple did not fall far from the tree!

Viraj got to his feet, grabbed his T-shirt and went inside his apartment. Being watched was his most hated thing, second only to talking! The only talk that interested Viraj was discussions on colonization of mars or quantum phase transitions. Unfortunately there weren't many people talking about it.

In his teenage years, Viraj had a few 'normal' adolescent traits—gawking at girls, especially the older ones, listening to nineties pop songs, flying kites and playing 'kanche', oiling the hair and combing it in different styles. The quintesstial 'normal'—sometimes he'd look up at the sky and holler, 'One day I will own you!' Unfortunately the 'abnormal' in his life always overshadowed the 'normal' for his father was a violent, and unemployed alcoholic. Poverty was their reality. His father was the type of man who felt that he deserved the best but never lifted a finger to achieve it. The only time he lifted his hand was to strike his wife and his younger son.

Viraj's elder brother who sucked at studies but excelled in mohalla cricket could do no wrong in their father's eyes. His father's favourite dialogue was, '*Bada sala* Sachin Tendulkar *banega aur yeh chota ration card katega!*' Ironically, now Bhai (as Viraj calls him) sells life insurance while Viraj made a million by the time he was twenty-one by selling his design of a toy that dispenses medicines to kids.

Viraj's father didn't live to see his success though. He had died of massive brain hemorrhage, quite contrary to the end that was expected—liver damage or getting hit by a truck as he roamed around drunk on the streets. Viraj had learnt of his father's death and cause of it much after it had happened. He had been surprised. He never thought his father had any brains.

'Omelette is ready and your dinner is in the fridge,' called out Viraj's mom from the kitchen. Kripa Dheer in her early fifties was small in frame. A thick bun of white hair hung over her nape and she always wore the plainest of cotton saris. Placing a glass of freshly squeezed orange juice, she beckoned him. Her smile showed more of her lower gum than normal. One day, in a drunken stupor, Viraj's father had hit her repeatedly in the face with a rolling pin and broken her jaw. Since they were poor back then, their visit to the local quack didn't help much. After all, he was no cosmetologist. So even though he mended her jaw, her lower lip continued to hang loose on one side.

Viraj had offered to have a cosmetologist, a rich man's cosmetologist, fix it now. But his mother preferred her loose lip as it was—a reminder of what she had been through.

'Maa, you don't have to come here to fix me breakfast every morning,' said Viraj as he chugged the juice.

'I live close enough to do this.' She held out the plate to him. 'Stop overfeeding the poor sparrows. Their feet and wings won't be able to support abnormally big bodies.'

'How is Keshav sir?'

'The usual, can't control his sweet tooth. Binged on gulab jamuns at dinner, had an uneasy night. He will probably wake up around ten,' she grumbled while wiping the counter clean.

'Who made the gulab jamuns?' Viraj asked, cutting into his omelette.

'I did—'

'Stop overfeeding your sparrow!'

'Sit on the table and eat,' his mother ordered. 'How is your work coming along?' She followed him to the table.

'It's boring!' Viraj grunted, brushing his hair back.

'You need a haircut.' Kripa patted her son's head and grabbed her purse from a nearby cane chair.

'I could walk away from my work.'

'They'll sue you!'

'What do I have to lose?' Viraj shrugged chewing.

'All the money they have given you!' she reminded him, walking to the front door.

'Like I said, what do I have to lose?' Viraj gazed at her with his usual solemn expression.

His mother sighed. 'One day you will find your drive back. Something or someone will help you finish what you started!' She opened the front door, giving him a final warning, 'Don't binge on gulab jamuns.'

'Hope your boyfriend feels better!' Viraj called out.

'You just love teasing me, don't you?' Her smile reflected the contentment within.

Viraj put his plate in the sink. 'What? Not every woman is cool enough to find a boyfriend at fifty-five.'

'See you tomorrow!' his mother said, closing the door behind her as she left. Viraj headed for a shower. He had to get to his lab. *She's right. It's my drive that's lacking.* His genius mind had begun to bore him. As the cold water poured down his skin, he closed his eyes and whispered, 'Luxemborg, you might be seeing me sooner than I had thought. Much sooner!'

Desperado

'Soon of course! Are you not bothered? Talk to him ASAP, Nik! You've got to save me!' The words might sound like a plea but they were delivered like an order of the empire. And it was ordered by the young woman clad in a light pink designer suit with a ruffled silk cream blouse, teamed with silver Ferragamo high heels. Her perfectly French manicured right hand fisted tightly in front of her chest. Her other hand adorned with intricate diamond-encrusted ring and bangles rested in her lap. Gayatri Dutta!

The order was being issued to an equally insurmountable force, Nikhil Chandel. He was the thirty-three-year-old M.D. of Diamond Design Inc. His persona was very much like the immovable carbon atom structure of the diamonds he imported and exported. However, there were a few chinks in his molecular structure and Gayatri was one of them. And unfortunately for him, she knew it.

Nikhil picked up his cell and glanced at the time. 'Can't do it now, Guy, I have to head home for Advey's swimming class.' Nikhil was talking about his three and half-year-old stepson who was now as much his own child as one could ever be.

Advey's mother, Sneha Gupta, and Nikhil had married a few months ago. Corny as it may sound, Sneha and Advey made Nikhil a better man. Nikhil's show-no-emotion-feel-nothing days were now a distant memory. The cover was more or less the same, but the book had been rewritten.

'Your son is adorable! But aren't you the one teaching him swimming?' Gayatri crossed her feet and swung her chair. Though Nikhil shied from showing obvious signs of pride, Gayatri did notice how his lips eased on the side and his eyes shone at the compliment she had just given Advey. *Old Singham was now the new Prem.* Gayatri had an inherent love for Bollywood movies.

Most NRI's had their children watch Bollywood movies with the same vengeance the Zealots indoctrinated the children in their community. The NRI parents were promoting their culture and the Zealots, their cults. The children were screwed up one way or the other but at least the NRI kids knew how to dance.

'*Your* nephew is adorable!' Nikhil began gathering his things from his glass desk.

Gayatri pouted, shifting in her chair. 'But you have to help me, Nik. You have to talk to Dad!'

'What is he telling you to do now?'

'Same thing, get married ASAP! I don't even get to choose the guy!'

Nikhil rolled his eyes. 'It can't be that bad!'

It's worse! Much, much worse! Gayatri stayed quiet.

'Fine, I will talk to him. Come home. We'll have dinner together. Let's discuss this a bit more.'

'Your Hitler—' Gayatri was about to continue, but seeing

Nikhil's wary expression, she said instead, 'I mean your wife, doesn't like me much. You should ask her before you invite me.'

'Can you blame her? In the last five months since Sneha and I have been married, how many times have you come over to our place? In fact, the one time that you visited, you completely ignored her.' Nikhil reminded her and he wore his jacket.

Gayatri grimaced, stretching her neck as if she were straightening a crick. Conceding weakness did not come easy to Gayatri. 'I just feel very awkward around her. I messed up a few things. I know it happened a long time ago but—'

Nikhil logged off his computer. 'The past is in the past, Guy. Don't carry it around; it's nothing but excess baggage.' He picked up his cell. 'If you promise to try and get along with Sneha and Vey, I will help you.' He gave her one of his rare smiles.

Gayatri got to her feet and smoothed out her skirt. 'Only if I had an actual biological brother.' She clucked her tongue.

Nikhil raised an eyebrow. 'Emotional blackmail. Some things never get old.'

'Whatever!' Gayatri walked to the door. 'I guess I'll see you when I do... Probably in Amsterdam, married to some guy with a belly bigger than a halwai who sits outside his shop making jalebis.'

Nikhil called out. 'Fine! I will talk to him. However, in the meantime let us have the pleasure of having Your Majesty for dinner.' Unseen by him Gayatri smiled. *Definitely the new Prem. Old Singham was unyielding!* Nikhil walked over and stopped in front of her. Playfully, he pressed her nose to the side.

Gayatri grabbed his finger. 'Oww! Stop!' She met his eyes grudgingly.

'You can't avoid my wife forever, you know. You might end up avoiding me, Guy.'

Gayatri's kohl-lined eyes widened and her lips, outlined perfectly with a fuschia Urban Decay gloss, parted. 'You and Sneha are now a package deal?' Since she was ten, Nikhil was always around. Though not part of the family, he meant more so than those with whom she shared her last name. 'Your wife has you wrapped around her little pinky!' She grumbled, hiding the fact that a big part of her felt envious of Nikhil for having found rock solid love and friendship with a woman who would always have his back. They were the perfect family. Gayatri pressed her lips. *I could gag!*

'Come home with me and I'll surely talk to Sir Dutta tonight. Promise!' Nikhil's father had died when he was very young and Gayatri's father who had been an old family friend had taken Nikhil under his tutelage. *My dad found the son he never had and Nikhil found himself a father of sorts,* Gayatri had thought then.

Gayatri glared. 'And you called me the emotional blackmailer!' Nikhil shrugged. 'Fine, I'll come for dinner and even be nice!' Gayatri crossed her arms, staring down at the carpet.

Nikhil smiled at her affectionately. 'Deal. Let's go. I'll text Sneha.' Retrieving his phone from his suit pocket, he walked towards the door. Gayatri followed him to the elevator. They waited side by side.

'Just hope it's not contagious!' Gayatri mocked.

'What?' Nikhil asked.

'Whatever you and Sneha have caught. Just hope it is not contagious!' Gayatri rolled her tongue against her cheek.

Nikhil reached out and tugged Gayatri's sleek ponytail.

'Owww!' Gayatri smacked his hand.

'Yes, it's contagious.' Nikhil let go of her hair. 'We got it from Nandini and Aditya—' He stopped short. 'Sorry! I didn't—'

Gayatri did not let any awkwardness show on her face. She would have made a good poker player. 'I'm cool!' she retorted staring at the metal doors. Once upon a time, Gayatri was nearly engaged to the country's most eligible bachelor, Aditya Sarin. Aditya had dumped Gayatri for his homely and pretty neighbour, Nandini Sharma. Coincidentally or maybe because life had a sense of humor like AIB, Nandini was die-hard friends with Sneha Gupta, now Nikhil's wife.

A few months ago, wanting to avenge herself for being humiliated, Gayatri had plotted against Aditya and Nandini and tried to break their marriage. That is when Sneha and Nikhil (Gayatri's brother for all intent and purposes) had stepped in to curb Gayatri and her devious methods. Sparks had immediately sizzled between a recently-divorced Sneha and Nikhil. Sneha and Nikhil had been quick to marry after they met, and her son, Advey, from her previous marriage made it a perfect trio.

Nikhil had forced Gayatri to see the ugliness of her obsession in trying to humiliate Aditya. As both the couples— Nikhil and Sneha, Nandini and Aditya—moved on, Gayatri had stayed back in India but kept her distance from them. Nikhil had tried to reach out to her several times as had Sneha, but Gayatri had never returned the calls until today.

Because today, I'm desperate!

Gayatri realized Nikhil was watching her. With forced flippancy she exclaimed, 'Aditya and Nandini should be quarantined on an island!' She added a wink for effect.

'True!' Nikhil shook his head.

In less than an hour they were at Nikhil's apartment. He used his keys and led Gayatri in.

'Dad!' exclaimed Advey and jumped down from the sofa. The open book on his lap slipped off and landed on the floor. He ran to Nikhil who was quick to put aside his laptop bag so he could swoop him up and throw him in the air. Advey chortled and Nikhil's eyes crinkled in response. Nikhil caught Advey and tickled his sides. 'Got you, kiddo!'

Advey's chuckles reverberated straight through his tiny ribcage.

Nikhil pressed a kiss to the toddler's plump cheek and then instantly turned Advey upside down. Advey shrieked in delight as Nikhil laughed.

Gayatri felt a warmth rise inside her as she saw her usually cold-as-a-cod brother morph into a doting father.

Nikhil straightened and lowered Advey to the ground. 'More, Dad, more!' Advey grabbed Nikhil's leg and pleaded.

Nikhil ruffled Advey's hair. 'Later! Let's get you changed. It's time for a swimming lesson!'

'Wimming lessons, Bua!' Advey suddenly woke up to the fact that there was someone else in the room apart from his dad. Wobbling on his chubby legs, he launched himself on Gayatri.

'Whoa!' Gayatri caught Advey without losing her balance and pecked his cheek. He wriggled to be put down. Gayatri obliged him, but only after kissing him on his other cheek.

'Wimming lessons! Bud!' Nikhil reminded.

Advey gave them a beatific smile and stripped his pants right down.

'Vey!' Nikhil chuckled.

'You're a hoot, Vey!' Gayatri clapped her hand over a mouth. Going up to him, she pulled his pants up. 'Aren't you the cutest?'

'No pants! Wimming lessons Bua!' Advey immediately pulled them down again and this time he tried to wiggle his feet out of the pant legs.

Amla, his nanny, came to their rescue. She picked Advey up with his pants and underpants hanging around his ankles. 'Shame, shame, Adi baba! Bad, very bad!'

Amla marched away holding Advey in her arms, his pants trailing across the room

Nikhil loosened his tie. 'Have a seat, Guy!'

'Sure, if I can find my way to the sofa without falling!' Gayatri muttered stepping gingerly over tiny cars and dinosaurs toys littered all over the carpet.

'I'll be right back. I'll have the cook bring something out for you!'

'Just some coffee would be fine!'

'Sure!' Nikhil went up the stairs and disappeared into a room at the end of the hallway.

Another door opened and Advey came running out in a pair of red-and-blue swimming shorts. A pair of blue swimming goggles flapped in his hands. He stopped and looked at Gayatri. 'Bua, Daddy?'

'In there!' Gayatri pointed in the direction of the kitchen.

Advey took off again, his bums all puffed up and funny because of the swimming diapers. *Father and son! My dad's favourite combo except he never got a son, he got Didi and me! At least Didi always does as told.* A familiar ache arose in Gayatri.

A manservant brought a tray with a blue and white Khurja pot and matching cups from the kitchen. He placed the coffee in front of her.

'Thanks!' said Gayatri, taking a cup.

The doorbell chimed. Gayatri stiffened. *Must be Sneha!* Squaring her shoulders she pasted a forced smile on her face. Sneha was one of the rare people who could cut Gayatri to her size with her piercing looks and mind-reading techniques.

Someone came into the living room.

What the fuck?

Moscow Mules

'Uh…hi!' Nandini raised a hand slower than a railway track phatak. Nandini took the seat that was furthest from Gayatri. The smile on the faces of both the women were similar; the difference was in their eyes—Nandini's were nervous and Gayatri's frigid.

'How are you? Long time!' Nandini was never one to hold a grudge or silence.

'Good! And you and…' Gayatri trailed off awkwardly. She hated the guilt that broke out in her upon mentioning Aditya to Nandini. *A damp vamp I am!* That was one limerick Dr. Seuss would never use.

'We are good!' Nandini smiled even as she played with the strap of her handbag and then shifted uncomfortably in her chair.

Gayatri tapped her feet incessantly. *Savdhaan India, please frame me for murder, if that is what it takes to get away from this half-assed barrel of goodness, Ms Nandini.*

Nikhil emerged out of his room carrying Advey like a sack over his shoulder. Advey hung upside down. Nikhil stopped short when he saw the two occupants in his living room—

Gayatri and Nandini. His expression was that of petrified victims in horror films seconds before they were slayed.

Eggjactly, Nik! Gayatri smiled acknowledging his horror with a smile that seemed sweeter than a packet of Splenda.

'Where's Sneha?' Nandini blurted.

'Good question!' Nikhil eyed the front door as though he were calculating how much time it would take to get out should he make a run for it.

Don't you dare! Gayatri narrowed her eyes at Nikhil. Advey looked up and loudly squealed, 'Maathi!'

Just then the doorbell rang. Nikhil went to answer it.

'Literally saved by the bell!' Gayatri muttered.

'Aha! Full house! Everyone's here!' Sneha said, stepping into the living room. She had a laptop bag slung over one shoulder and a wide purse in her hand.

'Let's leave these two here, go for dinner and make our own movie!' Nikhil whispered into Sneha's ear.

'Tempting, but I'll pass!' Sneha giggled and shot a warning glance at her husband.

Gayatri noticed the ardor that lit Nikhil's green eyes. They twinkled with affection for the five-foot-something girl whose spine and spunk probably outdid an army.

'Lou birds!' Nandini called out.

'Shudd up, Kul-Nandini!' Sneha went up to her son who was engrossed on 'Maathi's' phone. 'Hey, Vey! Where's the hug for Mom?'

A distracted Advey gave Sneha a half-hearted hug. Suddenly the phone was taken from his hands. Surprised, Advey looked up as Nikhil held the phone in his hand now. Advey screamed 'Mom!' as he flung himself at Sneha who lifted and embraced him in a heartfelt hug. He then planted a big kiss on her cheek and gazed at Nikhil with his lower lip jutting out. The pleading puppy look combined with his innocent light brown eyes worked like magic. Nikhil handed the phone back to Advey. 'Like mother like son! Always pushing my buttons.'

'Then stop throwing the buttons in our face!' Sneha retorted, unloading her bags on the sofa. She smiled warmly at Gayatri. 'You are here! Finally!'

'In flesh and blood!' Gayatri's smiled gingerly.

Sneha turned to her best friend, sister and first love all rolled into one. 'So Adi is back tomorrow?'

'Yup! Tomorrow afternoon. How did the meeting with the Bhatias go?' Nandini asked. Sneha and she had opened an advertising firm a few months ago. They now boasted of one big client and a few small ones. Being a boutique company Sneha and Nandini were choosy about the companies they pitched their work to.

'It went well. Preeti impressed them. Have set up another meeting for next week. You should be there for that one. They will be sharing their ad budget in that meeting,' Sneha informed.

'Sure! Send me a meeting invite, I'll add it to my calendar,' Nandini agreed.

Gayatri felt out of place during all this work-talk. 'I just got a text. I have to go.' She held up her phone to show them the message.

'Nonsense! Ignore it! You are staying for dinner. Nikhil hardly gets to see you. *We* hardly get to see you.' Sneha flashed a big smile. She gave Nikhil the 'back-me-up-here' look.

Nikhil quickly came around and gently placed his hands on Gayatri's shoulders. 'You are staying, Guy.'

'But...I had...' complained Gayatri even as she watched Nikhil take her phone from her hand.

'We boys will leave you girls alone while we go and brave the wild waters of the west! C'mon, Vey, it's pool time!' Nikhil said.

Advey dropped Nandini's phone at once and wiggled his bum off the sofa. 'Later gators!' He trotted away behind his dad with some swagger.

Gayatri clamped her lips in what she hoped resembled a smile. *Now what? Will they force me to draw blood and be part of some shitty sisterhood?*

'Drinks anyone?' Sneha asked gazing at Gayatri.

Gayatri gave a polite smile, still not used to this disarming Sneha. The Sneha she remembered was a fire-breathing dragon.

'Moscow mules! The one Nikhil taught you!' Nandini chimed in.

'Make that two!' Gayatri nodded.

'Make that three! I'll make one for myself too.' Sneha gave a thumbs-up sign and headed for the bar in the dining area.

'Make yours light, you crazy cow!' Nandini called out to Sneha while winking at Gayatri. 'Sneha's a one-drink-wonder. The last time she got drunk we all discovered Nikhil's flair for poetry,' Nandini giggled.

I'll need ten. Gayatri straightened her ponytail.

'So how have you been?' Nandini was an effortless conversationalist. She was genuinely interested in everyone's business!

'Just been busy with work,' Gayatri fibbed.

'Where do you work?'

Gayatri bit her lip, caught in her own lie. 'A few projects here and there!' She brought back her I'm-better-than-you look. 'Have been traveling a lot, between Amsterdam and Mumbai.'

'Of course, you have family there, don't you?' Nandini asked. Gayatri nodded.

Sneha entered the room right then. 'Nik was telling me about the situation with your dad! Marriage market ready?'

Gayatri drew in a sharp breath. *Nikhil, you idiot!*

'Gayatri's dad wants her to move back to Amsterdam. He feels that she is doing nothing constructive here.'

Sneha, you are a bigger idiot! Gayatri's hands fisted as she positively bristled at having her Achilles' heel exposed to the two women she would never want to appear weak in front of. In her head a GIF kept playing on loop—a GIF of her dropping a piano on Nikhil's head.

'Gayatri could come work with us,' Nandini blurted.

Sneha and Gayatri simultaneously erupted in a resounding 'No!'

Like Tihar jail was never free of criminals, Nandini never lacked ideas. 'She could work with Nikhil.'

'Pass!' Gayatri took a long swig of her drink. Then glancing in Sneha's direction, she said, 'No offense meant!'

'None taken!' Sneha shrugged.

'Hmm, maybe you could start something new?' Nandini quipped.

Gayatri gave a brittle smile. Another long swig of the drink! 'Not an option. Dad won't allow it.'

'Why?' Sneha asked.

'Because he won't…' Gayatri felt a knot in her chest and took a deep breath. *In for a penny, in for a pound.* 'Dad doesn't trust me. I haven't been successful in a few ventures he started for me.' She sat back, gently stroking her bracelet, a distant look in her perfect almond-shaped eyes.

'So what? Everyone has more downs than ups. All it takes is one big successful "up" and all the "downs" are ancient history.' Nandini spoke passionately in her defense.

Now I'm a sad vamp! Gayatri raised her glass. 'This is nice! But when do we have dinner? I'm starving!'

'Sorry! Let me grab some snacks.' Sneha jumped to her feet and went towards the kitchen.

'I'll be right back!' Nandini excused herself and followed Sneha.

Finally by herself, Gayatri slumped her shoulders and leaned back in her chair. The drink was strong enough to loosen her tongue. 'Maybe I should just fucking marry whoever Dad wants me to marry. So what if I don't get to choose my spouse?' She twirled the glass in her hand. 'So what if the man turns out to be a jerk? Why fight the inevitable? I'm used to jerks. At least I'll have money, because Dad would never pick a "nobody" for his rich bitch!' Gayatri sat up straight and finished the rest of her drink in one gulp. The minty drink did nothing to erase the bitter taste in her mouth. She rose to her feet and walked to the windows of the high-rise apartments that overlooked the Pali Hill neighbourhood.

Unknown to Gayatri, Sneha had witnessed her tortured confession.

Jai Shri Krishna

Sneha retreated and then came back again into the living room, this time announcing her entry. 'Appetizers are ready! I'll set the table in the dining room!'

'Why the dining room? We can just eat here.' Nandini returned from the restroom.

'Because I paid fortune for that damn thing!' Sneha retorted.

Nandini chuckled. 'I have to make a call!'

'Gayatri, why don't we move to the dining room?' Sneha suggested.

Sure, Mom! Gayatri followed Sneha into the formal dining room.

'You have a seat. I'll set the table,' Sneha offered.

'Don't you have servants for this?' Gayatri asked pulling out a chair.

Sneha smiled as she opened the drawers on the side armoire. 'Nikhil and I like our privacy. Thus we manage the household chores ourselves. Less traffic in the house you see!'

'Hmm…this is a nice table!' Gayatri trailed her fingers over the carving on the chestnut coloured, mahogany dining table; it was crafted with rosewood and walnut veneers with brass accents all over for an imperial look. 'It's big and formal for sure!'

Sneha gave her a wry look. 'I did go overboard. It dwarfs the room! Wish I had thought of that before I bought this beautiful monstrosity.'

Gayatri swiveled her head a few times studying the room. 'Decrease the length of the chandelier hanging over it, place a few long mirrors on the facing walls and get a smaller armoire. The room will look bigger and the table smaller,' Gayatri suggested tucking her hair behind her ear.

Sneha thought about the changes Gayatri suggested and then peered around as if visualizing those changes. 'You are right. That could work!' she exclaimed. 'I'm impressed!'

'Ouch!' Gayatri gracefully linked her arms in front of her, 'I'm a jack of few things but master of none!' *Wow I'm over-sharing!*

Sneha paused for a moment, her eyes gleaming. Slowly she took a seat opposite Gayatri. 'Have you ever run a facility, managed operations...a biggish office?'

'I did manage a few of my dad's offices. What do you have in mind?' Gayatri asked, arranging the napkins in origami style.

'That neat!' Sneha pointed at the napkin.

'One of those innumerable lame classes I had to take when I was young,' Gayatri replied dryly.

'No woman should ever *have* to do anything.' Sneha said quietly.

'Slip of tongue! Classes I took and thoroughly enjoyed!' Gayatri made a quick recovery. 'You were asking earlier about some operations?'

'Hold on! I think I heard Vey and Nik come in!' Sneha abruptly exited.

'What did I do this time?' Gayatri shrugged and resumed setting up the table.

By the time Nikhil, Nandini and Sneha came back in the room, the table had been laid out.

'Very beautiful, Gayatri!' Sneha remarked noticing how Gayatri had used some potpourri from a nearby vase to decorate the napkins and the table.

'I was bored,' Gayatri smiled.

'Did know that a shark can smile, Guy!' Nikhil teased her.

Gayatri rolled her eyes. 'Yes, they can. Haven't you seen Shark Tale or yourself smiling?'

Nandini chuckled loudly. 'Oh I saw Shark Tale and I loved it! She continued in her animated voice, 'It was hilarious! De Niro as Don Lino and Jack Black as Lenny! OMG! They cracked me—'

'I was forced to see it and hear most of it because a kid next to me on a flight was dumb enough to forget his headphones!' Gayatri interrupted, her tone dripping with sarcasm.

'Oh!' Nandini decided to shut up and instead fiddled with a napkin on her lap. Just then the servant wheeled in a trolley loaded with food.

Nikhil cut a piece of idli and put it into his mouth.

'You eat idli with a knife and fork?' Nandini noticed.

'He even eats paranthas like that!' Sneha remarked.

Smiling, Nikhil continued to eat.

Dad eats like that! Gayatri thought as her hands hovered over the knife and fork by her side.

Sneha leaned over and pushed Gayatri's napkin closer to

her. 'Go for it!' She gestured at Gayatri's hand.

'Thanks!' Grinning, Gayatri picked up a piece of Chicken 65 with her hands and ate it.

Nandini and Nikhil both watched the exchange, the former with a raised eyebrow.

'Nik, I was thinking, why doesn't Gayatri manage the lab?' Sneha voiced.

Nikhil continued to look down at his plate, hiding his frown. Gayatri turned her gaze towards Nikhil and Sneha.

'The lab?' Nandini asked. Sneha nodded.

Nikhil continued to frown at his plate.

'Frowning at your food won't make the question go away, Dad!' Sneha affectionately addressed him like Advey did.

'Please tell me what lab are you all going on about?' Gayatri asked.

'The lab where Viraj is overseeing the making of Adi and Nikhil's dream project. Adi's dad's started it. He discovered Viraj and his idea,' Nandini replied.

'So then basically this Viraj started it!' said Gayatri, wiping some crumbs from the side of her mouth.

Nandini became quiet and went back to breaking some of her idli and dropping it in her bowl of sambhar. Few drops of sambhar spattered on the white tablecloth near her plate.

'It's okay! Leave it!' Sneha said, trying to pacify a visibly horrified Nandini. Gayatri simply rolled her eyes.

'You are talking about the lab where Viraj and his team are working on a new kind of top secret battery and in which Aditya, I and eleven other investors have nearly invested all of our money in. Including Gayatri's father. The project which might reduce some of us to paupers if it is not implemented within the next six months,' Nikhil said, his voice even throughout.

'Yes! The lab, which is falling apart because of myriad management issues. Every two to three weeks the manager of operations keeps resigning or is fired because Viraj is worse than a stereotypical mad scientist. He is simply impossible to manage. A lab with a scientist who is nowhere close to beginning Phase 2 of the project when he should have been completing the final one—Phase 3 which involves testing!' Sneha reminded evenly.

'Why is he hard to manage?' Gayatri asked her interest piqued.

'Because he is borderline insane. Works odd hours, impossible to get through to and zero patience with people, including his financiers.' Then Nandini said pointing at Nikhil with her spoon, 'Actually, Nik is the only one Viraj can kind of stand.'

'I'm not sending Guy in a war zone.' Nikhil pushed his plate away from him.

'Ask her, don't decide for her!' Sneha persisted.

'No, Sneha! End of discussion!' Nikhil put down his fork.

'Her dad is one of the investors; he would probably feel good about his daughter overseeing something he has invested millions in,' Nandini suggested.

'True!' Sneha concurred.

Not in a million years! Gayatri focused on her food. *What are these two up to?*

Nikhil pushed his chair noisily and stood up. 'I'll make sure Vey has his dinner and then I'll join you guys back.' He planted a kiss on Sneha's cheek and left the room.

Nandini gaped at them. 'That is how you fight, a kiss on the cheek?'

'So I'm guessing this is not how all couples fight?' Gayatri smirked.

Nandini shook her head. 'Heck no! Most of us do it the good old-fashioned way. Shout, slam doors, don't answer calls, cold vibes in bed. Even a few broken plates!'

'Ignore her!' Sneha snorted. 'Nik and I are not fighting, we are just disagreeing!' Sneha got to her feet. 'Think it's time to feed Dad some dessert.' She winked and left.

Alone in the room, Gayatri and Nandini exchanged strained smiles and went back to eating.

Nandini put her spoon down with a loud clink. 'Why don't you call up your father. He won't say no to you. Use him as a leverage to convince Nikhil to work at the lab.'

Gayatri immediately shook her head. 'Let's leave him out of this.'

'What? No! Dads always help us daughters out.'

Not mine, bimbette! 'Pass!' Gayatri accidentally dropped her napkin on the floor, but quickly bent down to pick it up.

'C'mon! He'll help! We'll call him right now!' Nandini reached over and grabbed Gayatri's cell.

'No! No! Give it back!' Gayatri tried to get the phone back but in vain.

'Oh look, you have missed call from him!' Nandini squealed hitting the call number. Gayatri could only stare in shock.

'It's ringing. Here, talk. I'll put you on speaker,' Nandini gestured excitedly.

'How dare you!' Gayatri hissed, suppressing the urge to slap Nandini.

Her father answered, 'Hello Gayatri!'

'Hi Dad!' Gayatri leaned forward.

'When are you coming back home?' her father's sternness came through even on the call.

Gayatri grimaced. 'About that Dad, I was thinking...umm maybe...umm...'

Her father made an impatient noise with his tongue. 'Hurry Gayatri, I don't have all day. What is it this time? Another rich bloke or another bad business idea?' The words were accompanied by a mocking chuckle.

Nandini lost her buoyant smile.

Gayatri saw pity in Nandini's wide eyes.

I hate pity! And that too from her! 'Dad, I was thinking of overseeing the lab where the new project is being readied. I just—'

'Pagal ho gayi ho? Absolutely not! Get this crazy idea out of your head right now!'

Nandini started to get up.

Gayatri tossed an angry glance at her. 'Sit down!' she ordered. Nandini sat down looking guiltier than a terrorist caught with a live bomb.

Gayatri's father wasn't done yelling. 'You stay away from that project. Am I clear, Gayatri? It has cost me millions. You will not screw this up too! Am I clear?' her father hollered.

'I heard you!' Gayatri's face turned a dull red. Her nails dug in her palms.

'Good! Now get back here to your mom. And stop bothering Nikhil, he has enough on his plate with work and a new family.'

'Fine!' Gayatri glared at Nandini who studied the ceiling,

then her fork and then the wall.

'Jai Shri Krishna!' Gayatri's father added.

Gayatri stayed quiet.

'Jai Shri Krishna, Gayatri!' His voice was curt and demanding.

'Jai Shri Krishna!' Gayatri ended the call. She turned to Nandini, 'Are you happy now, Princess? Are you done humiliating me or do you and your damn husband have more in store for me.' She stood up and flung her napkin on the table.

'Don't curse, Adi. And I was only trying to help!' Nandini spoke quietly.

'More food!' Sneha entered with a dish in her hand. Nikhil followed behind, with Advey piggy-ridding on his back. Gayatri walked up to them, her face reflecting her emotions far too clearly.

'Thank you for your hospitality.' She looked at Sneha squarely in her eyes. 'I'm sorry, but I'm in no mood for food or...' she glanced over her shoulder pointedly at Nandini and concluded, '...or the present company.' Gayatri exited the room, her head held high, shoulders taught. Sliding Advey down Nikhil went after Gayatri.

Sneha put the dish on the table and decided to question the 'present company'. 'What did you do?'

Nandini shrugged as she pulled up Advey who was trying to get on her lap. 'Nothing! Don't look at me like that. It was her father!'

Sneha sat down, her mouth puckered. 'Her father? Then

why did she give you the evil eye.'

'Maybe I look her like dad!' Nandini avoided Sneha's eyes and reached for the Hyderabadi biryani Sneha had just placed on the table.

Sneha narrowed her eyes. She recalled Gayatri's father with his florid face, double chin, weak jaw line, over-exposed pores around his nose and under his eyes, and the white hair spotting his ears and temples. 'You look nothing like him! But I know you did something because you are stuffing your face with food and reeking of guilt, Sethani!'

Sneha waited for Nandini to finish the morsel that was twice the size of her mouth.

'We need to help Gayatri!' Nandini said handing Advey what he wanted—her cell phone.

'I was trying to!' Sneha sighed. 'Why do you think I convinced Nikhil to let her manage the operations of the lab?'

'Good, so you have a plan?' Nandini sat back.

Sneha raised an eyebrow. 'So you did do something!'

Nandini winced. 'Yes, but with good intentions!'

'As always!' Sneha helped herself to some biryani.

'Aren't you going to stop Gayatri from leaving?'

'Only Nik can convince her to do anything!'

Advey, who was sitting on Nandini's lap all this while, turned around and planted a big kiss on her chin and then snuggled against her. Nandini hugged him tight. 'I so badly want one of these. Where can I get one?'

'From your vagina!' Sneha quipped. Nandini and she exchanged a look and then burst into laughter. Advey laughed along without understanding a word of what had been said. Sneha leaned over the table and tickled him under his chin.

'Buddhu!'

'So if Gayatri doesn't listen to anyone besides Nikhil, how will *we* help her?'

Sneha flashed a grin. 'By doing what we do best!'

Nandini nodded. 'Ah! You put the fear of god in her and scare the crap out of her?'

'Yes ma'am!' Sneha raised her glass of water. And you emotionally blackmail her, kulta! Milk it!' Sneha squeezed her fingers.

'Aha good times!' Nandini said dreamily.

Sneha reached out with her glass and the two best buddies clinked their glasses. 'The best!'

Country Wants to Know

Gayatri's hotel
7.00 a.m.

Squatting on the floor, Gayatri rolled up her yoga mat. Beads of sweat, like water drops on oiled skin, lined up her forehead and upper lip. Sunlight came through her window and lit up the room, highlighting her unmade bed and the purple chair laden with clothes from the night before. There was a knock on her door.

Frowning, Gayatri grabbed a loose singlet and pulled it over her sports bra and calf-length tights. The single knock had now altered to a series of staccato beats.

'Hold on man, what's the—' Gayatri trailed off on seeing the visitors, 'this is unexpected.' She leaned at the door.

'Hiee!' Nandini waved at her.

'Morning!' Sneha nodded pulling the shades out of her hair.

'Morning!' Gayatri did not open the door fully, purposely blocking the entrance.

'May we?' Sneha asked.

'You are more than welcome!' Gayatri spoke stiltedly. In spite of all the good endorphins slamming inside her after a workout, she was finding it hard to forgive the stunt Nandini had pulled on her the other day.

Sneha stayed where she was, a polite smile on her face. 'It has to be both of us!'.

Gayatri wiped her forehead. 'Sure!' she grunted, leading them in.

Sneha and Nandini entered the hotel suite that served as Gayatri's place to stay whenever she was in town. They stepped into a tiny living room dominated by a red-and-beige sofa set and a metal coffee table. Behind the living room was the bedroom. On one side of the living room was the bathroom with gray marble floors and on the other side a small kitchenette full of shiny stainless steel appliances.

'Sorry about the mess!' Gayatri said standing behind the sofa, still uncomfortable with what could ensue.

'What mess?' Nandini whispered, eyeing the tidy surroundings.

'Beats me!' Sneha said looking around for a place to park her oversized handbag.

'You haven't seen a mess yet! Check out our Schumacher's car's glove compartment sometime,' Nandini snickered hinting at Sneha's love for speed.

'I have a kid,' Sneha reminded her.

'That can be your excuse for only so many things!' Nandini shot back.

'So what brings you here?' Gayatri asked sliding the door shut between the bedroom and living room.

'You!' Nandini blurted. Sneha grabbed her hand and pulled

her down onto the sofa next to her. 'Hey! I was going to sit,' Nandini protested as she brushed the hair off her face. She was spying on something lying on the kitchen counter. 'Oh my god! Cupcakes! May I?'

'Sure!' Gayatri murmured.

Nandini slipped off the sofa heading for the cupcakes!

'You are such a jughead!' Sneha quipped.

'Sneh, come here, you have to check out these amazing cupcakes. You must!'

Slightly irritated, Sneha still got to her feet and went over. 'Wow!' she exclaimed admiring the tiny pink, green and blue cupcakes sprinkled with silver balls and edible confetti. Sneha and Nandini each took a bite. 'These are amazing.'

'Umm…I could finish this whole tray in minutes! Where did you get these from, Gayatri?'

'A sweet lady on the second floor, Mrs Perez. She gets them from somewhere. I just order from her,' Gayatri replied, still standing.

Nandini grabbed the tray and placed it on the coffee table between them. 'Hope you don't mind!' she said.

'Go for it. I'll simply order some more from Mrs Perez,' Gayatri replied graciously.

Luckily for Gayatri, Sneha or Nandini did not explore her fridge or the contents of her kitchen sink.

Sneha came straight to the point. 'Nandini told me about yesterday's conversation between your dad and you.'

Gayatri pursed her lips.

'Which would have not happened if she,' Sneha pointed accusingly at Nandini, 'hadn't butted in.'

Turning back to Gayatri, Sneha said, 'You need to focus

on the real problem and it is not Nandini.'

'Why do you let your dad rule your life?' Nandini asked.

Gayatri acted as if she had not heard her question.

'Ya, why do you, Gayatri? You are educated, intelligent and confident. You have the right to make your own decisions. You are an adult for god's sake!' Sneha did not mince her words.

Gayatri gritted her teeth. 'What I do or don't do is only *my* business.'

'Why fight small battles and loose big wars,' Nandini spoke up again.

Exasperated, Gayatri looked at Sneha. 'What is she talking about?'

Sneha smoothed her skirt over her knees. 'Look, as a profession we make ads. Advertising is about knowing your market, the product and your audience.'

Bull! Gayatri's resisted the urge to roll her eyes.

'We're constantly observing people. Consciously or unconsciously!' Nandini added.

Sneha took over. 'We think you do annoying things simply because you want attention. That is a childish way of facing your problems. It's time to grow up! Take responsibility, make your decisions but do it right!'

Gayatri, who was trying to keep calm all this while, was getting pissed off. 'You might be Nikhil's wife but that does not give you the right to talk me like that.' She fought to came her voice even.

'Nik is worried for you too. Especially after the stunt you pulled with Aditya several months ago. When you drugged him and took compromising pictures of you two hoping to break his and Nandini's marriage.' Sneha used the Brahmastra.

And it worked.

Gayatri lost it. She slumped down on the couch and her face, free of makeup, was tinged a bright red. 'That was stupid. I have already apologized for that,' she mumbled.

'And it's all forgotten and forgiven,' Nandini quickly added.

'Aren't you tired of all this? Don't you want an actual career? Have a purpose in life. Earn a regular paycheck?' Sneha grilled.

Nandini smiled sweetly at Gayatri. 'Making big decisions is scary and going against your family is even scarier, especially when you have played by their rules most of your life.'

Exasperated, Gayatri covered her face with her hands.

'C'mon Gayatri, this is your last shot. If you don't do something now, even Nik won't be able to convince your dad anymore. You will have to move back to Belgium or wherever he is and get married to a man of his liking who could be a complete jerk for all we know.'

'Or a terrorist!' Nandini whispered.

Sneha and Gayatri gaped at Nandini.

'What?' Nandini put her palms out. 'Don't you guys read the papers? ISIS is recruiting in Europe and they are looking for brides.'

'Thank you, Arnab Goswami!' Sneha smirked.

Nandini blew a rasberry. 'I don't have the whole nation calling me 24/7, wanting to know things. You may call me Barkha Dutt. Sometimes, I think Arnab Goswami's spot boy is called Country and is an inquisitive sort. He probably bugs his boss with questions, thus because Arnab keeps telling everyone, 'Country wants to know! Country wants to know!'

Sneha shook her head. 'What will I do with you Sethani?'

'I have to take a shower!' Gayatri said dismissively getting to her feet.

Sneha crossed her arms. 'Perfect. And then we will take you to see the lab. Seeing won't hurt.'

Gayatri appeared unconvinced.

'What do you have to lose? Remember,' Nandini held out both her hands as if weighing things, 'lab or bride, employee or terrorist?'

Gayatri gazed at Nandini's hands and expression for few second. And then she burst into a chuckle that soon blossomed into 'doubled over body shaking kind' of laughter. Sneha grinned and said to Nandini, 'Kulta, you are certified crazy! Stop it!' She knocked Nandini's hands down

After a few Gayatri sobered as she wiped her eyes. 'My dad will never agree, Nikhil also said no,' she said glancing at Nandini, 'even your husband will disapprove.'

Sneha shook her head. 'Gayatri! In your whole argument not once did you mention yourself. Dad, Nik, even Adi… and you? What about you? What do you *really* want to do?'

'I want, I want…' Gayatri trailed off. *My dream is stupid enough in my head, I'm definitely not saying it out aloud to these two.*

Nandini turned to Sneha. 'Oh my god, she really does not know what she wants to do.'

Gayatri felt like she had swallowed nails. Sneha did not ease up. 'You are not getting any younger! None of us are!'

Gayatri grimaced. 'I need to take a shower.'

Sneha retorted. 'You need to get a job. A job that will exhaust you, drive you up the wall, pull you in several directions and yet leave you with immense satisfaction and earn the respect of others. Like you absolutely deserve! Go take a shower and then we are going to the lab. On that list of people making decisions for you, add my name.' Sneha sat back, her lips clamped tight, her expression determined.

'Temporarily, of course. Right, Sneha?' Nandini added smiling.

Sneha shrugged. 'Ya, of course, I can carry other people's crap only for so long. We are going to make you Miss Independent for real, Gayatri!'

Gayatri slack jawed stared at Sneha. Nandini waved her hand. 'She can be scary I know, but she is right. Please come with us!

Gayatri studied her manicured nails. 'I can take a look at the lab, I guess.' She capitulated.

Sneha and Nandini nodded.

'Why are you both doing this for me?'

'Because you are family...to me!' Sneha replied, easily as she hunted for her cell in her bag.

'And if Sneha is in, I'm in! We are like the "har tyohar dhamakedar". Buy one get one free, package deal!' Nandini continued, 'You have my condolences!'

Tackle Your Boss

Two hours later, the three women pulled into the parking lot of a warehouse-like structure that was all fortified glass and steel on the outside. Short, bushy trees added a splash of green to the austere white exterior and also concealed the entrance and exit doors of the structure. The parking lot housed a few cars and a motorbike.

'The lab?' Gayatri asked stepping out of the car.

'The lab,' Sneha remarked doing the same from the driver's side.

'Wish it was more colourful,' Nandini added getting off from back. 'It's so pennnhh!'

Sneha and Gayatri exchanged an amused look. The three walked towards the main entrance.

'Allow me!' Sneha said, swiping a card through the machine next to the door. She swiped the card twice and then keyed in a seven-digit code. 'Security' was all the explanation she gave. The green light blinking on the door handle indicated that code worked.

'In you go!' Nandini pulled the door open.

'Thanks!' Gayatri walked inside a large hall with an

unnamed reception. The walls were painted a light shade of green and the inside of the building was as quiet as the outside. Gayatri noted the large double-paneled metal doors on either side of the empty foyer.

The metal door opened on their left. A tall, bespectacled man came out on a hover board. His attention was on the tablet in his hand. Not slowing down, he headed straight for the doors on the other side. Extending one foot, he swiftly kicked open the other set of metal doors and disappeared behind it.

Gayatri peered at Sneha and Nandini. 'What was that?'

Sneha shrugged her shoulders that were wrapped in an indigo-coloured silk blouse. 'That was the crazy scientist. And he was not even at his weirdest!'

Deep in thought, Gayatri pursed her lips. She was expecting the crazy, mad scientist to be different—someone older, with greying hair, owl glasses, faded and mismatched shirt tucked in worn trousers. The tall, lean man who had just passed by appeared close to thirty, with dark hair that fell to his shoulders, looking more of a rake than boor.

Nandini looked at them quizzically. 'What's so weird about a man on a two-wheeler? It's India!'

The three went in the same direction as the scientist. They entered a long, sterile-looking corridor. As they walked on, they saw rectangular glass windows with light gray walls on either side that eventually revealed rooms fitted with large machines, computers on portable tables, all sorts of charts and graphs drawn on whiteboards, littered steel tables and people in lab coats wandering between them. The place smelled strongly of bleach and grease.

'If it looks like a lab and feels like a lab, it must be the lab!' Gayatri murmured looking closely through the glass in order to get a better sense of what the people in coats were doing.

'Why don't you wait here? We'll be right back,' Sneha said to Gayatri.

'Where are you going?' Gayatri asked, seemingly reluctant to be left alone.

'To negotiate or beg, whatever it takes!' Nandini replied confidently.

Nandini and Sneha disappeared behind a door to their right a room with no windows.

Gayatri felt left out. Bored, she walked the entire length of the corridor. At the end of the corridor she came upon a door with a sign 'No Entry! With or without a badge.'

Needless to say that piqued her curiosity. Gayatri put her ear to the door, trying to decipher any sounds she might hear. All of a sudden the door opened from the other side and Gayatri lost her balance. She made a garbled sound as she fell face down. 'Oof!' Instinctively, she put out her hands to hold onto something but her fingers closed on air. The person she fell on did nothing to help her. 'Ughhh!' Gayatri felt her cheek smash into a corduroy-ridden thigh as her knees scraped the floor. Her startled face was inches away from the stranger's crotch. Gayatri let herself tumble completely. *Rather the floor than someone's genitals!* Stunned she lay in an inelegant heap on the floor with her legs bent awkwardly. She felt the cool air on her thighs and realized that her skirt had nearly ridden up to her bum.

The man who she fell on had taken a few hurried steps back to protect a cylinder in his hand. *The man on the hoverboard!*

Mortified, Gayatri sat up and quickly straightened her clothes. Her dark eyes shot a furious look at the idiot who had caused her to fall. 'Are you freaking blind?'

The man's expression wasn't even remotely apologetic. 'You could have broken this.' Reverently, he held out the cylinder in his hands.

Gayatri shot to her feet. 'Really? THIS ONE?!' She grabbed the cylinder from his unsuspecting hands and raised it above her head ready to hurtle it on the floor.

A strong arm wrapped itself around Gayatri's waist and turned her around.

'Hey!'

His other hand shot to Gayatri's fingers clasped around the cylinder. He was much taller than her and even though she was in heels he towered above her.

'Oh no, you don't!' Gayatri bent her wrist and dropped the cylinder in her other hand. Simultaneously, she turned her back to him and drove her heel in the man's foot.

'Damn it!' The stranger reacted by pulling Gayatri forcibly against him as he tried to reach the cylinder she now held in front of her. 'Don't drop it!' The man yelped.

Gayatri instantly registered three things—as her body pressed against his from head to toe, she realized that the man's loose clothes covered a tight, hard body; he smelled of clean musk soap; thirdly, the man was totally oblivious to their proximity.

'Give it to me!' The man again made an attempt to grab the cylinder.

'Ha!' Gayatri bent her waist and leaned further, moving the cylinder further away from the man. 'Get it, buster!'

Bending down, the man with his sneaker-clad foot swiped Gayatri's feet off the floor with practised ease. Gayatri lost her balance again. The man deftly caught the cylinder with one hand as he outstretched the other hand to stop Gayatri's fall.

'Gayatri!' Sneha's horrified voice caused Gayatri to freeze.

The stranger used Gayatri's surprise to put her back on her feet, clumsily of course. Gayatri's mouth felt dry and her heart felt like it was bouncing around in her rib cage. *SHIT*! She had an audience.

Sneha wasn't alone. Nikhil, Aditya and Nandini were there too. All their faces held similar expressions of shock. 'It was all his fault!' Gayatri took a step forward and stopped. 'What the—' The infernal man still had his arm wrapped around her.

With an impatient push she freed herself. 'I, I was...only trying...' The tough expression on Nikhil's face caused Gayatri to fumble.

'Good news!' Sneha was first one to break the silence.

'Ugh!' Gayatri floundered. Her hair and clothes were a mess and her usual composure had evaporated faster than liquid nitrogen.

Nandini stepped around Aditya and Nikhil and came forward. 'Yes! We have just settled the matter with Adi and Nikhil. Congratulations!' She took Gayatri's limp hand and shook it lightly. 'You are this lab's new manager of operations.' Nandini slyly pinched Gayatri's palm forcing her out of her stupor.

'Oh! Thank you!' Gayatri flashed a relieved smile. 'I'm won't disappoint—'

'NO!' Came from the man holding the cylinder.

The emphatic word resounded like the crack of a whip.

Everyone looked at him.

Gayatri swallowed anxiously as realization hit her. *Shit! The mad scientist I just tackled is the boss. I'm so effing stupid.*

'No?' Sneha moving curiously towards the man who still had the cylinder hooked under his arm.

'To her,' the man said pointing at Gayatri, 'working here. I am going out. I will be back by 3.00 p.m.' He turned towards Nikhil and said, 'I want everyone gone by that time.' Having said that the man coolly weaved his way through those standing at the door and walked out.

'Nice going, Gayatri!' Nikhil crossed his arms and glowered. 'Dr Viraj! He owns and runs this lab. He was the only one you needed to impress!'

'But I thought you all were the bosses around here. Aren't you financing all this?' Gayatri's blurted.

'Viraj's word is what carries weight here. Rest of us just hop around like a bunch of bunnies trying to keep him happy!' Aditya said gruffly over Nikhil's shoulder.

Gayatri closed her eyes. *I just blew my last chance.* She turned to Sneha. 'Can't you do something? Please!' Gayatri hated the plaintive timbre in her voice but she was desperate.

'You should have been more tactful around Viraj instead of wrestling with him,' Nikhil answered with his usual hard-to-read expression.

'Why don't you guys sort it out? Nandini and I should be leaving,' Aditya interrupted.

Nandini nodded. 'Good luck!' she said, looking at Sneha and Gayatri.

Nikhil waved a quick bye to Aditya. 'I'll call you!' said Nikhil.

Sneha waited for them to be out of earshot. 'Nik, can I speak with Gayatri alone please?'

Nikhil peered at them. 'Sure! But not in his office. Talk somewhere else please.'

So this is the I'm-so-mad-I'm-so-important scientist's office? Gayatri gave the room a closer look, wrinkling her nose in the process.. The office was an unexpectedly small room. It had a square window with stained glass and had an attic-like feeling. A desk drowning under strewn papers, styrofoam cups full of pen, pencils and markers placed haphazardly all over the room. The room smelled of dust and reeked of neglect. On a smaller table shoved in the corner of the room was a precariously placed lcd monitor hooked to a keyboard. Under a table was a worn red-coloured plastic stool—the kind tea vendors keep around their thela. *I wouldn't even use this room to store my shoes.*

'Let's go outside,' Sneha beckoned her. The two walked out of the building. Gayatri leaned against Sneha's car, adjusted the purple hobo bag on her shoulder.

'Beg, grovel, do whatever you have to do to change Viraj's mind. You have an MBA degree in advanced management, so you definitely possess the skills for this job. But what you are lacking is a common sense and drive. And you have to figure a way out of this yourself. No one is coming to rescue you except your dad, with a wedding planner on one side and a groom on the other.'

'That's a little harsh,' Gayatri mumbled.

'But true. If you can convince Viraj to hire you, Nikhil will convince your father to let you stay here. You know Nikhil considers you family.'

'I'll try and talk to Viraj.' Gayatri gave a Sneha a weak smile.

'Without tackling him, please. Currently, there is no one more precious to Nikhil than Viraj.'

'Please!' Gayatri scoffed.

'Oh, I'm important to Nik but only when he is thinking from a certain part of his anatomy. It's a joke. Smile.'

Gayatri bit her lower lip and looked evidently anxious.

Sneha patted Gayatri's shoulder. 'FYI if Viraj says yes, then you will be the fifth operations manager to be hired in the last two months.'

Gayatri's jaw dropped. She recovered quickly though. 'What happened to the other four?'

'Number one was fired because he bought chairs. Number two for—'

Gayatri held up her hand. 'Hold on. Chairs?'

'Viraj allows no chairs in his lab. He feels that sitting down hampers efficiency.'

Gayatri felt a slight hysteria flood her body. 'Okay. And the second manager was fired because?'

'She put a coffee machine and snack vending machine in the break room.'

Gayatri quickly added, 'The scientist is against food and beverages too.'

Sneha bobbed her head. 'And he is against break rooms.'

Gayatri smacked her forehead aghast. 'Oh teri!'

Sneha grinned.

Gayatri fumbled. 'And the third?'

Sneha winced even as she said, 'He caught him talking on his cell twice during work hours!'

'Really! Wow! And the fourth manager?'

'The fourth quit on his own and that too within a week!'

Gayatri leaned back on the car, her face raised to the sky. 'And this is my only option.'

Sneha pursed her lips. 'You are missing the bigger picture. If you snag this job and by some miracle are able to keep it, by default you become irreplaceable. Currently, Viraj is their new god—Nikhil's, Adi's and your dad's. It's simple. What Viraj wants, Viraj gets.'

Gayatri sighed. 'So what should I do? How do I get that man—'

'That I do not know. That is your problem to solve,' Sneha said with a sense of finality. 'I have to get to agency now.' She gave Gayatri a thoughtful glance. 'Are you coming or staying?

As Gayatri ran her eyes over the road ahead, her brow furrowed. 'Staying. Definitely staying!'

Sneha opened her car door. 'Will you be able to get back to the hotel on your own?'

Gayatri nodded. 'Yeah! I'll take a taxi. I know the way back.'

Sneha started her car and cautioned, 'Please don't blow up the building or kill the man!'

Gayatri's smiled wryly. 'And please don't forget to pray for a miracle.'

Neither of them knew that eventually a tragedy would do the needful.

Selfies

Once Sneha left, Gayatri did a quick recce of the building. *Gosh! It's quieter than a cemetery around here.* She spied a coffee shop some distance across the busy and dusty main road. She walked inside the café that smelled of freshly ground beans coffee and baked savouries and ordered a cappuccino. She took a table that gave her an unobstructed view of the warehouse entrance and parking lot. In some time, Gayatri saw Nikhil drive away. *One less person to worry about! Where are you, Mr Madhatter?*

Gayatri stayed in her spot, observing the lab compound from a distance. Fifteen minutes turned into an hour and then another hour. No one came out of or went inside the building. Mid-morning turned into late afternoon and then evening. She had had copious amounts of coffee, polished off a blueberry scone, a sandwich and was now on first-name basis with the staff.

'Madam, we close at eight!' informed Raju, the young boy clad in staff uniform—bright pink shirt and brown pants that were most unbecoming on him and the other male servers in the shop. Either the company management was the secret benefactor of Gulaab Gang or they were all four-year-old girls in pigtails.

Startled, Gayatri glanced at her watch. It was 7.45 p.m. 'Thank you for letting me know. I was just about to leave.'

It was dark outside. Due to the poor street lighting, she did not have a clear view of the warehouse. *Where the fuck is he?* She banged her fist on the table.

Reluctantly, Gayatri left her stake-out and got ready to cross the main road. Being an industrial area, the traffic had now dwindled to trucks and state buses. She waited near a pan stall as a long line of trucks drove passed her. A few people were standing around the stall. One of them—a burly, swarthy man wearing a stained kurta and pajama, with pock-marked face and bloodshot eyes—passed an obscene comment about her backside. Gayatri glared at him over her shoulder. Some of the men had the grace to duck their heads. One or two even walked away. The burly man met her eyes and licked his lips crudely. Two other men standing with him tittered and added to the filthy conversation, boldly looking at Gayatri lasciviously. The trucks continued to cross in front of her.

'Madam! *Aap jaiye*!' The old stall owner urged.

The burly man spun around and slapped the stall owner, hurling abuses at him. Shocked, Gayatri froze. One of his cronies began to trash the counter of the tiny pan stall. People standing around them just stared at the ongoing violence. No one came forward to help. The burly man made a disgusting sexual gesture at Gayatri and started to moved in her direction.

Shit, this is getting out of hand. I need to get out of here! Gayatri took off, swiftly weaving through the slowing trucks in front of her. She reached the other side of the road which was pitch dark and totally isolated. She swiveled her head around. The lit warehouse was some distance away from where she stood.

Gayatri heard footsteps behind her. She glanced over her shoulder. Her face went pale and her body cold. She saw the silhouette of three men behind her. Snickering, they advanced on her, their body language threatening. They had covered the lower portion of their faces with woolen mufflers. All that was visible were their dark, beady eyes trained on one thing—her.

Gayatri's breathing became shallow as she turned around and increased her pace to head for the warehouse. Sweat trickled down the side of her forehead as the footsteps chasing her came closer. Gayatri could hear them describe her body parts in the most vulgar of terms. Goose bumps broke out on her arms and legs; her heart pounded in her chest and her ears started to throb. *Have to run!* The thought never became an action.

A rough grip landed on her shoulder. Gayatri opened her mouth to scream when suddenly a rough smelly hand covered her mouth, ending any attempt to call for help. A pair of hands grabbed her waist and pulled her away forcefully. She flailed her arms and legs wildly as she was dragged off the ground. One of the men came in front of her and snatched her thrashing legs. *Fuck, they are going to take me somewhere.* Fear made her tremble. *These pigs are going to rape me.* The thought pushed her to react. With one backward kick, she hit the knee of the man gripping her waist.

'Oof! *Sali kutiya!*' The man yelled in pain and pushed her.

Gayatri lost her balance and fell face forward against the hard cement. 'Arrgh!' Her cheek crashed into the sidewalk. Her eyes stung. She tasted something metallic in her mouth. Blood!

Just then she realized one of the men was about to level a kick at her stomach. Gayatri instinctively brought her knees up in order to shield her stomach. The man ended up delivering a hard kick to her knee. Gayatri's eyes rolled back in her sockets as pain exploded in her body.

'*Kutiya ko maar ek aur laat!*' One of attackers yelled, adding some heinous abuses. '*Sar par mar! Behosh kar issko!*' Another attacker hollered dropping to his knees, his hand fisted to land blows to her face.

Gayatri understood their plan in a flash of a second. They were going to beat her unconscious or to death and then brutalize her. A sudden calm descended upon her as she exhaled sharply and closed her eyes. *This is it!*

The man on the ground yanked Gayatri's face up by her hair. The sting from it was so intense, she felt her scalp would come loose. She bit down on her lips causing herself more pain. *I need to focus. Focus on the pain!* The man crashed his fist into her face. Gayatri ducked and his fist slammed in the back of her head. Her head felt like the first pin the bowling ball hits. Gayatri saw stars in front of her eyes. She howled like a kicked dog. Sharp rocks and pebbles on the ground jabbed her back as she was pinned on the ground.

Her attackers now clustered around and moved closer to her, snickered at her.

Perfect position bastards, all in a fucking line. The man again yanked Gayatri up by her hair to punch her in the face, his white teeth bared against his dark skin in a maniacal smile. He brought his fist down again but Gayatri dipped at the last minute. She felt the swish of the air as his fist sailed past her and hit the ground. He yelped and his grip on her hair loosened. In that moment, Gayatri grabbed his collar, pulled him down and used the momentum to push herself upright.

Gayatri brought her elbow down hard on his vertebrae near his L1 and L2—the area with the most nerve endings, thus the easiest spot to inflict most pain and disable the opponent. It all went down in seconds. She grabbed the right hand of the man standing closest and, grabbing his wrist, twisted his arm as she pulled at it with all her body weight. He yowled in agony and went down on his knees even as Gayatri jumped up to her feet.

The burly man, the ringleader, backed a few steps. Gayatri saw the confusion on his face. *Save the best for the last! Vanessa Williams definitely wasn't thinking of this as a situation for her song.* Gayatri grinned. Her teeth was stained with blood that flowed freely in her mouth. She spat some out even as she circled the ringleader, her limbs loose but her senses sharply attuned to the smallest movements of each of her attackers. Screaming, the burly man came at her, fists flying. Gayatri nimbly dodged and caught his outstretched arm closest to her. She knew he was off balance and he would totter forward. Gayatri's leg was ready. She kicked him squarely in the face and the tip of her shoe crashed and broke his nose. Warm blood spurted from his face and sprayed her leg. The man passed out before he crash-landed on the ground.

Cursing and abusing her, the two men on the ground jumped up and came at her. Gayatri was quicker than them. She noticed one of them was limping. 'Take this, bastard!' She ducked the first man and pushed him so he staggered past her. She grabbed the other attacker (the one that limped) by his hair, brought his face down with force and her bent knee was ready for him. She smashed his face into her and knee and simultaneously slammed her fists hard on both sides of his head. The man whimpered and fell at her feet.

The only attacker left rushed at her from behind. In a flash, Gayatri dodged and whipped around, wrapping her arm around his neck in a classic choke-hold from behind. He was taller than her. She kicked his leg from behind. He fell down. Gayatri caught his free hand and twisted it behind his back and increased the pressure around his neck. He whimpered and flopped like a fish out of water. He sobbed, '*Maaf kar do, behenji!*'

Gayatri ensuing laugh was cruel. '*Behenji? Kutiya nahi?*' she said in his ear. Her rage was darker that the blood that tricked down her cut lips. Adrenalin ran amok in her broken body, keeping her strong and focused. She maintained the pressure around the attacker's neck till he passed out and went limp on her. She dropped his body on the ground with a loud thud. *Hope he broke his fucking spine!*

Bruised and battered, Gayatri stumbled on her feet. She could only open one eye. The other eye was swollen and stung when she tried to open it, so she let it stay closed. Her cheek felt like it was on fire and she could still taste the dust from the pavement mingled with dried blood in her mouth. She looked down at her bedraggled state. Her arms and legs were bruised in several places; dark stains covered her clothes and bare skin. Some was her blood, some theirs. With her one working eye she looked for her bag and found it. The pain was now washing over her in waves, making her fight for her breath. With her bruised fingers, raw and bleeding, she took out her cell, somehow managed to open the camera on her phone, turn the flashlight on and clicked several pictures of her broken face and that of her attackers who lay on the ground. '*Saalon, har ladki kamzor nahi hoti*!' she kept muttering. She landed a kick or two on their prone bodies. But her adrenalin was gone and the pain of her battered body swarmed her senses. *I can't pass out here! I have to get somewhere safe!* She swayed and the phone slipped from her hand.

Someone caught her. Gayatri swung her only open eye up. *The mad scientist!*

'Shh...you are safe now. Let's get you to a hospital,' he said in a gentle tone, holding Gayatri protectively.

'They attacked me!' Gayatri croaked, unable to stand without support.

'I know. I'm so sorry I couldn't get here in time.'

Gayatri thought she was imagining things. She could not see his face clearly, yet he seemed genuinely concerned and contrite. She moved her lips but no sound came. Her body grew weaker by the second.

'It's the shock. Don't try to talk. I'm taking you to the hospital. I'll call the police and Nikhil as well.' Viraj picked her up in his arms.

'I...I was looking for you...the job...I need...' Gayatri struggled to her keep her head up and speak coherently. Her body was hurting and the man's arms under her felt solid and comforting. She fought the soothing blackness that was fast closing in on her mind.

The mad scientist looked down, meeting her one opened eye. 'Shh...the job is yours. Now close your eyes and rest.' He walked steadily even as he held her.

The shock is making me hallucinate! I'm imagining things. The scientist isn't mad...he's normal...and 'handsome!' Gayatri exhaled the last word and then embraced the blackness. Her head fell back over the broad shoulder under her.

Isaac Asimov

Carrying Gayatri in his arms, Viraj took her inside the warehouse. He had to lay her down somewhere safe before he brought the car out. He took her straight to the lab. Making sure there was nothing combustible on the table, he cleared it in a single sweep, letting the things fall over the floor. He then gently laid Gayatri, who was still unconscious. Her head lolled on the table.

She needs support! Viraj looked around and grabbed a few notebooks. Carefully lifting her head, he slid them under.

He felt his jeans pocket. *Dammit! Where's my cell?* Viraj hated those pesky things. His eyes fell on the cell already in his hand. It belonged to Gayatri. Some of her blood had smeared over the phone and onto his fingers as he held it. Rage seeped into every pore of his six-foot frame. If only he had reached the warehouse minutes earlier...

Gayatri's cell wasn't locked. Viraj first called the police and then Nikhil.

'Nikhil...your sister was attacked by some men outside the lab.'

Nikhil fired some questions right away.

'No, she fought them back. Gave them quite a beating actually. She is umm...unconscious at the moment. I'm taking her to St Mary's hospital. I'll see you there.'

Viraj rushed out and drove the company car to entrance of the warehouse and then laid Gayatri down in the backseat. While driving, he kept checking on Gayatri. Seeing her bruises and one side of the face swollen, Viraj's hands tightened around the wheel. *Dammit! Minutes! Just minutes!* He shook the steering wheel in rage. *Only if I had arrived five minutes earlier!*

'You are one heck of a fighter,' Viraj murmured glancing at her unconscious form in his back seat. Impatiently, he brushed back his dark hair that hung over his shoulders.

Viraj knew he was somewhat of a genius but he also knew better than to trust anyone. His eccentric quirks allowed him to be rude, abrupt yet the genius of his mind forced people to put up with him. *That equation works just fine for me.*

Today, the violence with Gayatri had brought up memories Viraj had long suppressed. Memories of his violent childhood.

Viraj looked at Gayatri again. She lay motionless. The sight left a bitter taste in his mouth. He despised violence against women. It reminded him of his mother who always sported bruises on some or the other part of her body.

Viraj was much like his mother. She was a mathematician whiz and so was he. She loved to read; libraries held more fascination for Viraj than video arcades. She liked adrak ki chai; Viraj drank nothing but that. Like her, he was nothing more than a punching bag to his father. Mind makes it own map!

Viraj's mouth turned at the ends as he remembered the time he was subjected to physical abuse by his father. His seventeenth birthday was the last time his father had hit him.

His mother seldom had a chance to celebrate anything as her life was full of struggles—the struggle to run a house of four on the little money she earned from her math tuitions; the struggle to go one day to the next, suffering physical abuse; the struggle to shield her pain from her young kids; the struggle to go to bed often on an empty stomach. So for a change, she had decided celebrate this occasion by preparing a cake for him.

The plan was to cut the cake before his dad or dad's pet—his older brother—came home. But that night Viraj never did cut the cake. Instead, he cut off a relationship that had died a long time ago.

His father came home early that day, reeking of cheap alcohol as usual. Viraj had backed away into a corner, frightened by his father. If there was a devil, it would look like what his father did in that moment—raised fist ready to attack without provocation; an ugly mouth, and eyes that were red slits filled with rage Knowing the ugliness that was about to unfurl, his mother rushed to save the cake as if it were the last shred of sanity remaining in her otherwise shattered life. She almost managed to save it, but his father grabbed it from her and smashed it right into Viraj's face.

As if this wasn't enough, his father then turned around and slapped his mother. The force of the slap was so strong it made his mother fall to the ground, bawling in pain. That is the moment when something stirred in Viraj. He didn't even realize when his hand tightened to a fist and landed a punch on his father's face. Viraj's anger, which he had suppressed for nearly two decades, had finally surfaced and how.

Viraj pushed his father against a wall that had more cracks than paint. His father futilely struggled to free himself and eventually collapsed, wheezing.

'Let go of your father. Let go, Viraj!' his mother yelped, desperately striking her bony fists at his back. 'Let him go! You will kill him!' His mother's final words got through to him. Viraj immediately let go of his father who now lay on the ground, making blubbering sounds as he struggled to breathe. Viraj ran to the bathroom and threw up.

When he came out, his mother slapped him across his face. 'How could you?' she cried out.

Viraj staggered in disbelief. 'You're protecting him? This man who beats both of us black and blue. Why would you protect him?'

'He is the animal, not you!' was his mother's stoic reply even as she bent down to offer her husband a hand—the same hand that he must have bruised countless times before. Without saying another word, Viraj turned around and walked out of that house and that life.

Without much deliberation, Viraj headed straight to the house of someone who he had trusted for years—the quirky Manohar Keshav, his chemistry teacher. He had been Viraj's guide, friend and mentor since the eighth grade. He was a bachelor who had devoted his life to chemistry and his students.

That day was a turning point in Viraj's life. Mr Keshav took Viraj into his home, no questions asked. For the next few years Viraj shut the door on his former life and worked hard on finishing school. After that, he pursued a bachelor's degree on full scholarship at the University of Massachusetts.

And finally, Viraj made up for all the lost years. He travelled, earned his first paycheck, sold his first invention, bought his first car, had sex for the first of many times to come. He stayed back in the US and pursued two master degrees simultaneously. And after almost nine years had passed, he came back to India, ready to work on his dream project—a high density, ultra-capacitor battery that would enable small planes to fly several thousand miles on a single charge.

On his second day back in India, Viraj had gone home, nervous and unsure. Just as he was about to climb the dusty steps leading to the tiny apartment on first floor, his nosy neighbour Maninder Arora stepped out of his house on the ground floor. The years had not been kind to this man.

'You! We thought you were dead!' were Maninder's first words as he hitched his thin cotton pajamas that revealed more of his anatomy than anyone would prefer to see.

'Well, I'm not!' Viraj's foot hovered on the first step.

'Your father is!' Maninder announced with little tact, all the while pulling the ends of his sleeveless vest that revealed his hairy arms and chest.

Viraj felt like someone had landed a blow to his gut. He put his hand against the wall to steady himself.

For some sick reason, his reaction seemed to have pleased Maninder. 'Your brother doesn't live here. He married some bar dancer and moved to Meerut. Has a son with her. Your mom lives here all alone.'

Viraj forced himself to climb the steps even as guilt flooded his heart. His mother was all by herself, deserted by all the men in her life.

Maninder wasn't done yet. 'She won't live long. If you

want to sell your apartment, let me know!'

Anger mottled his face, yet Viraj continued to climb the steps. His hand was unsteady as he reached out to knock on the familiar front door that had lost most of its polish, but still sported the scotch-taped picture of Ganpati. The tulsi beside the door was dead, its pot broken. He remembered his mother watered it every day, and sometimes Viraj did it for her.

With a low and long creak, the door swung open to his touch. Viraj stepped inside. The smell of stale food and dust was palpable. The room was poorly lit. The blue paint on the walls were peeling in big patches. Sounds of a dripping faucet came from the tiny kitchen in the corner of the apartment. This was not the house he remembered. Cleanliness and order were his mother's obsessions. It was like she maintained order in the house to somehow make up for the chaos in her life.

Viraj quietly walked towards the kitchen. The sink was full of dirty dishes. The single counter was spotted with food stains and there were more empty jars than full on the shelves.

He sensed some movement in the room.

A frail figure shifted on a cot nearby. *Mother!* Earlier black and luscious, her hair now was grey and appeared unkempt in a lopsided bun. Her skin had wrinkled and her arms and face were full of age spots. She lay in a fetal position, her bones jutting out of her paper-thin skin. For a second, Viraj thought that this painful sight would cause his heart to explode. 'Maa!'

Though in her forties, his mother seemed like a sickly woman in her nineties. Her face was haggard and gaunt. Her eyes were glazed and half-closed like she was still trapped in her sleep. She raised her hand. 'Viraj!' her voice was a hoarse whisper.

Viraj held her close, unmindful of her foul body odor. She was as light as a feather.

'It's a girl's name!' Viraj said, choking on tears that he had held back for ages, and repeating one of their favourite jokes.

Within an hour, Viraj packed her clothes, locked the house and got her admitted to a hospital. Over the next few days he found his brother and his new family that were living in squalor. There was an awkward five-minute reunion between the two, after which Viraj handed his brother the keys of a new house and the relevant documents. 'It's all yours!'

His brother broke into tears and tried to hug him. Viraj withdrew, because even though his brother was a victim much like him, he had done nothing to protect his mother or younger brother. 'Be a better father to your children than the one we had.'

In the following months, Viraj concentrated on caring for his mother and giving a 100 per cent on the job. Soon, his mother's health improved radically as the gloom of her past life faded from her body and mind. She finally found happiness with none other than Manohar Keshav and was now living with him. They felt they were too old to be married, but young enough to find love. Viraj supported her in this unconditionally. He bought them an apartment in an upmarket area and showered his mother with materialistic comforts that she'd only dreamt of until now. She accepted the apartment but returned everything else as she thought that they were an excess. So Viraj bought her something else—a pot with a healthy tulsi sapling. His mother did not return it.

Viraj was pulled back to the present when he heard a groan from the back seat. Gayatri was coming around. 'Where am...,' she tried to talk, but her voice was weak.

'I'm taking you to the hospital. Your brother and the police will be waiting there. You are going to be fine. Just stay with me,' Viraj assured her while keeping his eyes on the road. Gayatri went quiet, as did he. He knew little of Nikhil's sister, but he did know one thing—she was a handful. The advantage of him being quiet was that people dropped their guards around him when they spoke on their cellphones. They assumed Viraj wasn't listening. Wrong! Like Isaac Asimov said, 'Your assumptions are your windows on the world. Scrub them off every once in a while, or the light won't come in.'

Gayatri made hoarse sounds. 'It hurts!'

Viraj winced as if someone had head-butted him in the chest. 'You are very brave. You know Krav Maga?' he asked, trying to distract her.

'Yes…' Gayatri wheezed. 'Been doing it...for ten years...' She gasped, 'Watch out…the bump!'

Viraj slowed the car down, 'Sorry! I'll drive more carefully. We are almost there!' He heard her move and her breathing slowed down. 'I wish every woman could fight for herself the way you did. But next time I hope you have a gun.'

'Nexxxt tiiiime…'

Viraj was pleasantly surprised on hearing the amusement in her laboured voice. 'Sorry, I just…'

'Why didn't…you help?'

Viraj's guilt made it harder for him to speak. 'By the time I got there, the fight was over. I did see you knock some impressive punches.' His words were rushed. 'You are so brave!' Viraj blinked rapidly his mother's bruises flashed in front of him.

'You have witnessed violence against women before, haven't you?' Her voice sounded stronger.

Viraj glanced at Gayatri in the rear view mirror. She was propped up on her elbow. Her dusty hair hung limp on one side her face. The other side of her face was swollen. There was blood smeared around her face and neck. He muttered, 'My mother. My asshole of a father hit her often, sometimes till she passed out.'

Viraj sensed sympathy in her. *She's feeling sorry for me!*

Gayatri winced as she hesitantly touched her lower lip. 'I must look frightening I suppose?'

Viraj clamped his mouth shut. *She is Nikhil's sister. Why the hell am I'm telling her all this?* 'You should rest! We're about to reach the hospital.' His voice sounded sharper than before. Viraj focused on the road and the grating traffic. He heard Gayatri fall back on the seat. He took a quick peep. She was back to lying down.

'You promised me the job!'

A wry smile rolled over Viraj's face. *She doesn't forget!* 'Yes, I did. Once you get better, come back to the lab. Now rest!'

Viraj was rewarded with a soft sigh. He drove to the hospital, trying to channelize his thoughts on the new robotic exoskeleton by Korean researchers which could be controlled by users with their mind instead of thinking about the bruised woman on his back seat. She had found an opening in his mind, one which Viraj thought he had plugged forever.

Isaac Asimov waggled a finger.

National Hero

Gayatri regained consciousness in short, sharp tingles. She was able to grasp a few things immediately. The bed she lay on felt very different compared to what she was used to. Her body felt rested, as if she had been asleep for a long time. And lastly, her nose was picking up a strong smell of medicines and nail polish remover. Gradually, the memory of that fight and the faces of those men came back to her. Gayatri's eyes opened with a jolt as she strived to get out of wherever she was. Her body, however, could not match the briskness of her mind. She struggled to sit up.

'Guy! It's okay. It's okay!' Nik's supporting hand helped her sit up.

Gayatri was still blinking her eyes, trying to adjust to the light. She realized she was in a hospital room and hearing his voice calmed her down. As long as Nik was near, she was okay! Looking around the room, she saw Nikhil on one side and Sneha behind him. She tried to talk, but her mouth felt like cotton. 'What is going on?' Gayatri's voice was hoarse.

'You are in a hospital. You were attacked, remember?' Sneha spoke gently, offering her a glass of water.

Sneha held the glass to her lips and Nikhil assisted Gayatri as she took small sips. Her raspy throat felt much better. 'Thanks!' she nodded.

Nikhil helped her lie back. Sneha walked over to the end of the bed and cranked it up until Gayatri was sitting up in a comfortable position.

'Was I, was I...?' Gayatri asked the first question that came to her mind.

'No, Guy!' Nik squeezed her hand.

Sneha came back to her side and held her other hand. 'You are a national hero! We are so proud of you! You gave it back to those bastards. They are all behind bars now. The mad scientist brought you to the hospital, remember?'

Gayatri felt a much needed relief. And then something hit her. 'National hero?'

'I'm gonna go call the doctor. I'll be right back,' Nik said letting go of her hand. Then he did something Gayatri had never seen him do. He bent and hugged her, holding her tightly, as if she were precious. Gayatri welled up with tears. 'I'm just glad you are okay!' he said and kissed her forehead. Then he walked out of the room clearing his throat.

Gayatri wiped her eyelids. 'So that's what it takes to get a hug from him.'

'He loves you a lot. So do...' Sneha squeezed Gayatri's hand reassuringly. 'Anyhow, coming to the national hero part. A woman who happens to be a construction worker recorded the whole attack. News channels got it and have been running it on air all day. You are a hero to all the women in the country. Nikhil made sure your face and identity stays hidden. No one knows it's you! The video just shows a well-dressed woman taking a beating and then giving those assholes what they had coming. You are so brave. Where did you learn to fight like that?'

'On TV?' Gayatri tried to process everything she had just been told.

'Look there!' Sneha pointed at the side of the room. Gayatri turned and saw two big jute sacks. 'Just some of the letters and cards dropped off at one of the news channels within a day! You are famous, Guy!' Sneha in her excitement used Nikhil's nickname for her.

Gayatri asked, 'Does Papa know?'

'Of course! Your parents caught the first flight and came here.'

Gayatri slumped back on her pillows.

'They are waiting outside,' Sneha said.

No sooner had she said that than the the door opened. A number of people walked in. A female doctor and a nurse, Nik and her parents. Before the door closed, Gayatri caught a glimpse of Nandini and Aditya in the corridor. Nandini managed to give a quick encouraging wave before the door shut.

'Good lord, please tell me none of these ugly bruises are permanent!' were the first words out of Gayatri's father Mr Dutta's mouth.

Before Gayatri could react, a pair of arms embraced her. The fresh, floral scent was familiar.

'Mom!' Gayatri lowered her face only to be showered with more affection. She felt tears fall on her cheeks. 'I'm okay, Mum, I am!'

'Oh stop embarrassing yourself. Gayatri is okay! In fact, I feel sorry for those men,' Mr Dutta chuckled as he hitched his fingers in his vest pocket. He only wore three-piece suits.

'You feel sorry for whom?' Sneha blurted.

'Well, Mrs Nikhil Chandel,' Mr Dutta smiled at Sneha, 'I know my daughter is brave and strong. I'm very proud of her.'

Gayatri hid the surprise in her eyes by pretending to look elsewhere. Her mother sat down next to her, stroking her face.

'Gayatri is on TV for the right reasons after all. I couldn't be more proud,' Mr Dutta's voice dripped with condescension.

Gayatri cringed.

Her mother was a reticent person. Even her smile was measured just enough to look like a smile. 'It's okay, laddo! You are fine and that is all that matters.'

'Yes, yes, you are fine. The doctors said so. Thankfully no rape!' Mr Dutta's voice was loud and clear. Wincing, Gayatri closed her eyes. A comforting hand found hers. Gayatri opened her eyes. It was Sneha who pulled a stool and sat down next to her bed.

'Once your brusies heal we will reveal your identity. Let her do some TV interviews and radio talk shows and then we'll fly Gayatri home.'

'Yes, that would be perfect!' Her mother got up and gently tucked Gayatri's hair behind her ear. 'You need a shower.' She turned to her husband of thirty-five years. 'Why don't you go back to the hotel, dear, and I'll stay with Gayatri. Let me stand by the window and pose for the photographers hanging outside the hospital, like your publicist recommended,' Gayatri's mother suggested.

'Mom, what—'

'Gayatri, don't interrupt your mom!' Her father's booming voice silenced her.

Gayatri saw Sneha narrowing her eyes at Dutta Senior. *She's crazy enough to jump my dad! Don't stop her, Nik!*

'That's a great idea. Make sure to touch-up your hair before you go anywhere near the window. Balding spots are not pretty on a woman of any age!'

'Dad, please!' Gayatri croaked embarrassed for her mother.

'You should go now.' Nikhil's voice came out sharply. 'We will stay here with Aunty and Gayatri. You should go.'

'Yes! The humidity in this place is killing me.' Mr Dutta fanned himself. 'All right, bye everyone!' He blew a kiss at Gayatri who responded with a smile. 'Don't smile yet. It draws attention to the bruises on your cheek!'

Gayatri fisted her hand under the sheet and lowered her eyes.

'Your father is right. I'm sure your bruises must still hurt. Did the doctors give you painkillers?' Gayatri's mother airily addressed the room even as she took out a brush and started combing her light brown hair.

Gayatri's eyes met Sneha's. 'I'm so sorry!' Sneha whispered.

Nikhil shut the door behind Gayatri's father. 'Aunty, can I get you something to eat. Anything you need.' Nikhil's face was stiff and his words, clipped.

'Yes, there is something you can do for me,' Gayatri's mother said, putting the brush back in her bag. She pulled out the gloss next. 'Whatever happens, make sure Gayatri stays here and does not fly back with us.'

Gayatri gasped. 'Maa!'

Nikhil's cocked his head to the side as Sneha's mouth formed a small 'O' of surprise.

'Her father has some boys in mind for Guy! Especially

after she's become famous! Like her father said, "on TV for the right reasons".'

'It will be a pleasure to keep Gayatri away from all that.' Nikhil gave one of his rare smiles.

'Maa!' Gayatri felt tears flood her eyes.

Her mother came to her and patted her cheek. 'I love you so much, Guy. You are braver than your sister or I will ever be. You have so much spirit in you. And I can't let it be killed bit by bit like mine was thirty-five years ago. Live your life free of us.' Her mother planted a soft kiss on Gayatri's cheek.

'Mom!' Gayatri hugged her mother tightly. 'I'm sorry I misjudged you!' The two exchanged a long quiet embrace.

Sneha got up and walked to where Nikhil stood, near the door.

'We'll figure out something to keep Gayatri here, right?' Sneha spoke softly.

'Absolutely! She is not going back anywhere near Sir Dutta,' Nikhil replied.

'He is awful!' Sneha said

'He was always brisk and patronizing. And I thought Gayatri raised enough rabble to deserve it. But I was wrong. It was the other way round. She was rebelling because of the crap she was taking.' Nikhil's gaze was pensive.

'I could throttle him for the way he spoke to his daughter!' Sneha blurted.

'I might just!'

Gayatri's mother cleared her throat. Sneha and Nikhil turned to her.

'So how are you going to keep Guy from going back with us?'

Nikhil and Sneha exchanged blank looks. Nikhil walked to Gayatri and patted her cheek. 'Don't worry, we will come up with something. You are not going anywhere.'

Sneha joined him and smiled warmly at Gayatri. 'Yes, don't you worry! We will come up with something.'

'I'm sure they will. Don't worry, Guy!' Her mother added.

Gayatri gazed at them one by one and then said, 'I have a job offer!'

A New Beginning

Two weeks later
Warehouse parking lot

Gayatri stepped out of her car. Instead of looking at the warehouse in front of her, her gaze locked sideways. At the pavement few yards away! The place where she was the victim of violence and where she lashed back with more violence! *An eye for an eye! A scream for a scream!*

A hand on her shoulder startled her. 'Are you okay, Guy?'

Gayatri gave a quick firm nod. 'I am fine, Nik!'

A hand slipped through Gayatri's elbow. 'Of course, she is. Our Guy is one tough cookie. Nothing fazes her.' Sneha smiled reassuringly.

'You have my vote too, Gayatri!' Nandini still in the car made a clapping gesture.

Gayatri shook her head. 'Thank you! I could not have done this without you all.'

'Eh! Filmfare award speech!' Nandini teased.

'And keeping the filmy momentum going, *ja* Guy *jee le apni zindagi*!' Sneha slipped something in Gayatri's hand. 'Your official access card.'

'And your badge!' Nikhil handed Gayatri her a laminated picture badge.

'And your khana. Don't forget your khana!' Nandini held out a purple insulated lunch case.

'I'll drop her inside,' Nikhil said.

'I would like to go by myself,' Gayatri suggested taking her lunch case. She drew in a big breath. 'Onwards and upwards!'

'Go tiger! I'll send a car for you. It will be parked here all day. The driver will text you his number,' Nikhil said getting back into the car.

'Eat your food, okay?' Nandini added.

'Bhukkad!' Sneha poked fun.

As Nikhil drove out, Gayatri could still hear Sneha and Nandini going at it.

Smiling wryly, Gayatri turned around to face the lab. Smoothening her navy blue sailor pants and satin polka dot blouse, she took her steps slowly. Her high, pulled-back sleek ponytail brushed her back. In the past two weeks since the attack, Gayatri's life and many of her personal equations with people had changed. But for the better! Her parents went back home without her. Two days after Gayatri was released from the hospital, Viraj emailed all his investors including Mr Dutta about the lab's new manager of operations—Gayatri Dutta.

Nikhil and Sneha had insisted on Gayatri staying with them while she recovered. And just like that Gayatri had found a new family. For the first time she was witnessing the kind of life a good, strong and educated woman could create for those she loved. *Sneha! I have a new mum and this one kicks ass! And adorable little Vey. It's fun being around a kid you aren't responsible for. And Nandini is the perfect mom's aunty-friend.* Gayatri smirked.

She felt her nerves shudder and shake. Her perfectly manicured fingers tightened around the card in her hand.

She stopped at the opaque front glass door and took a few deep breaths to refocus her thoughts and channelize them in an optimistic direction.

Gayatri was, however, completely unaware of being watched.

Text Me!

So Ms Dutta, you did show up! Viraj studied Gayatri on the CCTV camera fixed above the front door. *Though injured, you were persistent, and I, momentarily, an idiot.*

She looks nervous. Viraj smirked and adjusted his glasses. *Nervous is better. Nervous is easy to control.*

In the past weeks, the video of Gayatri being attacked and then defending herself had gone viral. It was all that the news channels aired for days on end. Countrywide marches were held celebrating the brave woman. Women in every city were rejoicing for the unknown woman who fought back single-handedly against three serial rapists and won. The attackers who were recently released on bail were arrested again. There was a long chargesheet of assault, domestic abuse and rape against their names.

The country discovered a new hero, and the media, a solution to achieve higher TRPs. Politicians, celebrities and the media were drooling to become best friends with the modern day Rani Laxmibai. However, Gayatri shunned all publicity. Nikhil's team of top lawyers came down hard on the matter of privacy and were successful in shrouding her identity. The law gave the woman the right to stay anonymous and Gayatri chose that route.

Two days after attack, Viraj was sitting on his balcony sipping some coffee when he decided to bring up a matter with some of his 'mates'. 'Why did she not take this opportunity to become famous? She probably thrives on adulation. Daddy's spoiled princess would have become a celebrity overnight! She wouldn't need this job or any other job then! She could make money off cutting ribbons. Not that she needs more money to begin with,' Viraj scoffed, chugging his coffee. The fat sparrow cheeped, shook his wet furry body and went to sleep. The other two sparrows followed suit. 'I gave her the job because I felt bad. But that is where this ends. She is on her own when she starts, *if* she starts.' Viraj frowned in irritation. Just then a beep on his cell alerted him of a text. Viraj glanced down and muttered like a grouchy mother-in-law, 'She reads minds too?'

Gayatri had just texted him.

Hi! Hope you are doing well. I was wondering, when could I start?

'Where the heck did you get my number from?' is what he wanted to write back but he decided that would be childish. He exhaled and let his fingers type on impulse.

'Aren't you still in the hospital?'

She did not text for a minute or two.

Viraj kept glancing at his cell expectantly. Eventually, he grew impatient.

'When do you want to start?'

Gayatri's response was instantaneous.

'The sooner the better!!!'

Viraj quipped sarcastically to no one in particular, 'Of course, one exclamation point would not be exclamatory enough.'

Reaching out Viraj took a long big sip of his coffee. *Think it's time you met the crazy mad scientist.* His fingers flew over the keyboard.

Come when your bruises stop showing.

Viraj felt as tall as the directory lying near his feet for typing that rude message. But he was seeing the bigger picture. Keeping her at distance was crucial. That night Gayatri's injuries, her bruises had left a mark on him. Even though she was the one wounded, Viraj somehow became vulnerable. He was somehow connected to Gayatri. Viraj trained his eyes on the inky night sky. The city lights cast a warm, fuzzy glow on the dark ocean. Viraj refused to acknowledge his impatience which was more than evident in the way he shook his legs. He was waiting for Gayatri to text back!

He remembered her bruised face as if it were right there in front of him. Since the news had broken, he had followed the news closely eager to catch a glimpse of Gayatri. How did she look now? Were her injuries healing well? But mostly, he wanted to see if her chin was back to pointing up and her eyes were back to shining stubbornly. For someone he had met briefly he remembered a lot about her. Viraj recalled the swiftness with which she had grabbed the cylinder from him earlier at the lab. Her soft lips had curved as she smiled smugly, her coffee-coloured eyes held arrogance and the colour crimson stained her cheeks. And then she had found out who he was. How the mighty fall! Gayatri's expression had been comical. Viraj took another sip staring up at the night sky.

His cell beeped. Viraj looked down at it.

Sorry for the delayed response. I was trying to find a doctor. My bruises will be fully healed in two weeks.

Reading her text, something softened in Viraj's chest. His frown began to fade. He feigned anger at the excitement that sizzled in him at the thought of seeing her again. He squashed his urge to text her.

'Dumb, dumb machine!'

Curses uttered in a courteous voice brought Viraj back to the present. He blinked and focused back on the monitor that reflected the image of Gayatri through the CCTV at the gate. She was swiping the card up and down and smacking it with her hand.

She's going to break the 'dumb' machine! Viraj opened the door and walked out as fast as he could. He swung one of the exit doors open and went around the side of the warehouse. By then, Gayatri had fisted her hand and was banging the machine with all her might.

'Stop!' Viraj ordered. He saw her shoulder jerk under her blouse. She turned, fixing her large brown eyes on him.

'Morning!' Gayatri's voice was low and smooth.

Viraj stood for a few seconds as his eyes surveyed her face. He exhaled contently. Her face was free of all bruises. Then he saw her hazel eyes blink uncertainly. Viraj realized he was staring. He moved forward and stopped in front of the door which had the machine attached to it. He put out his hand. 'Card!'

'What? Yeah, sure!' Gayatri put her card in his hand.

Viraj noticed that she dropped the card in his hand rather than hand it to him. *Good! Be scared of me!*

'I tried swiping it several times. Up and down! Up and down and—'

'Then you decided to punch it!' Viraj held the back of the card to the machine.

'What? No...I...' Gayatri trailed off. The machine made a beeping sound and flashed green twice.

Viraj opened the door. Gayatri was about to enter but he stopped her and handed the card back.

'First learn to use it, then come inside.' Viraj moved inside and shut the door on her face. Till the door the closed Viraj and Gayatri were locked in each other's gaze. Two opponents inside a boxing ring!

As Viraj turned to walk away he heard a thump on the wall outside. He winced thinking of Gayatri punching the machine. The thump was followed by a soft bristling, 'fuck this shit!'

After years, Viraj felt the urge to whistle. And so he did as he treaded back to his office.

Hyde Turns Jekyll

'I can do this, I can do this, I can...' Gayatri wound her fingers tightly around her cellphone as she made her way to the cubbyhole Viraj called his office. *I did not expect a freaking hug, but a polite 'how are you' wouldn't kill that man.* She rapped her knuckles on the door.

Viraj swung the door open. 'What?' His brows were furrowed and his lips, pursed.

Gayatri remembered what Nikhil had said to her once. *Dr Viraj owns and runs this lab. He was the only one you needed to impress!* 'It's my first day here!' Gayatri could hear her voice shake. 'Could you tell me—'

Gayatri scuttled out of Viraj's way as he leaned out. 'Find an empty room, do your work there. You are free to leave any time you want. You are free to come or to not come.' The door shut on her face.

Flabbergasted, Gayatri kept staring at the door. *What just happened?* She cleared her throat. *I should not piss him off anymore.* 'Thank you for this...this job.' Her voice was as uncertain as the look on her face.

Viraj tugged the door open again. Gayatri flashed a smile

at him and opened her mouth to speak but he stopped her short. 'I don't like talking. Find a room and stay there.' He shut the door on her again.

Asshole! Gayatri fisted her hands and retreated. *I can do this! I am doing this! Bigger picture, please!* Gayatri paused and peeped inside the first lab that she stumbled upon. The place was quiet except for a low hum of machines. Gayatri pushed the doors open and walked inside the lab. It was empty. 'Does anyone else work here besides the mad scientist?' She leaned against one of the steel racks. The door flew open behind her. With a big grin she turned to greet the person coming in. 'Hi! I—' she froze. It was the mad scientist with a bunch of papers in his hand.

Viraj noticed Gayatri at the same time. A familiar irritation flashed in his eyes. 'Not this room. Not my lab! Find another room!' He spoke with cool authority.

'I was just looking!' Gayatri smoothed her ponytail trying to mask her nervousness. He had her in knots.

Giving an indifferent shrug, Viraj walked past her. Gayatri got a whiff of his aftershave; it smelled clean and crisp, like water with a twist of lemon. *At least he doesn't stink like his manners!* Gayatri stood there quiet and confused.

A loose paper slipped from Viraj's hand and landed on the floor.

'You dropped some paper!' Gayatri said, her voice friendly.

'Ignore it. Like you, it is not going anywhere.' Viraj pulled a portable stool and took a seat in front of an electronic panel fixed to a bigger panel.

Gayatri gritted her teeth and grinned with the ferocity of a wild animal that could pounce any moment.

Unknown to her, Viraj gave a similar smile except his was more like the wild animal that had pounced and won.

'I'll go and find a room. Thank you!' Swiveling on her heel, Gayatri headed for the door.

Something stopped her—her father's face and the realization that two weeks ago she had physically fought for herself, and now she had to fight again but with her mind instead of hands. *I have to win over Mr Madness. Maybe I could wear a beaker over my head and tattoo the periodic table on my arms!*

'If you are trying to open the door telepathically, let me be the first to tell you it is not working!'

Gayatri exhaled noisily. *Scathing and sarcastic, what more could a woman ask for?* Taking a few calming breaths, she slowly pivoted to face Viraj, specifically his back as he sat hunched fiddling with the panel in front of him.

'I'm sorry if I have offended you somehow. I really need this job. And also, I'm qualified for it. I can show you my degrees. I can really make a difference here.'

Hearing Gayatri's words and her apologetic tone, something melted inside Viraj...again. But to keep up appearances, he turned rude. 'I'm busy!' he barked.

'Please Mr Viraj, give me—' Just then, without warning, someone swung the door open. Gayatri wasn't prepared for the push. 'Ouch!' She toppled. Her desperate hands grabbed the first thing in the vicinity—a steel rack. The rack shuddered violently and some of its contents landed on the floor.

'What the hell!' Viraj bellowed jumping to his feet.

Gayatri winced. A large electrical component had crashed into her hand 'The door just opened, pushing me in,' she said shaking her arm in pain.

Viraj glared at the door. He instantly lost the frown and his mouth eased at the ends. 'Oh it's you! Come inside!'

Huh, Hyde turns Jekyll! Gayatri spun around.

A timid, bespectacled, five-foot-nothing girl, her long hair in a tight braid, clad in a pastel-coloured salwaar kameez, stood at the door. Her skin was smooth and her hands kept tugging at the dupatta around her neck 'Sorry to interrupt! Dr Kalra wanted to show you some tests he is about to run in lab 2.' She then glanced at Gayatri. 'I'm sorry if I hurt you. It was an accident.'

Gayatri was about to speak but Viraj cut her off. 'She's fine. Let's go!'

Viraj went out with the girl, not even sparing a glance at Gayatri.

Astounded, Gayatri watched them leave.

Urghh…the shit-faced scientist actually smiled and that too at that *girl!* Gayatri kicked the steel rack. It shuddered again! *Shoot!* Before anything else would fall on her, Gayatri went after the scientist and the simpleton.

The particular lab that Viraj and the girl had gone to required a retina scan as well as the access card. *Bloody Fort Knox!* Vexed, Gayatri hastily went over to the lab window. She noticed Viraj and an older man confer over something that looked like an engine. The simpleton stood to their side, listening intently. Gayatri noticed Viraj glance sideways at the girl. The girl, oblivious to Viraj's stolen glances, kept nodding at whatever the other scientist, Dr Kalra, was saying.

Just then a minor accident happened in the lab. Dr Kalra coughed vigorously causing an electrical chip with jagged edges to fly from his hands and hit the girl's arm. She let out a shriek and gripped her arm, her face creased in pain. Viraj grabbed her hand and bent down to blow over it. They stood closer than tied branches.

Gayatri cocked her head to the side and smiled the smile again. *Interesting!*

The girl yanked her hand from Viraj's grip. Her face was the shade of a freshly washed beetroot as she walked out of the lab. Gayatri noticed the surprise on Viraj's face, but he went back to his discussion with Dr Kalra.

The girl came out and treaded quickly past Gayatri. Stroking her chin, Gayatri's nutmeg-coloured eyes sparkled as she watched the simpleton head towards the women's restroom.

'Mera tujhse hain pehle ka nata koi...' Humming that song, Gayatri ambled to the women's restroom.

Pimp I Am

A round 8.00 p.m. that day, Viraj came out of his cubbyhole, helmet in hand. He checked the doors of the labs. They were locked. He peered inside through the window. Everything that he and his teams had been working on was in the vaults inside. He slipped the helmet on and walked towards the main door. Reaching in his jeans pocket, he took out his access card.

Before he could swipe the card, the night guard stationed outside opened the door for him with a salute. 'Good night, Sir!'

'If you will open the door for anyone and everyone, then what is the point of having an access card?' Viraj barked. The guard appeared nervous and guilty at the same time. 'Everyone enters,' Viraj lifted his forefinger warningly, 'or exits with their cards only. You are here to ensure the place stays safe, not have it robbed.'

Viraj left the bumbling guard feeling uneasy. He walked towards his motorbike—a black Enfield parked at the last spot in the parking lot. He halted momentarily, speechless for a few seconds.

'You again?'

'Yes. Me...again!' Gayatri waved, leaning against the bike.

Viraj gestured at her to move away from the bike.

'Of course!' Gayatri immediately obliged. 'Did you think about what we spoke earlier?' Viraj skirted around Gayatri and sat astride on his bike. 'Did you?' she persisted. In response, Viraj shut the visor of his helmet, prompting Gayatri into rushed speech. 'It's very important to me…this job, I promise. Please give me a chance to actually work and not just sit in a room!' Viraj extended his foot to kick-start the bike.

Gayatri threw her head back and snapped her jaw shut. *Oh, all right! Let's do this the hard way.* Leaning closer, Gayatri put a hand on the steering of the bike and purposely brought her face in front of his helmet. Blood pounded at her temples and her face turned warm. She was petrified, but sometimes one just has to trust their instincts. 'Sana Kirloskar. Twenty-four, unattached, unmarried. Two older brothers. Father retired, mother housewife-type. I even know where she lives.' Gayatri held her breath. *Please don't let me be wrong! Please, please, please!* Viraj's foot came back to rest on the ground.

Gayatri waited for him to say something. He didn't. His onyx eyes clashed with hers. Viraj's gaze was mysterious like his thoughts, and Gayatri's eyes wide, hopeful and anxious!

'How do you know so much about her?' Viraj finally asked, lifting the visor of his helmet. His glasses got dragged along. Exhaling in irritation, he tried to yank them out the helmet.

'Here! Let me!' Gayatri helped him disentangle his glasses from the helmet. She was buying time. She was about to dive in deep now and she wasn't sure if she would make it back to the top. 'I know you like Sana. And you have probably liked her for a while because she told me you've known each other a long time.' Gayatri drew a breath discreetly.

Viraj wore his glasses. For several seconds he stared in the dark. Gayatri watched him, unblinking. It was too dark to see his expression. 'Does she know? Sana?' Viraj ran his fingers through his hair.

Gayatri did not know many men who had long hair and she always assumed it would make a man look effeminate. But she was wrong. Viraj's face looked more rugged, his profile sharper, his jawline more pronounced. 'Does she?' Viraj repeated.

'That you like her?' Gayatri asked, biting her lower lip. Viraj stayed mute. Gayatri immediately offered. 'No, she doesn't. In fact, she is doesn't like you at all. She is very scared of you.'

Viraj looked up in astonishment. 'Scared of me? You have got it all wrong.' He sneered and started to put his helmet back on.

Gayatri put her hand on the helmet. 'Hear me out. She told me that you were a visiting professor in her college. And you handpicked her to work with you on your "big idea".' Gayatri did the air quote gesture with her fingers. 'She took it though she was apprehensive of working with you and now she is thinking of quitting.'

'What did I do?' Viraj shot back.

Gayatri shrugged daintily.

Viraj hung his helmet on the handle of the bike and put his bike on stand. He got off and stepped close to Gayatri, so close that his chin bumped her forehead and their bodies were nearly touching.

'Excuse me!' Gayatri whizzed and stepped back. *Oh my god, does the weirdo think I have the hots for him?!*

Viraj towered over her. He was pissed at himself. A fleeting touch by her and he was all hot and bothered. 'What do you want?'

Gayatri raised an eyebrow. *Impressive! He guessed.*

'What do you want?'

'A real job in this place.' Gayatri gestured at the warehouse. 'Please!'

Viraj's expression was unreadable now.

'I'll hook you up with Sana Kirloskar. All I need is a job for six months tops. In this place. As the operations-in-charge.'

Viraj cocked his head to one side, his expression searching. 'Hook me up?'

'Hook you and Sana up. Make her fall for you. Get you both together!'

Viraj stared at his sneakers. 'Yes.'

Gayatri drew a breath. She could not believe her ear. 'Yes? Yes?'

Viraj simply nodded and got back on the bike. He raised his helmet to put it on.

'Wait! You won't forget this tomorrow, right? I mean, you will remember our deal, right?'

'I never forget anything important.'

Gayatri jerked her neck back and gave a bemused smile. Her eyes softened. 'Ohh!'

'Sana! Sana is important.'

'Ohh! Of course!' Gayatri bobbed her head. 'So see you tomorrow?' She stepped away from the bike.

'Where's your car?' Viraj asked, strapping on his helmet.

'There!' Gayatri pointed a few feet away from them to the car and the driver who waited obligingly.

'Tomorrow then!' Viraj started the bike and simply rode away.

Gayatri walked to her car with a broad smile on her face. 'I have a job. The pimp I am. Gonna get the scientist laid, hot damn!'

The far right corner of the parking lot still lacked proper lighting. Otherwise, Gayatri and Viraj would have noticed the person standing there, listening to every word they exchanged.

Southie Guantanamo Bay

Next day sharp at eight in the morning, Gayatri and her driver pulled into the warehouse parking lot. She was casually dressed—indigo harem pants, teamed with a pale pink, short-sleeve top tucked in, showing her tiny waist. Her hair was tied high on her head in her signature ponytail, drawing attention to the twinkling solitaires in her ears. Her make-up was sheer and her lipstick the colour of blooming bougainvillea. A black Michael Kors handbag and black and silver gladiator sandals completed her look.

Gayatri spied Viraj's bike parked in its usual spot. Confident, she walked inside the warehouse. The lab was completely silent, save the muffled sound her shoes made on the floor and the low hum of the machines.

Gayatri knocked on the door to Viraj's cubbyhole. No answer! Gayatri put her ear to the door. She heard soft, shuffling sounds come from inside. *Is he having a heart attack?*

Tentatively, she opened the door. Viraj was on the floor doing push-ups, bare-chested and in jeans that hung low on his waist. Sweat beads formed on his upper back adding sheen to his smooth skin. Gayatri stared, not moving. *Scientists are not supposed to look like that!* Viraj was tough, all muscles and sinewy.

She watched his shoulder muscles move under his skin as he heaved up and down. His arms were strong and his jeans were suggestively low. Gayatri felt a heat wave passing through her.

Viraj glanced over his shoulders. He wasn't wearing glasses. With sweat glistening on his face and long hair sticking to his face and neck, he looked dangerous. Gayatri's pulse quickened.

'Get out!' Viraj was breathing heavy from the workout.

'Gladly!' Gayatri immediately backed out, shutting the door behind her. *Crapshoot, he caught me staring!* She rested her head against the wall and closed her eyes. Instantaneously, her mind produced a jpeg. The smooth and glistening skin, the straining muscles, the buffed chest rising and falling, the narrow waist and the low-slung jeans that sat snug on the curve of his hips. 'Oh my!' Gayatri jerked her eyes open and swallowed.

The door to the cubbyhole opened and Viraj walked out, his shirt and lab coat back on and his face free of sweat. He turned left and headed to the lab door, completely ignoring Gayatri.

She hurried to his side trying not to breath in the crisp, salty fragrance coming off of him. He reminded her of rugged mountains. *I need an effing CT scan!*

'Hi! Morning! So what should I do first?'

Viraj stopped short and gave Gayatri a blank stare as if he didn't even know her.

Gayatri felt her heart plummet down her ribs. 'You hired me last night?…Sana Kirloskar.'

'Sana is not here. Why are you?' Viraj barked, resuming his brisk tread.

They were at the doors of Fort Knox. 'I have to do some real work. It will look strange if I continue to just hover around here.'

Without replying, Viraj went on to complete the retina scan and then disappeared inside. The door shut with a loud bang. To Gayatri it sounded like the bang of a gavel announcing her sentence. Gayatri's shoulders slumped as she stared at her sandals. Her bag suddenly felt heavy on her arm and her blouse stifling.

Gosh, this is how he is when he doesn't get periods. Gayatri grumbled and walked past the empty reception to the side of the facility she hadn't seen yet. She opened the other set of steel doors and found two or three unoccupied rooms, bare except for few boxes and some spare equipment. Gayatri started poking around, opening the boxes and testing their weight by pushing them with the tip of her sandal. Approaching footsteps made her stop. Curious, she turned around. It was Viraj.

Now what? Gayatri braced herself.

He stopped in front of her and his hand shot out. Spooked, Gayatri jumped back.

'What?' Viraj was watching her closely, his gaze sharp and assessing. He wasn't wearing his glasses.

'Nothing!' Gayatri glanced down at his hand. He was extending a business card toward her.

'For me?'

'No, for the box behind you!'.

Gayatri took the card by its tip.

'Write a number—your salary.' The instructions were brusque.

'Can it be seven figures?' Gayatri mocked.

'Make it ten! Your brother and his rich friends are paying. Also, write whatever designation you want it to be.'

How about the Prime Minister of the country or your boss? Gayatri nodded, her lips parted in a demure smile. Viraj wasn't done yet. 'In front of the card is the number of Chandel's payroll manager. Tell him you're the one I sent the email about. He'll add you as a new hire'

A relieved smile flashed across her face. Gayatri just stopped short of hugging him. 'Thanks. Thank you so much.' She curled her fingers around the card. 'This is amazing. You are very k—' Viraj turned around and walked out of the room.

'Weirdo!' Gayatri mumbled, a smile still playing on her lips. She hugged the card to her chest. Unmindful of her clothes or the dust around, she sat down on one of the taped box near her. Wriggling her bottom to a more comfortable position, she fished her phone out of her bag. She called the number on the card. The conversation was brief but fruitful. 'Finally! The pimp is on the payroll!' Gayatri whispered after ending the call.

Next, she opened the blinds partially to let in more natural light. Taking her ipad out of her bag, she sat down again.

An hour later someone came looking for her.

'Hi Nik! Guess what? You will be paying me big bucks!' Gayatri winked at him. She slyly closed the candy crush she had been playing on her ipad on mute.

Nikhil extended his hand for a high five. 'So I heard. Congratulations! I'm surprised. I thought you would take us to the cleaners!' Nikhil sat down next to her. 'Now focus on your work here. Viraj is a bit off his rockers. Genius, but off his rockers!'

Gayatri rolled her eyes. 'You don't say!'

'So you don't plan to sit in this room all day, right? What's first on your agenda?'

Gayatri had a serene smile on her face.

'I have seen that smile before. It scares me!'

Gayatri pinched him lightly. 'First thing on my agenda is to get chairs!'

'Absolutely not! He bloody fired a well-qualified chap just for that reason!' Nikhil frowned at her.

Gayatri made an impatient clicking sound. 'Oho! Quit being such an aunty. All izzz well!'

Nikhil got to his feet. 'You are mad. Be careful where you tread, okay?'

Gayatri nodded. 'Okay!'

'So, Viraj and I going out for a while. I'll see you later! Join us for dinner tonight!'

'Okay! I'll coordinate with Sneha.' She smiled at him.

Gayatri waited for fifteen minutes after Nikhil left and then went to the labs. She introduced herself to the seventeen people who worked there describing her role in vague terms. Finally, she sought out Sana Kirloskar. Today, too, Sana was clad in an ordinary salwar kameez with her long hair in a braid. Her footwear was simple and a common wristwatch circled her wrist. Oblivious to Gayatri's presence, Sana was absorbed staring into a tablet in front of her. She wrote on it with a thin stylus.

'Morning, Sana!' Gayatri spoke softly so as to not startle her.

Sana looked up. 'Oh hey!' She glanced around as if double-checking to make sure where they were.

'Hi! I just started working here.' *All thanks to you!*

'As what?' Sana asked softly.

Did she just slight me? Nah! She is too simple. 'I'm the fifth operations manager.' Gayatri winked conspiratorially at her.

'Good luck! Viraj Sir is different!' Sana said, going back to her work.

'Yes, yes he is. I won't take much of your time. I'm asking everyone around here what are the two things they would like to change in this facility if they could. I'm sure you have some valuable suggestions.'

Sana spoke with no hesitation. 'I like it the way it is.'

Gayatri was stumped for a second, but she did not push her. 'Okay sure! Great! Then I'll leave you to your work.'

Gayatri spied on Viraj and Nikhil passing through the corridor outside the lab. Viraj looked inside. Gayatri made it a point to lean closer to Sana right at that moment and ask, 'We are going for lunch today? My treat, you name the place.'

'But…' Sana hesitated.

'We girls have to stick together!'

'So then all of us are going together, all the girls!'

Dammit! 'Sure! Great idea, scientist! Name the place.'

'There is a South Indian restaurant nearby. We'll go there. Around 1.00.'

Gayatri gave her thumbs-up sign certain that Viraj was watching them. 'Awesome! See you then!'

At lunchtime Gayatri came back looking for Sana, who was waiting with three other women.

Gayatri politely nodded as Sana introduced her to each of them. She was introduced first to a plump lady in her mid-forties, Lata Verrapan. Next was a woman closer to Lata's age, Suhani Hussain; the last was an anglo-indian aunty, Christina Mendoza, in a maxi with floral print. They were all scientists who were part of Viraj's team.

Gayatri insisted on driving them.

'Every time I see that pavement I get goosebumps. That is where that girl was attacked. So close to us!' Christina pointed out leaning over the back of the seat. 'There were so many media guys asking around but no one knew her. She must have just been passing through. Car breakdown ho gayi shayad.'

Gayatri kept her eyes away from the spot as best she could, but the strain appeared on her heart-shaped face.

'Wonder why she never came forward? Lagta hai uska rape ho gaya!' Lata gave her input.

Gayatri took in deep breaths trying to calm her thumping heart. Her fingers wrapped around the steering were now trembling. She felt some pee leak into her panty liner even as she pressed her knees together. While she was in the hospital, Sneha and Nikhil had tried to convince her to talk to a therapist. But Gayatri had waved them off. 'I won, right? I beat them! I don't need therapy, I just need time.' And an unlimited supply of panty liners and a bottle of wine every night!

Sana turned around and said, 'No, no, she beat them. The girl is very brave. Not every girl can fight back. I can't!'

'I can teach you!' Gayatri regretted the second the words left her lips.

For a second there was silence in the car and then the aunties in the back burst out laughing. Sana, too, smiled.

'You are funny!'

Gayatri's laugh was forced.

The South Indian restaurant was just a five minute-drive away. The tables were wobbly, plastic chairs were haphazardly placed around and the servers wore lungis and seemed to be teleported straight from Meena Amma's village in Chennai Express.

Gayatri perched her bum on the edge of the chair, kept her elbows in her lap and did not dare to glance at any surfaces. *I'm just here to interrogate! And what better than a southie Guantanamo Bay.* Gayatri ordered some filter coffee and idlis. The lunch was nearly an hour long—an hour in which Gayatri spoke the least, nodded more and schemed the most.

Take My Blood! Happy Friday!

Once they got back, Gayatri went back to her office—the one with boxes and dust. She wasn't alone for long. Twenty minutes or so later, the door swung open. Sighing, Gayatri closed the Candy Crush game again.

Gayatri glanced up at the visitor. *I was expecting you!* She tucked her arms around her knees. 'Hello!'

Viraj shrugged his shoulders and slid down on the floor to join her. He stared at the box on which Gayatri sat.

'Chairs are overrated,' Gayatri voiced. She waited for him to speak. Viraj fidgeted with his glasses, then with the pen in his hand. After clicking the pen on and off several times he finally said, 'You went for lunch with them!'

'We did!' Gayatri confirmed, putting her Ipad down. 'She's sweet.'

Viraj nodded and touched his nape. *I was right! He does have a hard on for behenji.* 'But I'm sorry, I don't think it is going to happen. You and her!' Gayatri fake-cringed. 'Sorry!'

'Why?'

'Because she is...' Gayatri paused as if searching for words. 'Chairs!'

'Chairs?' Viraj raised an eyebrow.

'She likes chairs. You don't. She likes a normal work place, you don't. So you both are very different even though in the same profession. She doesn't finds you wierd...'

Viraj stayed quiet from some time and then got to his feet.

'So should I tell Sana to stop whining and just deal with it.'

'Don't bother!' Viraj muttered without much conviction. 'I guess it's not going to work.'

Gayatri panicked and jumped up. 'You don't give up on an invention just because the first test did not work. You keep at it, smoothen out the chinks. Test again? Right?'

Viraj did not appear convinced.

'Are you going to give up on the love of your life just because things like chair and tables? C'mon!'

Viraj gave her meaningful look. 'She is not love of my life or whatever. I just I think we are compatible because we are from the same field. Commonality.'

You just killed Devdas with that one sentence! Gayatri squirmed. 'Still the pursuit of commonality and compatibility requires effort. Like arranged marriages. That is why they work beautifully.' *I'm talking such crap!*

Viraj rubbed his cheek and stared at his sneakers. He was mulling. Gayatri watched him with fingers crossed behind her back. *Please don't give up on Sana Aunty!*

'Fine, she can get a chair!' Viraj turned around, ready for a quick exit.

Gayatri could only stare. *Did he just agree for a chair? In for a penny in for a pound.* 'You can't just get one chair. Please get just a few more. I'll place them randomly around the lab or in some other room...'

'Not in the break room or food room or coffee room. That is just not acceptable.' Viraj's flaring nostrils and furrowed eyebrows made a better point than his words.

Gayatri hesitated, measuring him for a moment. 'We were talking about chairs.'

Viraj straightened his lab coat. A grunt was only his answer.

'Do you want one for your office?'

'NO!' The word rang out like a brick dropped on a glass plate. Viraj left the room.

Gayatri kept her gaze fixed on the door in case the scientist popped back again. When he didn't, she finally relaxed. 'Compatibility and commonality khaas, baki sab bakwaas! What crap!' She quickly texted Sneha.

'About to order CHAIRS!'

Sneha's reply was prompt.

'Congrats! Just telling you what I tell Nandini and will be passng on to Vey in a decade: think before you act and not the other way around.'

One more gyani! Grinning, Gayatri texted back.

YES MA'AM!

That evening several chairs were delivered to the warehouse. Gayatri played her own Game of Thrones or khel kursi ka and placed them randomly in the lab, ensuring that no more than two were laced in any room.

Encouraged by the devil inside her, Gayatri left one outside Viraj's cubbyhole door.

Next day, Gayatri checked on that chair specifically. It was gone. *The mad scientist probably burnt it.* She went back to her room and the faithful quiet boxes.

For the rest of the next week, Gayatri stuck to sitting in the empty room far from the lab. Some of the scientist tiptoed to her room and thanked her for the chairs, in quiet tones of course.

Gayatri shushed them and sent them back to the dark side. Hers was the dusty side!

The following Monday, Gayatri came into the lab and headed straight for the dusty side. A pink post-it was stuck to her door. On it someone had scrawled, *Coffee Maker*. Next day another post-it, another request. *Microwave*! Third day, third request! *Vending Machine* ☺ *Please*!

Frowning, Gayatri went inside her office. 'Why don't I just give you all my blood?' The rest of the week passed in Gayatri sitting quietly among her boxes and working on her own personal project.

Come Friday afternoon and she finally had some company. Her boss! In his usual attire—jeans, plaid shirt and lab coat flapping around his knees and the usual sneakers.

'Is she happy with the chairs?' Viraj demanded standing at the door.

'I agree, polite talk is overrated just like chairs!' Gayatri murmured from her side of the room.

'What?'

'Nothing! Yes Sana the scientist is very happy with the chairs. She and I are going for movie this Sunday.'

Viraj contemplated Gayatri for a few seconds. There was no denying Gayatri's prettiness in her dark blue jeans, white shirt and her face made up lightly. The way she sat cross-legged on the floor amongst all the boxes made her appear younger and fragile. She had not taken a chair for herself. It surprised and impressed him. Again Viraj somehow felt like a cad. 'Should I come for the movie?'

Gayatri puckered her nose and shook her head. 'A bit too early. Sana hasn't completely warmed up to me yet. Let me figure her out a bit more. I'll update you on Monday?'

'Okay!' Viraj left the room as abruptly as he had come.

'Happy Friday to you too!' Gayatri reached out for her iPad.

This time the scientist popped back again and he brought goodies. Gayatri got to her feet slowly. 'Chair!' She tilted her neck, amused and curious. 'For me?'

Viraj stopped a few feet away from her. He rolled the chair toward her. 'For you!'

Gayatri stopped the chair just it was about to roll onto her. She pushed it back. 'Thank you, but no thanks. I do appreciate the gestu—'

'Why?' Viraj's tone's was curt.

'Just saying' Gayatri gestured, 'like a door needs a room, a car needs a driver, a chair needs a desk. So...' She waved her hands at the boxes. 'No desk! But it's okay! Boxes work for me.'

'Then get a desk,' Viraj shot back.

A smile grew on Gayatri's face bit by bit. Viraj stepped back to see it in its full glory. Then he left without a word.

'Mission Impossible 6 just happened.' Still smirking, Gayatri quickly ordered a desk for herself. 'Happy Friday indeed!'

Monkeys and Manuals

On Monday morning, Gayatri entered the warehouse and went straight to Viraj's cubbyhole. She knocked on the door. 'Morning!'

'Come in!' he hollered.

On entering his tiny office, Gayatri's eyes popped out. The scientist was sitting on a chair. *The one I left outside his office. Mission Impossible 7, 8 and 9!*

'Sana and I spend several hours yesterday. The movie was good.' Gayatri opened with that.

Looking up from the papers in front of him Viraj gave her a penetrating look. When he wasn't wearing glasses, Viraj's gaze could be unnerving. And he wasn't wearing glasses today. He had a look that could transport one from the ground to a petri dish in seconds.

Gayatri noticed some water dripping from his wet hair onto his forehead. It slowly trickled down his forehead and into a cheek. The drops then fell on the papers in his hand. 'Bloody shit!' He ground his teeth as he waggled the papers to shake off the drops.

'Hold on!' Gayatri clucked her tongue and grabbed the

box of tissues wedged in the corner. Swiftly taking out a few tissues, she began patting his hair, using the tissues to absorb the excessive moisture. 'You ran out of towels at home?'

'What do you think you are doing?'

Gayatri paused. 'What? I am just...' She flickered her eyes from the napkin in her hand to his wet hair to his eyes.

'You are touching me and I did not invite you to do that!' Viraj's voice grew deeper. His cold words did not match the fire in his eyes. Confused, Gayatri's fingers strayed further down his cheek. His skin was warm and smooth. Her fingertips tingled. Gayatri quickly withdrew her hand and put some distance between them.

'Sorry!' Embarrassed, Gayatri moved and the tissues stayed glued to his damp cheek. She wiped her hands on her designer trousers leaving damp patches on them.

'Why did you want to see me?' Viraj asked even as he plucked the damp tissue and tossed it in the bin.

'You were dripping. I was only trying to help!' Gayatri tried to not to appear as flustered as she felt. She rubbed her palms against her trousers again to erase the feel of his skin from her fingers.

'Asking again, why did you want to see me?'

Gayatri blurted, 'I want to help you with Sana but I'm not a pimp.'

That got Viraj's attention. Very slowly he got to his feet.

Gayatri's pulse shot up. However, she did not back down from her assertion. Viraj stretched, rolled his shoulders and then sat down continuing to wipe his hair and nape.

'You missed a spot near your left ch—side of your face.' Gayatri gathered her thoughts. 'I want to help you with Sana—'

'You will help me with Sana,' Viraj cut her off. 'That's the only reason you have this job.'

Wish I could vapourize you! Gayatri smiled a big wide smile that was more fake than boobs made of silicon. 'You did not let me finish!' she cooed. 'I am going to help you but with some conditions.'

'Go on!' Viraj got up and reached out for the coffee cup kept on the other table. He tripped over his open laces, but steadied himself by grabbing the corner of the table in the nick of time. The coffee sloshed in his cup and splattered on the papers on his table.

Way to go, genius! Coffee stains are better than water! Gayatri hid her smirk staring at the ceiling, as Viraj tried to contain the spill.

'You can look, it's decent now!' Viraj quipped sarcastically.

Gayatri blinked her eyes. 'I was just…I was—'

'You have wasted my ten minutes already. Either get to the point or get out!'

Jerk! Gayatri took a deep breath. 'Look, Sana is a nice girl, but if it is to truly last between you both, which I hope it does, then you really should get to know her. Not just know her because of the things I tell you. It's simply not right. Not for you or for her. But more for you.' Gayatri's fingers curled in her palm and she bit her lower lip. *Please don't fire me!* What seemed a very logical speech when she had delivered it to the mirror, now sounded to her like a drunk skeleton dancing on a tin roof.

'I'm not even using 0.00.'

Now who's wasting time? Gayatri rolled her eyes.

Viraj nearly grinned at the eye roll, but he contained

it. '0.00001% of my brain trying to decipher what you just alluded to. Either speak now—'

'Or forever hold your peace!' Gayatri finished. 'I'm sorry! That's just a part of a western wedding vows.' Gayatri saw him frown thickly and a muscle ticked in his cheek.

Gayatri had no idea that Viraj's clenched cheeks were not a reflection of his impatience but a mechanism to stem his smile, similar to a curtain obscuring the light.

'Sorry, I'm digressing!'

'Yes, you are!'

Gayatri felt rushed. 'If I tell you everything that Sana likes, where is the fun in that? How do you really get to know her? It's like I give you a book on monkeys and you read it cover to cover. But there is no interaction with them. No practical knowledge!' Gayatri noticed Viraj's blank gaze. 'Oh c'mon, would you like to drive a car or do you just want to read a manual?'

Viraj turned away from her and wrapped his arms across himself. He tucked his chin under trying to kill the laughter bubbling in his throat. Gayatri had so naturally compared the alleged woman of his dreams to monkeys and car manuals. In that second, Viraj knew he should never trust his love life to Gayatri. The girl did not have a romantic bone in her body. And thankfully neither did he. But he did like to laugh.

'Are you okay?' Gayatri stretched her neck. *Oh my god! Is he crying? He is making weird sounds and his shoulders seem to be twitching.*

'I'm fine!' Viraj cleared his throat and bought some time as he picked up his glasses and cleaned them with an end of his always untucked shirt. 'All this might take time. I am focused on my project. The product has to be sent out to testers in two months.'

'I'll make it easy for you. Twice a week, an hour at lunch with me. That's all! You do eat, don't you?!'

'Even monkeys need their food!' Viraj murmured, removing the last bit of amusement from his face.

'I'm sorry, I didn't hear you!'

Viraj put his glasses back on and faced Gayatri. 'Why lunch with you? I don't want to know you.'

'Ditto moron!' Gayatri muttered under her breath.

'I'm sorry, I didn't hear you!' Viraj mimicked her words and tone.

'I'll just be telling you stuff about Sana. You wouldn't be getting to know me! You gave me a job and I'll give you Sana.'

Virak smirked and sat down on the stool. He crossed his arms and two of his top shirt buttons popped open. Gayatri averted her gaze from the smooth brown skin above his muscled chest. She remembered how he looked doing push-ups. Her body felt warm. She needed some air.

'My planner is somewhere under the papers on the other desk. Add whatever days, whatever time you have in mind. But I don't do lunch before 3.00 p.m.'

Planner? He is into such antiques! Gayatri rummaged in the direction he had pointed. 'Found it!' She picked up the planner and flicked it open. 'So day after tomorrow around 3.30 p.m.!'

Viraj grunted.

Gayatri penciled in the appointment, closed the planner and put it back on the desk. 'See you around. Thank you!' She had her hand on the doorknob when he called out.

'Stars!'

Gayatri stopped and turned to look at him. 'Excuse me?'

'Next time when you want to make a romantic point, mention stars not monkeys,' Viraj paused, 'and definitely not manuals.'

Go to hell! Flushed, Gayatri nodded. 'Ohh okay, sure!'

Viraj gave his usual grunt.

Gayatri blew a frustrated sigh. 'You will have to do more than grunt with Sana.'

'You are not Sana, are you?' Viraj replied without even bothering to glance at her.

Gayatri could not think of anything smart comeback, so she quietly exited his office without stomping her foot or slamming the door. She missed Viraj's mischievous grin and his soft whistle.

A New Star System

Once Gayatri left the room, Viraj stared at the door. A benign smile sat on his face. Getting up, he stretched his arms above his shoulders. *Monkeys and manuals!* A deep chuckle burst in him. Pushing a lock of hair off his forehead he walked over and took out his planner. He opened it to the day after and studied Gayatri's neat handwriting on it. He put it back, still whistling. His eyes snagged on his open shoelaces snaking around on the floor. He placed each foot on the table and nimbly tied the laces in neat bows.

Next, he unbuttoned his low hanging, hip-hugging jeans, tucked in his red-and-blue checkered shirt and buttoned his jeans back. He walked over to a stained window that overlooked the adjoining building. Seeing his hazy reflection in the glass, he took out a small comb out of his back pocket and combed through his rakish long hair. Then he took off his glasses and placed them on the chair. A look through them and one would find that they had no power. They were merely there to complete his look. Viraj then smoothed the bridge of his nose under his eyes to alleviate the red mark his glasses left there.

The last bit of transformation came when his usual dour, distracted look vanished from his face. Instead he smiled an astute, wicked smile and his eyes, which had abstractness in them, now twinkled with humor. 'If Ms Dutta is a con, then so are you!' Viraj said to his reflection.

His gut told him not to trust Gayatri. There were many layers to her beneath the façade she presented. And Viraj trusted his gut and instincts! Shifting the table back, Viraj created more space on the floor. Growing up around an abusive father who could flare up in seconds, Viraj knew how to read people, observe telling signs and preempt their actions. Having to watch his back constantly had sharpened his instinct over the years. And it screamed that Gayatri Dutta was nothing but TROUBLE. Unbuttoning his shirt, Viraj flung it on the seat of the stool. 'You are using me, Gayatri! Why are you doing this job, taking crap from me? Why are you so desperate?' Viraj murmured, rotating his wrists and flexing his shoulders.

Over the weeks, Viraj could not help but feel respect for her, albeit grudgingly. He had thrown a lot of curve balls at her but she had taken it all in her stride. His high-handedness, his utter disregard for her background or connections, the dusty room where she spent her days sitting on boxes! *She is tough!* Viraj would give Gayatri that. She had observed his sly interest in Sana but she was foolish to think that Sana Kirloskar was his weakness. *People were never his weakness!* Viraj got down on the floor and started doing his pushups.

The years had piled up on him and he now felt it was time to settle down—enter a marriage of convenience, have a kid or two and break the vicious cycle his father had started as an abusive parent. He wanted to pass on his genius gene and give the world a few intelligent people. In his opinion, the world had more than its fair share of idiots!

Thirty-seven! Thirty-eight! Thirty-nine! He intensified his workout. However, Viraj's whole marriage-plan hinged on one thing and one thing alone—his partner had to be a fellow scientist. He had slept around with women of various ages and backgrounds. *The test tube had been thoroughly tested.* Viraj smirked at the analogy. Scientists were the intelligent and non-violent bad boys! Their eccentricities were adorable at least for a few rounds of dates and sex. And they never came after their exes with abusive calls and violent visits.

Fifty-three! Fifty-four! Fifty-five! Sweat was trickling down his back. Another must have! The woman should not have an expectation of love! In fact, Viraj welcomed every emotion but that. He wanted nothing that forced him to stay in a relationship that wasn't working. Under no circumstances would this rule be broken.

And Sana Kirloskar fit the bill. She was a scientist, she was intelligent, reasonably pleasant to look at and she had no arrest record. Her family was a normal, blue-collared family, no visits to asylums of any kind. *No crazy relatives!* Oh yes, Viraj did extensive background checks on the people he hired. Not just because of the secret nature of his work but also because he felt background checks could uncover all there is to know about a person. Yup, scientists can be stupid too!

Viraj started his eightieth push up. As he exerted his shoulders and hands, his breathing became laboured. Gayatri trickled into his mind.

She is as much a manager as I'm a bumbling scientist. Viraj was playing a part—a part that was now second skin to him, a stereotyped version of eccentric traits and unkempt appearance. He drew a line at constantly holding a bubbling beaker. A chuckle escaped his lips even as he exerted his shoulders to push him up. 'The things I do!'

Couple of months ago, Aditya Sarin had been acting all friendly with Viraj. He got into the habit of dropping in unannounced, armed with books on various scientific subjects, hoarding Viraj's time with repetitive questions. After a week, Viraj had enough of being stalked by the billionaire.

One day, like the piper, Viraj led Aditya into his lab, which he knew was empty during lunchtime.

Aditya followed him with a new book and the same old questions. Viraj then lured him into a corner and as Aditya talked, Viraj put on his safety goggles and gloves. Aditya was too busy being a scholar to notice Viraj's new accessories. Discreetly filling a test tube with small amounts of potassium chlorate, he added a few drops of sulphuric acid. Aditya was about to step away because of the foul smell when Viraj dropped a pen from his pocket. As a reflex, Aditya bent down to pick it up, when Viraj dropped a piece of candy in the tube. Abracadabra! Long dancing flames popped out of the tube, with loud sizzles and cracking noises and there was a burst of grayish fumes. The pungent smell filled the room faster than smoke from a smoke machine. An alarmed Aditya grabbed Viraj's shoulders. 'I got you.'

Viraj had not accounted for Aditya's quick reflexes. 'Let go!' Viraj hollered, trying to hold on to the beaker that was now smoking profusely. *I should have paid better attention to the portions!*

Aditya bolted. As Viraj was about to self-congratulate

himself, Aditya came back with a fire extinguisher. Another thing Viraj hadn't accounted for!

'Don't! Stop! Stop!' Viraj could only sputter as Aditya sprayed him hand to head and back with a fully topped fire extinguisher. Foam and its bitter, soapy taste permeated his every orifice above the shoulders. 'Bloody fool!' Viraj screamed as he walked to the restroom, not giving a damn about the messy trail he left on the floor and unsure of who he was cussing—himself or 'The Extinguisher Man'.

The incident didn't go as Viraj planned, but the outcome was exactly what he was hoping for. From that day on, Aditya Sarin kept his distance.

'Hmmphh! 108! 109! 110!' Viraj could not help but wonder how stupid most people could be. A person like him who understood concepts like Casimir effect, quantum field theory, thermodynamics, and even parts of nuclear chemistry, 'will nott understandddd basic,' exertion made Viraj stress out the words, 'basiccc ruless of societyyyy and personal groommming. 121! 123! 124!' The hum of the computer and his breathing filled the otherwise quiet room.

The concept of a 'proper' society made Viraj think of Gayatri again.

From her perfectly tied hair, to her coffee-coloured eyes that covered an entire spectrum of emotions in seconds, to her smooth cheeks with high cheekbones which were always either flushed in anger or awkwardness around him, and her mouth that often broke into a smile was spectacular. Two things came to his mind when he thought of her lips—peaches and rose buds! Viraj tumbled down to the ground; his arms and shoulder felt like they were on fire, much like the candy he dropped in the test tube.

Peaches and rose buds!. Viraj smacked his head with the palm of his hand. *Who are you? A scientist, a farmer or a bad poet!*

Huffing and puffing harder than a steam engine, Viraj rolled on his back, uncaring of the dust on the floor sticking to his back. 'I know what it is!' Viraj sat up and flicked the sweat form his forehead. He finally understood his interest in Gayatri, who was so different from the women that he usually found attractive.

A newly discovered star system or any new breakthrough fascinated Viraj but not until he had read all about it, cross-checked the facts, debated and analyzed it to its last letter. *That's why I find Gayatri interesting!* Relieved, Viraj got up, mussed his hair, wiped his face and neck with some tissues. He sprayed on some deodorant, wore the glasses followed by the plaid shirt loose and hanging around him. Bending down he untied his laces and then glanced at the chair in his cubbyhole. 'I'm keeping you!' Viraj frowned at the possessive tone in his voice. 'For now!' he added and then grabbing his laptop left the office.

The scientist did not realize he had just used stars as an analogy!

Asswipes

On Wednesday morning Gayatri took special pains in getting ready. Her stomach was uncharacteristically knotted and her eyes seemed over-bright. By the time she reached the lab around 8.50 a.m., she had already consumed four cups of coffee. Today was the day she lunched with her boss. Her boss from Mars!

Gayatri looked up at the sky as she swiped her access card. *Why couldn't I think of some idea to save the world instead of constantly having to save my ass or get my ass out of trouble? Be positive, Queen Antoinette! Be positive!* She opened the door to her office. 'Ohh! Hi Nik! What are you doing here? Everything okay?'

'You tell me?' Nikhil straightened away from the desk he had been leaning on. His face held its usual deadpan expression but his green eyes had a focused look that made Gayatri anxious. She bought some time as she took off her bag and put it in the drawer of her spanking new desk.

'You are going for lunch with Viraj I heard?'

Gayatri swung around, with an expression of being hurt. 'Are you spying on me, Nik?'

Nikhil shook his head. 'Drop the act, Guy! Why?'

With affected casualness, she lowered herself in her chair. 'Don't you go out for business lunches with your team as a boss!'

Nikhil came closer and stared down at her. Gayatri avoided his direct gaze. 'I have known Viraj for several months now. We've met on a regular basis. I have worked with him closely and still do. I even wrote him his first big paycheck. But he has never agreed to go for so much as a cup of coffee with me or any of his other partners. And here you are, barely three-weeks-old in the company and he is going for lunch with you!'

Gayatri shrugged her shoulders and fiddled with her computer. 'I have my charms, Nik!'

'Are you sleeping with him?'

'Are you mad?' Gayatri jerked.

'Sorry!' Nikhil raised his hands. 'Just testing all my theories!'

Gayatri grunted. 'I'm busy!'

'Whatever you are planning please don't mess with his head, Guy. It's messed up already! There is too much at stake here.'

'Why don't I carve that on my forehead!' Gayatri grumbled, narrowing her eyes.

Nikhil gently pulled her earlobe. Gayatri brushed his hand away.

'Remember, you are an adult. Adults are expected to act responsibly. So act responsibly.'

'Okay, Nikhil aunty!' Gayatri stuck her tongue out at him.

Nikhil went towards the door. 'Actually, your boss is an

eligible bachelor. He's intelligent and now he is loaded.'

'And he's mad!'

'You are not perfect either, Guy!'

Gayatri tossed paper clips at Nikhil. Giving her a small smile, he left.

Just then the door opened again. 'You want more papercli—' She froze.

Viraj came in shrugging into his lab coat. He stopped abruptly, glancing at her desk.

'You said I could get a desk,' she blubbered nervously, unable to decipher his expression.

Viraj transferred his cryptic gaze at her. 'I did?'

'Yes! You did!' She nodded hastily. 'The other day, you came in and saw me sitting on the floor.'

Coming closer to her, Viraj tripped over his laces. Gayatri couldn't help but roll her tongue in her cheek. *Klutz!*

'Can we go now? I'm busy later.'

Gayatri glanced at her watch. 'The restaurant where I was planning to take you won't be open right now.'

Viraj pivoted and walked out of the door. 'Outside! Ten minutes!'

Gayatri could only stare at the door till it shut tightly. Then in anger, she flipped over the penholder on her desk. 'Brilliant! Just fucking brilliant!'

Viraj purposely waited outside her door and heard her curse. His smile was one of deep satisfaction. *Threw you off your game. Less time for plotting!* Donning his usual distracted expression, Viraj sauntered back to his lab. Showing her that she is not in control made her angry. 'And angry people says things and reveal more!'

Completely unaware of Viraj's devious scheme, Gayatri spent the next four minutes anxiously perusing her short hand notes on Sana. Yes, she had made notes on Sana. *I'm an educated pimp.* Gayatri glanced at her wristwatch. She was already minutes past her ten-minute deadline. Grabbing her bag, Gayatri trotted outside. There was no sign of Viraj.

'What the? Kya rubbish!' Gayatri muttered glancing around the parking lot.

The low hum of a motorbike became audible. Gayatri glanced around and she saw Viraj approaching her on his bike. His lab coat billowed around his legs.

Viraj idled in front of her and gestured Gayatri to hop on.

'I'm wearing a...a...' Gayatri fumbled pointing at her knee-length black skater-skirt.

Viraj kept his helmet on and opened the visor. 'Let's do this some other day.'

'No! No!' Holding Viraj's shoulder, Gayatri scrambled on. 'I'll manage.' She quickly withdrew her hand. A courteous smile glued to her lips, Gayatri crossed her ankles and sat with her legs dangling on one side. The back seat was elevated to an angle that had her titling uncomfortably and holding the back guard of the bike. Her skirt kept riding up.

Gayatri gritted her teeth and said, 'We can go now!'

Viraj shuffled the bike a bit. He opened the visor and asked her over his shoulder, 'Comfortable?'

For a second Gayatri could only stare at him. 'More comfortable than I was in my mother's womb,' she said with her teeth clenched.

Viraj hid his smug smile. 'Where are we going?'

'Because it's so early in the morning and on such a short notice, I—'

'I didn't ask why, I asked where!' Viraj cut her off impatiently. *There are a million things for me to do and here I'm baby-sitting Nikhil's spoiled little sister.* He tried not breathe in any more of her perfume—floral and citrusy—which he was beginning to recall from their previous meetings. Viraj quickly started the bike and drove away from the lab.

'Just keep going straight. I'll tell you when to stop.' Gayatri gave him a bright smile in his rearview mirror. Inwardly she groaned and sulked. *I should have said yes to the first marriage proposal that came for me. So what if I was only sixteen?*

Gayatri's problems seemed never-ending. Her skirt kept riding up, showing an indecent length of her thighs. At the red light Gayatri felt herself turn the colour of light as all the men around her ogled at her legs. 'Asswipes!' To her utter humiliation, she felt a familiar sensation in her bladder.

Clamping her legs tightly, Gayatri closed her eyes trying to block out the autorickshaw nearby full of men with sleazy leers. They were raping her with their eyes. Another man in car behind them, old enough to be her father, was nearly standing in his driver's seat to check her out. Mindlessly, her fingers dug into Viraj's back.

'What!' Viraj squirmed at the pinch he felt. He adjusted his side-view mirror to see Gayatri. His forehead wrinkled when her saw her eyes tightly shut and her mouth twisted as if she were in unbearable pain

I Look like Sana

'What the hell?' Viraj turned around. And then he saw them—the men with the frenzied lust in their eyes! Hungry, rabid wolves would make a prettier sight! Viraj glanced down and saw the why. Gayatri's skirt was riding up her thighs and she was desperately trying to pull it down.

Viraj felt furious enough to explode. In a flash of a second, he hopped off the bike, a bit awkwardly, and parked it. Gayatri opened her eyes. She tried to balance herself. 'What are you doing? The signal is about to turn green,' she sputtered.

Viraj shrugged out of his lab coat. Swiftly, he covered her legs with the coat and tucked it firmly under her legs on either side.

Viraj glared at the autorickshaw and its occupants. The men continued to violate Gayatri with their eyes. Viraj landed a tight slap on the face of the puny weasel of a driver hanging half out of rickshaw. The man winced and rubbed his cheeks.

Then Viraj yelled something obscene at the men.

The tips of Gayatri's ears burned. She grabbed Viraj's arm. 'Please, let's go. We are holding up the traffic. Please!' she pleaded. The traffic light had turned green by then and there were horns going off like firecrackers in Diwali.

Still standing firm, Viraj glanced at her and took off his helmet, completely oblivious to the cacophony around them. 'Aren't you going to smack these perverts?'

'Please don't create a scene. I just want to go.' Gayatri started coughing because of the dust rising from the slow, grinding traffic.

Viraj watched her press her chest with one hand as she coughed and wave her other hand in front of her face.

'Fine! Let's go!' Resigned, he took Gayatri's arm. As she was about to sit on the bike she sensed someone coming towards her. She instinctively glanced sideways. The autorickshaw driver Viraj had just slapped was coming straight for him with a iron rod in his hand.

Gayatri acted on instinct. She grabbed the helmet Viraj was holding. Just as the driver raised the iron rod to smash into Viraj's back, Gayatri slammed the helmet in the driver's face. Her helmet hit him first. As the driver fell down, Gayatri hit the side of his head. With a tiny squeak, the man went down and the rod slid out of his hands, falling with a thud at Gayatri and Viraj's feet.

The traffic came to a halt. Everyone stared at them.

'Atta girl!' Viraj looked at the fallen driver and then at Gayatri. 'You...!' It was then that he noticed the urine running down Gayatri's legs and how hard she was trembling, hunched forward, her mouth twisted as if she were in pain.

'Hold on! Hold on!' In a haste Viraj got back on the bike. 'C'mon sit!'

'But I...but I...' Gayatri glanced down at herself soiled. She wanted to shrivel up and die in the loneliest corner of the earth. Cars were milling around them, some people was shouting at them in the distance. The men from the auto had jumped out and were helping their fallen buddy.

Viraj leaned forward and looked directly into her eyes. 'It's okay, Gayatri! You are very brave. Now let's get out of here. C'mon! Here, take this!'

Gayatri peeked down. Viraj was offering her his helmet.

'Thanks…' Gayatri slipped the helmet over her head and hopped behind him even as her limbs shivered. Closing her eyes, she hugged Viraj tightly from behind .

Viraj took off. It took some time for them to make their way out of the throng.

Having gone some distance, Viraj stopped the bike. Gayatri raised her head. They were in front of some small shops that were just opening up. 'Stay here!' Viraj parked the bike and went inside one of the shops with glass doors. Gayatri watched him go inside and talk to the owner. Viraj turned to look outside and Gayatri immediately glanced at her lap. She could smell her soiled state. *I'm such filth!*

Within minutes, Viraj came outside. 'Go inside! They'll take care of you.'

Gayatri got off. Taking a deep breath she went inside the shop avoiding eye-contact with him, keeping the helmet on. Viraj didn't question her.

Inside, Gayatri was greeted by a small framed, dark-skinned young girl. She seemed fifteen or so. 'Hi Didi! I'm Anna Matthews. You are Viraj bhaiya's friend?'

Gayatri nodded and took off the helmet.

'Go to the back! That door leads to the bathroom. I will bring you your new clothes.'

Gayatri hesitated.

She glanced at Gayatri's skirt. 'It's okay! I'm a med student. It's just body fluid, Didi!' Gayatri did not know whether to cringe at that comment or hug her. 'My father owns this shop. We live above it. My grandfather used to be Keshav chacha's driver.'

Gayatri gave her a blank look.

'You don't know Keshav chacha? You know Viraj's bhaiya's Ai?'

Gayatri shook her head and replied softly. 'We work together. Viraj is my boss.'

'He must be such a sweet boss na!'

Gayatri shifted from one foot to another.

'Sorry! Sorry. I talk too much. Go, go!' Anna moved to the side and Gayatri hobbled to the tiny bathroom. She left the helmet on a nearby counter.

The bathroom had a mosaic floor and was just big enough to accommodate a commode, a sink and a bathing area.

'I have hung a fresh towel for you on the door. I have fresh clothes too! When you have washed yourself just call me and I'll pass them inside.'

Gayatri quickly stripped and stepped over her clothes leaving them in a heap on the floor. She filled a red bucket and soaped her lower extremities. 'I love you, lifebouy!' Gayatri muttered to the pink bar as she put it back in the soap dish.

Having bathed, Gayatri used the towel to her dry herself. Then she hesitantly knocked on the door.

'I have your clothes,' Anna replied.

Gayatri opened the door a few inches and took the clothes.

'There is a plastic packet underneath them. You can put

your used clothes in that.'

'Thank you!' Gayatri replied, her voice hushed. She got into the simplest of simple chikan salwar kameez in pale blue. *I look like Sana!* She stuffed her stinky soiled clothes in the bag including her damp shoes.

Barefoot, Gayatri came out of the bathroom. Anna waited with a broad smile on her round face. She wasn't alone.

Smoking Marijuana

Gayatri's colour ran high as she saw Viraj there.

'Didi, you are so beautiful. Blue suits you. Viraj bhaiya chose it for you.' Gayatri heard Viraj make a strangled kind of sound. She could not bring herself to look at him or say a word. Her tongue was frozen and she was planning to keep it that way for the rest of her life.

'Here!' Viraj tossed something at her. A pair of ghastly bright and sequined silver slippers replete with multicoloured pom poms!

'That was all I could find. Hope they fit!' Viraj said.

Gazing at the slippers, Gayatri blinked her eyes as her voice thickened. 'They are perfect! They...' She couldn't complete her sentence her throat choked.

Making sympathetic sounds, Anna embraced Gayatri. 'It's okay, Didi! Kya hua? Hota hai yeh sab!'

Over Anna's head that came up to her shoulders, Gayatri met Viraj's eyes. Her dark brown eyes swam with gratitude and a plea of mercy. Viraj's gaze swept over her features. He looked away and then met her eyes again as if he was drawn to them. Something passed between them at that instant.

Gayatri saw him draw a breath and then he smiled. Not a broad grin but just a small one—the reassuring kind.

'Can I get you some tea?' Anna asked letting go of Gayatri.

'No thanks Anna, not today. We are leaving,' Viraj replied and then said to Gayatri, 'I'll be waiting outside.' He pivoted to go and then stopped and looked at Anna. 'Your exams start next month. No more movies or TV. Just study. I know you'll do well. Just focus.'

Anna's grin was ear to ear. 'Yes, Bhaiyya! Thank you for—'

Viraj waved at her and exited the shop.

'Bhaiyya is too much. He never lets me thank him,' Anna complained shaking her head.

'Thank him for?' Gayatri asked sliding her feet into the slippers. They were at least two sizes bigger but she did not care. She would sacrifice a thousand of her designer footwear for these right now.

'Oh Viraj bhaiya paid for my education. He pays my medical college fees, book expenses and everything else. He does that for many people. He has helped people set up their businesses, paid the school and college fees for many children. Hospital bills, marriage costs, even funerals.'

Gayatri forgot to slide her other foot. All she did was stare at Anna.

'His Ai runs a shelter home for abused women and children. And Keshav chacha is Ai's boyfriend. Cool na? And he is also Viraj's bhaiya's guru. He teaches the women in the shelter. And Viraj bhaiya helps whoever he can in any way he can.' Anna sighed. 'Amazing family, Didi! God's children, all of them.' She made a cross sign.

Gayatri's head reeled with information overload. *I'm*

manipulating a saint! She felt sick to her stomach. 'I should... go!' Gayatri gave a quick hug to Anna. 'You are god's child too. Thank you and good luck with your education. Quickly become a doctor so I can come to you. And if I can ever do anything for you, let me know. Let me give you my cell...' Gayatri panicked. 'I dropped my purse. It had everything, my wallet, cell—'

'Viraj bhaiya got it. That's where he went after you came inside.'

'Oh!' Gayatri smiled weakly.

Anna walked her out of the shop and then, waving goodbye to her and Viraj, went back inside. Gayatri's cheeks turned crimson when she saw what Viraj was doing. He was wiping the seats with some bleach and wipes. 'Oh please, let me.' She jerked forward and as she wasn't the steadiest in the big slippers, she tripped and landed square and centre on Viraj's back. Her arms went around him in trying to balance herself. Heat seared though Gayatri as her breasts pressed into his muscular back. She felt shivers run through her body and a strange burning sensation between her legs. *Not again!* Gayatri swiftly backed away.

Viraj turned to face her. 'You're okay?'

Gayatri nodded. 'Can I have my purse?'

'Sure!' Viraj passed it to her. Gayatri took her bag avoiding contact with his fingers like he had a highly contagious disease. 'I'll drop you home.'

Gayatri felt her throat choke. 'No, it's fine, thank you. I can go home by myself.' She evaded his gaze by pretending to look inside her bag. *Shit, I'm going to cry.*

'I know your parents live abroad. Do you have a roommate,

a boyfriend or a husband?' Viraj asked walking to the other side of the bike.

'No.'

'Should I call Nikhil or his wife?'

'NO. Please no!' Gayatri was quick to answer.

Viraj sat astride his bike. 'Then I'm dropping you home. C'mon!'

Finally Gayatri looked up at him. She found him observing her. Nervously, she licked her lips. She hated letting him in on her private life! Even though she was covered head to toe she felt exposed under his scrutiny.

'Let's go, Gayatri!' Viraj urged.

Gayatri walked around to take a seat behind him.

'I have GPS in my bike. All it took was a bit of re-wiring of the front panel, adding a WiFi signal catcher and an LCD panel over the odometer. Use my phone as a hot spot and that's it!'

Gayatri glazed at him blankly. 'That's the longest I have heard you talk.'

Viraj's eyes shone amused. 'That was me asking for your address.'

Gayatri exhaled and some of the tension left her shoulders. '32 Mahavir Road, Lokhandwala!'

While Viraj spoke the address into his phone, Gayatri climbed on behind him. The drive to her hotel was uneventful. Viraj left his bike with the valet. Combing his hair, he asked, 'Do you mind if I come up with you?'

'No! Of course not!' Gayatri gestured him to follow her. They walked through the lobby. Using her keys, Gayatri let Viraj and herself in.

'You live in a hotel?' Viraj asked, putting down his helmet on the coffee table.

'Yes! For over four months now,' Gayatri replied unsure of how to handle his presence.

'Who foots the bill?'

'My dad, he...' Gayatri trailed off. She saw something similar to judgment pass Viraj's chiseled face. 'I'll go and change. Please make yourself comfortable.' Gayatri rushed inside her bedroom and shut the interconnecting door. She went inside the bathroom and collapsed on the floor. She placed her palms on the cold marble floor and let its cool seep into her palms. After a few minutes, she dragged herself to the sink and splashed water on her face. Her cheeks and lips were devoid of colour, her hair was bedraggled and her eyes held deep-seated pain. Gayatri took off her clothes. A part of her wanted to rip them into shreds and a part of her wanted to hold them and fall asleep. Her throat felt dry. *I need some wine!*

Donning a pair of jeans and a loose T-shirt, she opened the door and stepped out of her bedroom. 'What?' She froze.

No! Viraj wasn't smoking marijuana or standing naked in her living room. It was worse.

Cupcakes, Wine and Therapist

'Care to explain this?' Viraj asked, slipping a mini cupcake into his mouth. He was pointing at the coffee table which was covered with wine bottles, several of them.

'You went through my fridge?' Gayatri's eyes were wider than a pressure cooker cover.

'You drink a *lot* of wine!' Viraj said putting one leg over another. He continued to eat off a plate full of mini cupcakes. 'These are really good!'

Gayatri slowly sat down opposite Viraj, her eyes fixed on the bottles. Most of them were empty. 'I have guests over often.' Her stomach was beginning to cramp with anxiety.

'I can share this with Nikhil and he can corroborate with the hotel CCTV footage as to how many guests come over.' Another cupcake was finished.

Gayatri sat straighter. 'You have no business doing all this! I can...'

'You can what?'

'I can...I can!' Gayatri lost her indignation and lowered her eyes. *I will be fired! Nikhil and Sneha will be so disappointed! Mom will be hurt! Dad will have won again.* Panic pounded her chest. Sweat beaded on Gayatri's upper lip. She rubbed her chest but she still couldn't breathe easy. In seconds, Viraj was down on his knees in front of her, holding a glass of water. 'Don't panic! It's okay!' Viraj held the glass to her lips.

Gayatri took small sips. 'Thanks. I'm a mess.' Her voice broke. Tears dribbled from her eyes down her cheeks and then fell on their clasped hands.

Viraj gently held her face up to his. 'You have nothing to be ashamed of. You have PTSD. It's Post—'

Gayatri sniffed. 'I know what it is!' She pulled her hands away from his.

'Good!' He offered her some tissues.

'Thanks.' She wiped her eyes. 'You've come prepared.'

Viraj nodded. 'I am. I have cupcakes too!'

Gayatri mustered a smile. She shifted and sat back in her chair.

Viraj simply crossed his legs and sat at her feet.

'Oh please, sit on the chair. It must be uncomforta—'

'You sat for days on boxes and on the floor against the wall.' Viraj became quiet and his eyes studied her face but the look in his eyes was distant. 'My father was an abusive. He beat my mother merciless, couple of times inches away from death. He hit me, too, regularly until one day I ran away from home.'

Gayatri gasped, 'I'm so sorry!' Her hands reached out to hold his hand and then she realized his hand was no longer in hers. She curled her fingers in her lap.

Viraj reached out and took her hand out of her lap and held it. Gayatri liked the warmth of his skin. 'It all started with his alcoholism. He couldn't keep a job. All his frustration was vented on the family, especially my mother, for he knew she was more capable than him. She was a topper in school and college. Then she married a loser.'

'Why did she marry him?' Gayatri's voice was strained.

'Love! The worst of all emotions,' Viraj said without a hesitation. 'Anyhow, I didn't tell you this to gain your sympathy. I told you this because I see the start of a problem.' He pointed at the wine bottles. 'You have a problem. Obviously it's early because you can function the entire day without it. And the loss of your bladder control earlier indicates that it is probably an offset of the attack on you.'

'This is very embarrassing. I haven't talked to anybody about this!' Gayatri swallowed as she lowered her eyes again. She fisted her hand against her mouth.

Viraj took her hands. Gayatri resisted the tug but he pulled them out and smoothed the half-moons her nails made in her palm. Gayatri held her breath at the sensation of his lean fingers with their calloused tips against her soft skin. The room instantly felt warm. Gayatri raised her large eyes, parting her lips and breathing in spurts. Viraj's eyes started to blur and his strokes became harder and more insistent. Gayatri's body felt heavy, a tingle between her legs made her tighten them. This small movement alerted Viraj and he immediately pulled his hand away.

Getting to his feet, Viraj put some distance between them.

Gayatri blankly stared at the spot he had just vacated. Too much had happened in one day and she was desperate to be alone now. 'I appreciate you helping me out today. Especially the pep talk!' She raised earnest eyes at him. 'Whatever you said will stay between us, I swear. But you should go now!'

'I will soon enough.' Viraj picked up the wine bottles and emptied them into the sink. He began poking around in the cabinets, drawers, looking under the sink.

'What are you doing?' Gayatri demanded, getting to her feet.

'I'm looking for undiscovered treasures! Aha, found one!' Viraj brought out another bottle from under the sink.

Gayatri wanted to cover her face with a pillow. 'This is trespassing!' she declared. Viraj went into her bedroom. 'What the hell!' Her feelings of gratitude were fading quickly. 'I'll call security,' she threatened weakly, following him.

'I'll call your brother!' Viraj shot back, opening and shutting the closet.

After that Gayatri became silent and went back to the living room. Viraj returned empty-handed after investigating her bedroom and bathroom. 'Like I said, the problem is in a nascent stage. It can be broken as easily as a coffee or tea addiction.'

'That's the dumbest thing I have heard. I don't have a problem.'

'Yes, you do, dumbo.'

Gayatri opened her mouth but Viraj flashed a smile over his shoulder and her anger dissipated. Gayatri simply pouted as she settled back in her chair.

Flushing the last of the wine down the drain, Viraj removed his wallet from the back pocket and took out a card. 'That's my therapist. Or used to be my therapist for seven years. She is good. Talk to her. I'm going to call her tomorrow and find out whether you have made an appointment or not and then I will find out whether you kept it or not.'

And I thought Nikhil was bossy! Gayatri turned away and walked to the window of the living room.

'You will thank me someday!'

'I'm sure!' Gayatri could not contain her sarcasm.

Viraj chuckled. Gayatri frowned at her own reflection. His laugh was pleasant and it made a dent in her anger. *Wish he squawked like a duck!*

'These cupcakes are really good. Where did you get them from?'

Gayatri smiled at her own reflection. 'I'm not telling!'

She heard some sounds of crockery being moved around. She turned and asked, 'What are you doing?'

Viraj was putting all the cupcakes in a Tupperware. 'I'm taking them all. You can get them from wherever you do!'

Gayatri opened her mouth and then stopped. A thought hit her. 'You are a con!' Viraj paused. 'What do you mean?'

'You are normal. You are not eccentric or weird or socially-challenged.'

Viraj's guilty expression sealed whatever doubt she might have had. 'No one will believe you!' Viraj put the plate down, his tone defensive.

'I wasn't planning to squeal on you!' Gayatri came forward. Viraj gave her a grudging look and shut the box of cupcakes. 'You don't need me for Sana. You can do that on your own.' She said.

'Yes, but with you involved, it will be easier.'

'How?'

'You will fasten the process. You are my glorified pimp after all.'

They both exchanged a look. Gayatri was the first to

laugh, Viraj quickly followed. Soon they bent over laughing.

'Hey, don't laugh so hard. You might pee!'

Gayatri had to hold her stomach as her chuckles grew louder. 'Stop! I might just!' she said, wiping her eyes. And then she straightened and sobered. Viraj did the same. They both stared at each other, a frisson of awareness passed between them. Gayatri was the first to look away.

'See you tomorrow?'

'You still want me to come to work?' Gayatri perked up.

'You are not just going to stop at chairs, are you?' Viraj teased.

'Never!' Gayatri swallowed a lump in her throat. 'Poha with toast and cold coffee.'

Viraj raised an eyebrow.

'That is one of Sana's favourite breakfasts. Now I might as well—'

Viraj put his hand out. 'No, we have a deal. I will honour it. I will learn about Sana from what you don't tell me. Though you could tell me where you get those cupcakes from?'

'I will. See you tomorrow, boss.'

Viraj walked to Gayatri and, lightly tapping her chin, said, 'Anything but that! Viraj works fine!'

'Thank you!' Gayatri said, somewhat shy when he stood so close to her.

'We all need help, Gayatri. Professor Keshav helped a damaged boy of seventeen and now I'm just returning the favour.'

To quite a few! 'I would like to meet Professor Keshav.'

'Definitely! Soon.' Viraj walked out of her apartment.

Gayatri shut the door behind him and felt her chin on the

spot Viraj had fleetingly touched. She could feel an imprint of his fingers there.

Humming to herself, Gayatri went to the kitchenette and opened the fridge and took out the eggs and butter. Next from the cabinets she took out some baking flour, sugar and a few other ingredients.

'Today, the cupcakes are going to be lemon cream cheese and chocolate with raspberry filling!'

Hot Dreams and Cold Beer

Viraj was just in his low hanging jeans, moving over a supple and bare female-form, his hands stroking and squeezing the warm flesh. Two bodies lusciously entwined like two serpents moving over each other. It was hard to distinguish where one began and the other ended.

Viraj saw his hands hold her petite shoulders; her skin was soft and creamy and it begged to be touched, stroked and tasted. His skin was dark in contrast to her paleness. His hands moved to her soft breasts, its pebbled chocolate tips made his mouth drool. He gently rolled the nub between his fingers and was rewarded with a low moan as she surged against his demanding fingers. His body hardened. She sounded even more delicious. Growling, he brought his mouth near a nipple and blew on it. She arched her body, offering her glorious perfectly-shaped breasts to him. Just as he took the delectable mound in his mouth, suckling on it, he moved his hand under her firm bottom, cupping and lifting it against his hardness. He moaned as she rubbed her centre against his arousal. The harder he sucked and licked her breasts, the faster she rubbed herself against his hardness. Their bodies were a quivering mass, moving in a constant rhythm.

Viraj felt he would explode. He moved his mouth from her wet breast to her luscious mouth. He had to taste the mouth of this goddess who made him shake as if a lifetime of sexual tension was about to find its release in him. Her pink lips parted for him. He slanted his mouth over hers and slid his tongue straight in, bringing her closer to him. His tongue entwined with her licking and stroking and the vixen mimicked his movements. *I have to have her now. I have to bury myself in her wet nectar.* Viraj tore his mouth away and she whimpered. 'Just a sec, sweetheart!' He muttered as he was about to rip off his jeans. That is when he saw her face and froze. Gayatri!

Shit! Viraj woke up with a jolt, as if someone had dropped a live wire on him. His torso was covered in slight sheen of sweat and his sheets were in a frenzied mess around him. *I was having too much fun in the dream!* Sitting up with a jerk, Viraj stared in the darkness. His heart was thundering in his rib cage, his pulse was beating like he had run a marathon. He was rock hard and felt a deep dissatisfaction as his body craved fulfillment. Nearly all of him wanted to fall asleep this very second and finish that dream. *It was just getting to the really epic part!*

Viraj buried his head in his hands. 'What the hell!' Frustrated, he flung his pillow across the room. He fell back on the sheets and lay there staring at the ceiling. The dream had imprinted itself on his mind. Viraj closed his eyes and instantly saw her face again, wanton and stunning. Pink lips swollen from his kisses, thick and silky dark hair across her back—hair that he craved to breath in, locks he wanted to place around her sexy—*Oh for crying out loud!* Viraj got out of bed with a start and went into the bathroom. Within minutes he was in the shower.

Post a sudden cold, midnight shower, Viraj emerged out of the bathroom, a towel wrapped around his midriff. Heedless of the water dripping from his body, he walked to the fridge and took out a chilled beer. He opened the balcony door and let the humid, Mumbai air hit him and stir his wet locks. Viraj took a long swig of his cold beer. It cooled his heated insides. He pressed the bottle against his hot forehead. 'What is wrong with me?' His furry friends—the three sparrows—asleep on the balcony rail, opened their eyes and gave him dirty looks. 'Sorry! Can't sleep.' He pulled the cane chair and sat down watching the traffic on the road facing his apartment. It was less at this time of night.

He sighed. *This dream has to go away. I can't think of her that way. I have to focus on Sana.* Yet all Viraj saw was Gayatri's passionate and beautiful face in front of him. This morning's incident had brought them closer. Gayatri invoked feelings of protectiveness he had not felt in a long time. Her struggles seemed like his, her fears made him want to slay them for her. And today she had seen Viraj for who he really was. He rubbed his forehead. *In the light of the day everything will normalize. Balance shall be restored. All I need to do is focus on Sana and everything will be okay. From tomorrow I will meet Gayatri but only for Sana. And of course to help Gayatri fight her demons. Only as a colleague.*

The fat sparrow shook its body. Was it laughing?

Spice and Ice

Next day around lunchtime, Viraj weaved his bike through the busy streets of Malad. 'So this is it!' Leaning his foot on the side, Viraj stopped the bike in front of a restaurant. A two-by-ten-feet-board plastered above the entrance of the restaurant proudly read 'Swagat Naka'.

'We are eating here?'

His pillion passenger hopped off and removed her helmet. 'Yes, this is one of Sana's favourite college-time haunts. But you have to guess what Sana likes here!' Gayatri grinned, smoothing out her jeans. She waited patiently as Viraj parked his bike on the pavement.

After yesterday's incident, Gayatri was dreading coming into work today. She had hid in her office until 11.00 a.m. when Viraj came looking for her.

His opening words: 'Let's do lunch today?'

Thus, they were doing lunch.

Gayatri led Viraj up the few white marble steps. The atmosphere inside was simple but bustling. Sturdy tables with simple iron chairs spotted the floors. Nearly all of them were taken. Waiters in short-sleeved, red-collared shirts and white pants walked around taking orders. A bespectacled man sitting on a chair and table at the entrance gestured them towards an empty table.

The waiter arrived immediately, with a laminated menu card that had a spot of water which hadn't been fully wiped.

'So what am I having?' Viraj asked.

'Can you handle spicy?'

'Asks the NRI!' Viraj rolled his tongue in his cheek. His eyes shone when he was amused. He had ditched his glasses today.

Gayatri could only bring herself to steal occasional glances. Since yesterday, she was feeling very exposed around Viraj. And finding out about his helpful and generous nature made her feel small and insignificant. *Intelligent and philanthropic! Viraj was the Indian Bill Gates. And no one can not like Bill Gates!*

A waiter came to their table when Gayatri was ready with the order. 'One special vada pav and one regular vada pav. Thank you.'

Viraj squinted. 'So I'm confused. Sana does not like vada pav!'

'No. She does like *one* of the vada pavs I ordered. You have to guess which one—regular or spicy.' Gayatri fished out a small bottle of hand-sanitizer and smeared some over her hands.

Viraj watched her hands, her slender fingers and short manicured nails. She wore no rings, just a thin silver bracelet that caught light as it slithered up and down her delicate wrist. *She has beautiful hands...what would it feel like to have them glide over my body...* Viraj felt himself getting hard. *Dammit! This is supposed to work the other way round!* He raised his eyes to meet hers. Gayatri was uncharacteristically quiet and shifty. He picked up on her discomfort like an airport tower tracking an incoming plane.

The waiter came back with the order. He placed the two plates in front of them. 'Regolar and esphecial vada pav,' he said in a unique accent.

'The esphecial is spicy and regolar is not. Which one do you want?' Gayatri asked, simultaneously offering him the hand-sanitizer.

'Esphecial one!' Viraj studied her face. Even though Gayatri's mouth curved up in a smile, her eyes were dull today. 'Did you make the appointment with my shrink?'

'Yes, Mom!' Gayatri murmured losing her smile completely. She picked up the bun and parted it to let some steam escape.

'When is your first appointment?'

Gayatri exhaled sharply. Viraj clamped his lips. The feistiness was still in there and he was thankful for it. He liked her fighting with him. Esphecially with him.

'Tomorrow after work, at 5.00 p.m.! Why are you smiling so much?' Gayatri grumbled, pouting.

'I'll come with you.'

Gayatri narrowed her eyes and crossed her arms over her chest.

Viraj trained his eyes on her fierce expression and tried not peek at how her breasts got pushed up. *I'm such an asshole!* He grimaced. 'Look, I'm not doubting you. I know you are not lying.'

'Oh really, do you now?' Gayatri uncrossed her arms.

Viraj sighed and said without thinking, 'I checked with the therapist.'

'You did WHAT?'

Viraj was sure Gayatri would smack him now.

She did not smack him, instead she slid him some food. 'You are trying to help me here!'

She picked up her food.

'Yes I am!' Viraj nodded eagerly and watched her small white teeth bite into the bun. *What would it feel like to have her nip him as he thrusts repeatedly into her?* Alarmed by his thoughts, Viraj did the first thing he could think of. He picked up and ate a big chunk off his esphecial vada pav.

Gayatri sat back and smiled, watching him chew furiously. Viraj dropped the vada pav on the plate. Her smile grew sweeter as panic swam in his eyes. Viraj was reaching out for the glass of water, but Gayatri pulled it out of his reach. He opened his mouth gasping for breath. 'Give me the water! My mouth is on fire!' He kept shifting in his chair. He felt like he had swallowed flames instead of food.

The people around smiled, few even sympathized with his state. However, the woman seated across from him still held his water hostage. 'WATER!'

'No more monitoring me, you have to promise! You have helped me enough. Promise me! No more helping,' Gayatri said, holding the glass away from him.

'FINE! I don't even know you!' Viraj's ears were turning red. Gayatri thrust the glass toward him. He grabbed it and drank it down in one go.

Leaning over he grabbed the glass of water from the table next to them. 'Sorry bhai saab, emergency!' was all he muttered chugging water from someone else's glass.

A startled laugh escaped Gayatri's mouth.

Obviously just two glasses weren't enough. Muttering excuses and apologies, Viraj went around drinking water from the tables of complete strangers. A young girl few tables away snickered covering her mouth. Gayatri gave her a smile and a wink. The girl and her parents started laughing. A harried Viraj nearly traversed four tables, drinking water from other's glasses. It was quite a sight. Finally, one of the waiters came and handed him a bowl of ice cream. Viraj unloaded the bowl in his mouth.

Gayatri composed her face as Viraj, after thanking the waiter profusely, made his way back to their table. He gave her a stern look as he sat back in his chair.

'I told you it's spicy!' Gayatri rolled her eyes.

Viraj reacted neutrally to her audacity, even though he wanted to smile. She had made quite a spectacle out of him and yes she had warned him indeed. 'This can't work!' He delivered the blow. *Now my turn to watch the show, queen!* Satisfied, he watched as Gayatri chewed the insides of her cheek and her dark eyes fringed with thick eyes lashes grew wide and anxious.

'Why?' Gayatri asked leaning forward.

'If Sana eats that much spice, I'm dead already. My ideas will fry even before they germinate!'

Gayatri sat back and burst into roaring laughter. The hold-your-stomach-and-throw-your-head-back kind of laugh!

Viraj was captivated by the sound of her laugh. And then he noticed her throat. And of course how smooth her skin was and the hint of cleavage above the first button of her blouse. And then he saw the mole just above her cleavage. Viraj was mesmerized by it. He almost leaned forward. *How many more does she have all over body?* Viraj swallowed. *Dammit! I should not be thinking such thoughts. Fuck this!*

Viraj picked up the remaining I-will-fry-your-brains-out vada pav and stuffed it in his mouth.

Gayatri was surprised. 'Oh my! Are you okay?' Watching his speed of consumption, she shot to feet. 'I will go get some ice cream.' Viraj nodded and kept chewing. His face reddened and eyes watered. 'Oh god, I'll get a tub of ice cream.' Gayatri fled!

At the same time, in a land not so far away…
Nandini and Sneha's Advertising Agency

'Sneh! Any news of your sis-in-law?'

Sneha looked up from her laptop. 'Why do you roll your tongue and your eyes whenever you say her name?'

Nandini squinted her eyes thoughtfully. 'I dunno! Habit, I guess!'

'Heard Viraj has taken to liking to her!' Sneha said as she typed an email.

'Like liking liking? Or like real liking?'

'Kulta seriously, the eye and the tongue roll again?'

'You say stuff that begs the eye and tongue roll.' Nandini flexed her shoulders. 'You were saying?'

'Nothing! Just that Viraj and Gayatri are hanging out!'

'Hmm!' Nandini tapped her chin. 'Maybe we should visit the lab!'

'Maybe we should!' Sneha's look was equally contemplative.

Scientist and Sleazeballs

Next morning
The lab

There was a knock on the door. Viraj looked up from the 3D design he was improvising. 'Get out!'

'It's me!'

'Come in.' Viraj went back to working on his 3D design. A plastic box was thrust in front of him. He smelled them before he saw them. 'Cupcakes! For me?' He gazed up at Gayatri. She was pouting and her eyes were free of all shine. 'What?' Viraj asked, wanting to know what was bothering her.

'The spicy thing wasn't funny! I'm sorry!'

Viraj took his time to respond. He opened the box and looked at the delectable array of mini cupcakes, all frosted with different coloured icing. Today's theme was chess and there were sixteen cupcakes, with all the figures drawn artistically on the top. 'There's still some pain. But it's only my ego that hurts.' Viraj picked up the cupcake with the queen drawn on it and brought it close to his mouth. His eyes twinkled as he popped it into his mouth. He took his time relishing the cupcake. His mouth creased in a wide smile, one that was very Zen-like. 'These are bloody good!'

Gayatri hid her smug smile as she pretended to brush something off her sleeve.

Viraj popped another one into his mouth. Devouring the cupcake, he rolled it around his mouth. 'What flavour is this?'

Gayatri moved closer to look into the box. 'That one was banana pecan.'

'You know these flavours well!' Viraj remarked, lowering his head full of dense hair to choose another one.

'I should. I make the—' Gayatri gasped covering her mouth. 'I mean, I bake—fuck! Pardon my language!' Viraj looked up in surprise. 'I mean, I order them...so many of them all the time that I feel like I make them. I order them! I have to go!' She turned around and left abruptly.

A few minutes later, Gayatri's office door swung open. She looked up from the prize selection she was working on. 'Knocking is simpler than it looks!'

'Agreed, but it does not go with my image of crazy mad scientist,' Viraj retorted coming closer. He glanced around and spied a large box. Pushing it closer to her desk. Before she could ask why or what, he sat down across from her.

They had a staring match for a few minutes.

'Vending machine!'

Gayatri cocked her head to the side. 'Excuse me?'

'You can have a vending machine for the employees, if you tell me why you freaked out about the cupcakes earlier. You make amazing cupcakes and you should be proud of that, not embarrassed.' Viraj scratched his head but his eyes were fixed on Gayatri the whole time.

Gayatri was starting to get unnerved. 'That's not fair! You

can't mix the professional and the personal. Vending machines for employees have nothing to do with me making or not making cupcakes.'

'You are forgetting something—I am the crazy mad scientist, capable of anything, even firing employees without any notice or justification.' His dark eyes hardened behind the glasses.

Gayatri studied her nails for a few seconds and then she simply said, 'My dad! He thinks baking is for idiots or servants.'

There was silence for several minutes in the room. Gayatri looked everywhere except at him.

'Your dad pays for your fancy lifestyle, doesn't he? Hotel, clothes, car, etc.?'

Gayatri bristled. 'Yeah, so? He provides me with the standard of living befitting his family.'

Viraj rubbed the back of his head. 'Whoever provides for you, decides for you. Stop being a chicken! If you want to start a business, do it. I can give you a loan.'

Gayatri gritted her teeth till she felt her jaws would snap. 'Just like you have given money to all the other poor people you know!'

'They were born into poverty, yet they are working hard to do better for themselves and their families. They have an abundance of spirit and ambition. All they lack is money and I have more than I need. We all need a helping hand. Even I did! When my father would beat my mother and me black and blue, all I prayed for was help, even the teeniest bit.'

Gayatri closed her eyes at the image his words conjured. She felt a stab in her heart for the little scared boy he was. She swallowed painfully.

'And one day, I went out and found help. Professor Keshav. He helped me turn my life around and now I try and help as many as I can, not because I'm looking for awards, or recognition, but only because I want everyone to succeed, at least everyone who tries to.' Viraj paused.

Gayatri leaned forward on her desk. The cool wood felt good under skin. 'You are very kind. But please don't think of me as another one of your charity projects. I can manage my life on my own.' She did not understand why it pricked her when he clubbed her with the others. She labeled it pride.

Viraj cocked his head and studied her. Under his gaze, Gayatri felt something pricking her eyes.

Viraj got up. 'Let me know your answer.'

'Do I get my vending machines?'

'Do I get cupcakes every day?'

Gayatri bit the corner of her lower lip and smiled up at him. 'Deal!'

Viraj watched her small, perfectly aligned teeth gently bite lips that were painted a dull maroon. He treaded to the door. 'And don't think I did not hear the "machines" when all I offered was "machine",' he remarked as he walked out of her office.

Sneha answered her ringing cell. 'Hey! What's up?'

'What? Can't I call just to talk my wife?' Nikhil said on the other end.

'Yes, you can, but you don't!'

'Well, if you are going to be like that, then I'm not telling you what I called to tell you,' Nikhil retorted.

Sneha could hear the playful smile in his voice. 'Is it big?'

'Verrrry big! Just like my—'

Sneha quickly cut him off as she was at work. 'Okay then, what is it?'

'I was just going to say as big as my new phone. What did you think?'

Sneha stayed quiet.

'Okay fine, don't give me the third degree. The lab has a break room with coffee-makers, microwaves, fridge, toaster, vending machines, several chairs and tables and an ice cream machine!'

Sneha breathed heavily. 'Ohhh that is huge!' She paused. 'Me thinks the mad scientist likes Guy!'

Nikhil was curt, 'Don't be silly! Not him and Guy. That scientist girl there seems more his type.'

Sneha grimaced. 'Nah! She's so vanilla!'

'If women have flavours, you would be chocolate. Milk chocolate that can be devoured in so many ways, all night—'

'Okay bye!' Sneha hung up despising the fact that just with his words Nikhil had her all distracted.

'Husband?' Nandini asked, looking up from her laptop.

'Nah! Some sleazeball.' Sneha grinned.

Just then Nandini's cell rang too. 'Oooh my sleazeball is calling. Something big?'

Sneha bobbed her chin. 'Yup! It includes microwaves, toaster, vending machines.'

New Threads

Close to the end of the work day, there was a knock on Viraj's door. 'Get out!' he shouted his customary greeting even as he continued to heave above the floor.

'Coming in!' It was Gayatri. She poked her head through. 'Oh, you are naked! Why are you naked?' She grinned, entering the cubbyhole.

Viraj fell on the floor, smilin, his cheek plastered against mother earth. 'I'm wearing jeans in case you hadn't noticed, Ms Operations Manager!'

'Oh I had noticed.' Gayatri again peeked at the way his jeans clung to his firm butt. *HOTTIE ALERT!*

Viraj went back to doing his pushups.

'So I was thinking!' She walked further into his office and shut the door.

'You were thinking? I'm scared!' Viraj rolled on his back, wiping his face.

Gayatri saw his chest. It was hard, flat and some dust from the floor was stuck in patches on his skin. She had an insane craving to run her hands over his chest and see how it felt. Her cheeks turned pink.

'Why are you making that face? If you need to use the bathroom, then go!'

'What? Eww!' Gayatri crinkled her nose. 'I was thinkin…'

'And that word again!' Viraj started doing crunches.

'So do you have an hour or so to spare right now?'

Viraj paused. 'Why?'

'Umm…' Gayatri scratched her nape. 'I think it's about time we got different threads.'

'Threads? Now you are going to have my scientists embroider? Absolutely NOT!' The crunches resumed.

'What? No! I just think you need some new clothes.'

'NO!'

'I think Sana and you should go out for lunch or something. I spoke with her and she is okay with that.'

Viraj paused and sat up. 'Isn't that too quick? I just started getting to know about her in that roundabout way you suggested.'

'How about coffee? You have to talk to her. She is very awkward around you because she thinks too highly of you.'

Virak raised an eyebrow. 'You don't want her to think highly of me?'

'Of course not!' Gayatri rolled her eyes. 'I mean she needs to know the real you. Not just as her boss or someone famous in her field.'

'Fine!' Viraj abruptly stood up. He loomed over Gayatri. His smell, his nakedness and his eyes that seemed more riveting without glasses caused Gayatri to step back. Her mouth felt dry. 'I'll take her out for coffee but I'm not going shopping for clothes. I'm not changing for anyone.' Viraj turned around to slip on his T-shirt. Gayatri found an opportunity. She turned around and switched the objects on his desk.

'What are you doing?'

'I just bought you a new paperweight!' Gayatri held up the older one.

'Why?' Viraj asked, his eyes hooded.

'When I was here the other day, I saw the paperweight on your desk. Its side was chipped. So at lunch I went and got you a new one.'

'Thank you. Can I have the old one please?' Viraj extended his hand out.

Gayatri handed Viraj the old chipped paperweight. His eyes were lowered and devoid of their usual gleam. The side of his lips curved downward similar to the ends off an arc.

'Is something bothering you?'

Viraj sat down shifting the paperweight in his arms. His fingers stroked the chipped edge. He finally spoke. 'See this chipped area?' Gayatri nodded. 'My father threw this at my face.'

Gayatri gasped.

'It missed me. It bounced off on the wall and broke off. The jagged edge cut my cheek. I cried out reflexively. My father laughed at my pain.' Viraj met her eyes and saw his hurt on Gayatri's face. 'This paperweight is a reminder of my past. A reminder of why I have to succeed.'

Gayatri couldn't help herself. She clasped his hand that held the paperweight and hugged it to her chest. 'I am so sorry that you suffered so much. You were just a child…' Her voice shook. And then she straightened. 'You were strong then and you are strong now. Your past, your pain does not own your genius. Nothing or no one owns your brilliance except you. I'm a 100 per cent sure that you would have succeeded anyhow, anywhere.' She grabbed the chipped paperweight from his hand and trashed it.

'Why did you do that?' Viraj asked still holding hands with her. Her skin was warm and in this moment there was no other hand he'd like to hold but hers. Her hand fit perfectly in his.

'You don't need pain as a reminder of anything. Some memories need to be trashed. Your father was bad news and I hope he goes to hell.'

'He's there already I hope! He died few years ago.'

'Oh!' Gayatri blinked. They continued to hold hands.

Viraj tugged her closer, and Gayatri went to him. 'Thank you.'

Their faces were as close as their hands but not touching. It was the clasped hands against their chests that created the distance between them. Complicated! Welcome to Relationship class for Dummies!

'I like the new paperweight,' Viraj said softly. His gaze was bold.

'You…are welcome…' Gayatri's reply was a soft murmur. She was lost to the depths of his eyes; the salty musk from his body overwhelmed her. She was scared to breathe. They both stared at each for several seconds and then Viraj let go of her hand. The spell was broken. Murmuring incoherently, Gayatri went to the door. *I need to get out of here!*

'Wait! I like your coffee idea.'

Gayatri felt a prick of sorts in the whereabouts of her chest. 'Great! Let me know how it goes, if you want to of course.' Her mouth dry, she reached out to open the door.

'And your idea of new threads.'

Mulishly, Gayatri refused to look at him. 'Good luck with that too!' She heaved the door open.

'Wait, Gayatri!'

She stopped unable to resist her name on Viraj's lips.

'Will you have coffee with me and help me dress better?' The teasing tone was back in his voice.

Gayatri grinned down at her shoes. 'It will be my pleasure.' She tossed him a mischievous glance over her shoulder. She felt buoyant like a few knots in her heart had come undone.

Viraj's eyes sobered. 'We can complain because rose bushes have thorns, or rejoice because thorns bushes have roses. Abraham Lincoln.'

Gayatri was quiet for a second as she thought of a perfect comeback. 'They misunderestimated me. George Bush.'

Viraj laughed. 'Meet you outside in ten minutes in the parking lot?'

'Cool!' Gayatri walked out.

Viraj walked to the trash bin and stared at the paperweight. *You were strong then and you are strong now. Your past, your pain does not own your genius. Nothing or no one owns your brilliance except you.* 'Maybe she is right!' Whistling, Viraj walked back to his desk and tidied up. Opening the safe on the side of the wall he put his design prints in and locked it.

A twenty-five-minute drive got them to the mall. 'This place is bloody crowded.' Viraj held Gayatri's elbow as they weaved through the crowd at the entrance.

'It's the week before Ganesh Chaturthi. Everyone is out shopping,' Gayatri remarked. 'Should we just get our coffee to go and walk around window-shopping?

'We can get our coffee to go. But why are we buying windows?' Viraj glanced down at her.

'For your new office! I'm changing it all...' On seeing the visible irritation on his face she smiled mischievously.

Viraj noticed her teasing smile. 'Very funny!' He squeezed her skin where he held her and then as an afterthought he stroked that spot on purpose.

Butterflies broke out in Gayatri's stomach as his callused fingertips rubbed on her skin. On the pretext of moving faster, Gayatri removed her elbow from his grip. 'There's the coffee shop.'

Viraj and Gayatri got the same thing. Different treatments to the same products, Black coffee and cappuccino!

'So now we shop for windows?' Viraj asked paying for the coffee.

Gayatri giggled. 'Yes, now we shop for windows!' She saw the looks the opposite sex gave Viraj as he passed them. *He's mine, ladies! I mean he's with me!* Gayatri increased her pace. *What am I thinking?*

'Hey, hold up!'

Gayatri had calmed down her rabid thoughts and pulse by the time Viraj came looking for her.

'Are your pants on fire?' Viraj tried messing around.

'Crazy mad scientists are not supposed to be witty.'

'And women in heels are not supposed to run so fast!'

'Oh stop it!' Gayatri dragged him away.

'Before we shop for windows, can we go in there?' Viraj gestured at a store.

'A music store? Sure!' Gayatri followed him to the music store. They listened to a lot of music, sometimes even sharing headphones. Viraj had her splits, especially when he lip-synced to several songs, including Elton John's Can you feel the love tonight?

Next, they went to an ice cream parlor where they bumped into Double Trouble!

Split the Bannana

'How can they call this ice cream a banana split? It isn't like the banana is wearing black tights and doing splits to some beats?' Viraj voiced.

'Good, keep talking, then I can have more of the ice cream,' Gayatri said sliding a big chunk of the ice cream from the glass bowl into her spoon.

'It should be called banana butchered or banana murdered,' Viraj said taking the chunk off her spoon putting it in his mouth. 'Don't steal my ice cream!'

'Hey! All three are scoops of chocolate. Take any. And anyway good luck trying to feed kids an ice cream called banana butchered.'

Viraj put more ice cream in his mouth. 'Have you seen the video games children play these days? They like violence. Banana butchered might sell more than banana split. Nikhil has a son, right? Does he play such games?'

Gayatri laughed. 'Not Vey, he is too small! Nik and Sneha are very involved parents. They will bring him up right.'

'Gayatri!' A familiar voice interrupted them.

Shit! Speak of the devil. Gayatri closed her eyes for a second.

Then she gave an imploring look at Viraj and mouthed 'be nice!' Pasting a smile on her face, Gayatri turned sideways. 'Hi Sneha,' she paused, 'and Nandini!' *Someone shoot me! Now!*

Viraj continued to focus on the ice cream.

'Gayatri and Viraj!' Sneha bent down to give Gayatri a quick hug.

'Right! Viraj. I was thinking I had seen him somewhere. He looks different from the last time I saw him,' Nandini added, her look thoughtful.

Viraj just grunted. Gayatri gently nudged his foot under the table. He raised his gaze and saw the pleading look on her face. There was no way he could resist that. He gave the two intruders a quick 'Hello and hello!'

Both Sneha and Nandini's jaw dropped at the simple greeting.

'So what are you guys doing here?' Sneha asked.

Viraj left the talking to Gayatri.

'We came here for shopping,' Gayatri said, internally panicked at the gleam that appeared in Sneha's eyes. 'For employees, as a part of the service awards which appreciate a team member for their individual contributions.'

'Impressive!' Nandini. 'May we join you?'

'We were just leaving. We are almost done.' Gayatri grabbed her bag.

Viraj was already half out of his chair. 'Nice to you see you. Have a good evening!'

Bug-eyed, Sneha and Nandini both stared at him and then at each other.

Viraj took the empty bowl and went to throw it in trash.

'Gayatri! Is that Viraj's clone?' Nandini leaned forward.

'What did you with the original? Is this one as smart?'

'That *is* Viraj!' Gayatri hissed back. She glanced at Sneha. 'It's just work!'

'I'm sure it is. Congrats on making a huge difference. We heard about the break-room,' Sneha voiced. Gayatri puckered her mouth, her eyes suspicious. 'Nik is super impressed and proud.'

Gayatri perked, 'He said that?'

'I thought he told you. Anyhow, I'll make sure that you hear it from the horse's mouth,' Sneha quipped.

'Even my horse, I mean, Adi was praising all the changes you have made there,' Nandini chirped.

Standing behind Sneha and Nandini, Viraj gestured at Gayatri to come.

'Gotta go! Work work work! All right then, my boss is calling me. It's all work. So I guess it's back to work for me.' Gayatri slipped her bag over her shoulder. 'I'll see you guys later!' Waving at them Gayatri joined Viraj. 'Let's get out of here!'

'Out of the mall?'

'We'll go to a store at the very other end. Those two have seen us. I'm going to be hauled over coals,' Gayatri said.

Viraj and Gayatri walked away from the ice cream store. 'They seem harmless.'

'Harmless! You haven't seen those two in action. They can bring governments down.' Gayatri rolled her eyes.

Double Trouble

Nandini tapped Sneha on the shoulder. 'I'm getting the biggest sundae and then we'll talk about what we just saw.'

'Why do we have to talk about it?' Sneha narrowed her eyes.

'We just saw the biggest transformation of the century. T-rex has turned into a panda and you are not going to discuss it?' Nandini gestured.

'I don't like to pry in other people's business and somehow you always get me to do it. I'll always fall for your crap.'

Nandini moaned, 'It's just talking! And when did you fall for my crap?'

Sneha whipped her head around. 'Seriously? When? Okay, so what about the time in twelfth grade when you went to gather intel on the new neighbour's family because you thought the father was a serial killer.'

'Well he did keep odd timings!' Nandini reminded haughtily.

'Ya because he worked the night shift at a chemical plant. And how did it end for us, Nancy Drew, when we tried going from our terrace to his just to investigate as per your stupid instincts?'

Nandini squirmed for a bit and then she burst into peals of laughter. 'Well, of all the things to step on, you step on the old blind dog.' Nandini pointed a finger in Sneha's face. 'You simply jumped back to our terrace. I got smacked by the servant's slippers right here.' Nandini pointed at her forehead, smiling.

Sneha blew her a raspberry.

Nandini grabbed her purse. 'I'm getting ice cream.' In a few minutes, she came back with two sundaes and took a seat. 'So let's focus! Do you think Gayatri and Viraj are a couple?'

Sneha took a small bite. 'Just because they are hanging out outside office doesn't mean they are seeing each other.'

Nandini went through a few bites before she said, 'But T-rex has changed. The lab is a whole new place since Gayatri came on board. And today you saw Sneh, he spoke to us.' Nandini planted her hands on her chest for emphasis. 'He said hello and nice to see you and good evening.'

'She does have his ear.'

'And maybe his heart too!'

Sneha snorted. 'Why do you become Mills and Boons and Yash Raj Films at the drop of a hat?'

Nandini sighed. 'I love love!'

Sneha grimaced. 'Kulta listen. Gayatri is family to Nikhil. I don't want to experiment with her. Let's leave her alone. Why don't we pick on someone in our office? C'mon!' Sneha cajoled. 'How about that girl who is the head copywriter?'

Nandini clapped her hands. 'Tina! The one we have known for so many years. Your very distant relative. I thought you liked her.'

'I like my husband more!' Sneha asserted with mocking severity.

Nandini threateningly waved her ice cream-dripping spoon at Sneha.

'There aren't too many people Nikhil considers family. He is very protective of Gayatri. We should back off. YOU should back off!' Sneha took another bite.

Nandini poked her tongue at Sneha. 'Traitor!' She ate some more of her sundae but Nandini wasn't done by a long shot. 'Did you see the times Gayatri said "work". "It's all work! All right then, my boss is calling me. It's all work. So I guess it's back to work for me".' Nandini repeated Gayatri's rantings. 'That is such a basic giveaway. It's like wearing a lal chaddi and dancing in front of the bull.'

Sneha winced and closed her eyes. 'You are a bull!'

Nandini continued to enjoy her ice cream. 'No baba, we're the bulls!'

'And how do you know the colour of her chaddis?'

Nandini held her two fingers very close to her eyes and said, 'X-ray vision!'

Sneha snorted. 'So now you are Clark Kent, Superman?'

'No...Karamdatta! Amrita Singh and Mithun Chakraborty!'

Sneha grimaced. 'Howwww and when do you see such movies?'

'Try watching TV after 1.00 a.m. They show all these movies!'

'Why do you watch TV at that ungodly time?'

Because my husband has these crazy conference calls on some project or the other going on in some or the other part of the world.'

'Sane explanation for an insane hobby!' Sneha quipped. 'But I'm concerned for Gayatri. Viraj is very unpredictable. He is not normal like us.'

'You are normal?' Nandini scoffed picking nuts off her ice cream.

Sneha snorted. 'Normaler than Viraj.'

'Normaler is not a word.' Nandini rolled her eyes.

'So sue me, shabdkosh!' Sneha made slurping sounds as she licked the spoon.

'You know Sneh, I see sparks between those two.'

'Kulta, you probably see sparks between unborn babies also.'

'Sometimes!' Nandini shrugged. 'So we back off?'

'No!' Sneha gestured. 'We never back off. We watch from a distance. You know, Viraj is not the only one changing!'

Nandini tilted her head to the side. She read Sneha's face accurately. 'Bitch, you have been holding out on me. Kya news hai?'

'I just found out like day before! Gayatri got her first paycheck last week. And the first thing she did was to inform Nik that she wants to move out of the hotel and into an apartment. A small regular apartment, nothing fancy, very basic. She's returned the car Nik bought for her and cancelled most of the credit cards Daddy Darling gave her.'

'Most?'

'She just kept one for emergency only.'

'So no help from Nikhil or Daddy?'

'Well, Nik offered her money, told her to take it as a loan and pay it back as and when she wanted. But she refused point blank. She told him she is starting something new and has a generous amount as an advance.'

'She didn't tell you who gave her the money or for what?' Nandini asked. Sneha shook her head. 'Suspeeecious!' Nandini tapped her chin.

'Enterprising and brave!' Sneha replied.

Nandini sobered. 'True!'

'Let those two find their own way to each other.' Sneha smiled a kind smile.

Nandini pouted. 'Not even a teeny tiny bit?'

'No! We'll watch.'

Nandini grinned.

'Can we eat our ice creams now? It is starting to melt!'

'You are an idiot.'

'So are you! And a bull.'

'As long as I'm not the chaddi!'

Lunch Shunch

'**K**nock, knock! Anybody home?'

'Come in, boss!' Gayatri called out, her face lightened up.

Viraj came in a washed pair of blue jeans and a green and white shirt rolled up at the sleeves. He had ditched his glasses and lab coat.

'So now we are calling each other names?'

'I am! Don't know about you!' Gayatri's smile was cheeky. 'What's up?'

'I asked Sana for coffee. She said yes.'

Gayatri clapped slowly. 'Nice! When?'

'Tomorrow after work. She is still very nervous. Are you sure it's a good move? Just hope it doesn't change Sana and my working relationship.' Viraj picked up a pencil and twirled it between his fingers.

'Just keep it very casual! Talk less and listen more! You guys have so many common interests. It should be easy!' Her stomach felt uneasy but Gayatri blamed the spicy biryani she had for lunch.

'We'll see! I'll call you after that!'

Gayatri smiled. 'And do wear the new clothes we bought yesterday!'

'So what's with the four-day holiday next week?' Viraj leaned on her desk. He was reluctant to leave her office.

'The weekend is followed by Ganesh Chaturthi.'

Viraj grunted. 'So what are you doing for the four days?'

'Something big!' Gayatri sat back with a smile. Her eyes gleamed.

Viraj leaned forward. 'What are you not telling me?'

'I'm moving out of the hotel into an apartment, my apartment!' Gayatri's face lit with pure joy.

Viraj studied her face wanting to etch her expression in his mind. Hope and excitement filled her eyes and spilled onto her full lips. Her smile made him want to smile.

'Say something?' Gayatri prodded.

'When and how did this happen?'

'Once you said to me, "whoever provides for you, decides for you." That got me thinking.'

'So you were listening to me?'

'Don't gloat!' Gayatri gave him a mock glare. 'With my first check last week and some money I came into, I got myself a teeny tiny apartment. It's small but it is all mine.'

'Very impressive! So which of the four days are you planning to move?'

Gayatri tapped her chin, 'Whyyy?'

'If I'm the reason you are moving then I should be the one helping you move. I did my bachelors and masters in the US where we did a lot of apartment-moving parties.'

'What college did you study in?'

Viraj murmured something under his breath.

'What college?'

Again something incoherent.

'Why are you mumbling?' Gayatri asked exasperated.

'Fine, I guess you should know. MIT!' Viraj blurted.

Gayatri rolled her tongue in her cheek. 'Name dropping!'

'That's why I was mumbling. It was all through scholarship though.' Viraj got to his feet.

'I'm proud of you, my boy!' Gayatri deepened her voice to sound masculine.

Viraj went, 'Phhbbbt!'

Gayatri threw a paper clip at him. Viraj caught it. As he brought down his hand, his eyes flickered and his smile dipped.

Gayatri immediately sensed the change in him. Her insides melted. Viraj took a step forward and Gayatri grabbed her chair as if she was ready to be pulled out of it. Both of them couldn't look away. Just then,there was a knock on the door and Dr Julius stuck his head in.

'Dr Viraj, we want to show you something. The test results on the prototype came back.'

'Great! I will be right there.' Viraj turned his head to her. 'I will take your leave.'

After Viraj left, Gayatri was deep in thought. Then she hesitantly picked up her cell and dialed Sneha's number. It rang a few times before being answered. 'Hi Sneha, it's me Gayatri! Is it a good time to talk?'

Since Sneha and Nandini happened to be in the vicinity, she invited Gayatri to meet for lunch.

Gayatri accepted. She worked straight until 11.30 a.m. and then headed out. Viraj bumped into her in the hallway

'Where are you off to?' Viraj asked lowering his voice.

His regular avatar was still as big a secret as Salman Khan's engagement status.

'Meeting Sneha for lunch! Will be back soon.'

'Bring me back something!' Viraj turned around to tread back to the lab.

'Sure! Spicy?' Gayatri asked with a straight face.

Viraj narrowed his eyes which were mockingly threateninging. 'Don't misunderestimate me!'

Gayatri chuckled feeling warm inside. Happy and carefree, she drove away in her car to meet the Double Trouble.

Gayatri parked the car and hurried into the Chinese restaurant called Nanking. The Double Troubles were not hard to spot.

'Hi!' Gayatri gave a quick hug to Sneha and smiled at Nandini. It was a round table and she took one of the chairs across from them.

A bit of social chatter and having ordered food, Sneha asked the million-dollar question. 'What's going on, Guy?'

Gayatri, taking a deep breath, gave a tepid smile to Nandini and began. Double Trouble did not interrupt her.

When Gayatri finished Double Trouble stayed quiet for a few minutes, pontificating.

Nandini broke the silence. 'So you found the poor scientist's weakness and exploited it?'

I never thought of it like that. Gayatri's smile was strained.

Sneha thumped the table. 'Atta girl. I'm so proud of you!'

'I was just messing with you!' Nandini dropped the act. 'Smart and seeeexxy!'

Gayatri's shoulders loosened. 'So you are not mad at me?'

'For what?' Sneha raised an eyebrow. 'You are not breaking

any laws.'

'You got an opportunity and you took it! One has to be freaking smart to do that!' Nandini seconded.

'And look what you did with that knowledge. You have done so much good there. The scientist's happy, the project pace is not only back on track but Phase 3 will be completed before the scheduled deadline.' Sneha high-fived her. 'Do you know how big it is? The actual battery will be ready before its launch and there will be more time for testing and more time for last minute tuning! IT'S HUGE, GIRL!'

'You are uniting lovers and acquainting us with a new Viraj, less crazy more sane Viraj. And how generous and helpful he is. Helping so many people. Thanks for showing us that side of him. First I was scared of him, but now I'm in awe.' Nandini added. 'You did good, Gayatri!'

'Thanks!' Embarrassed, Gayatri hid her face in her hakka noodles.

'Okay so when do Sana and Viraj go for their coffee date?' Sneha asked.

'Tomorrow after work!' Gayatri replied.

'That hardly leaves any time for a makeover. Today is almost over!' Nandini quipped.

'How about this? Let's change the plan a bit. Today is Wednesday. Nikhil and Aditya throw a celebratory party for the team on Friday. We have Sana come over earlier and get her ready for the party,' Sneha suggested.

'So no moving-party at my new place?' Gayatri asked.

'We'll do that after a week or two. Another chance for those two to meet outside of work,' Sneha added.

'Cool!' Gayatri nodded.

'Are you sure Sana is right for Viraj?' Nandini asked.

'Ya!' Gayatri shrugged delicately. 'She is totally his type, scientist and all. They'll make a good pair.'

'Of course they will, kulta. Gayatri knows what she is doing.'

'Can this stay between us? The whole Sana and Viraj thing.'

'Oh yeah, absolutely!' Sneha and Nandini said together.

'Great! I'm glad you both are on board. Now I can breathe easy,' Gayatri said nibbling on a chicken lollypop.

How wrong she was!

Sneha and Nandini watched Gayatri leave the restaurant.

Nandini turned to Sneha. 'She has no idea!'

Sneha nodded, 'Nope! None!'

'So are we going to give her the breaking news?'

'No! We are going to make her feel it. In a very painful way.' Sneha smirked.

'Oh Gayatri is going to be heartbroken. She really likes the dude. Her face was glowing when she was talking about him. Her eyes lit up and she couldn't stop smiling,' Nandini murmured.

'Sheesha ho ya dil ho aakhir toot jata hai!'

'I thought I was the filmy one, Sneh!' Nandini grinned.

'So can you arrange for an extra date?' Sneha asked

'Absolutely! Have you forgotten how many blind dates I arranged for you before you and Nikhil!' Nandini smiled wide.

'Yes I do! You are a freak!' Sneha smiled spooning some food in her mouth.

'I want Gayatri to burn!' Nandini said adding some soy

sauce to her fried rice.

'Ohh she will!' Sneha raised her glass of water in a toast.

'Yeah baby!' She picked up her glass of iced tea as a toast. 'To breaking hearts.'

Coffee and a Call

Next day around to 7.00 p.m., Gayatri brought out a suitcase from the top shelf of the inbuilt closet. Wiping it, she opened it on the floor. Gayatri checked her phone. There was no new text or missed call.

She packed her coats and jackets first. 'Bringing a coat to Mumbai is like wearing weights while swimming.' Bending her knee on the suitcase, she zipped it shut. Gayatri again checked her phone. It was 7.15 p.m.! No missed calls on new text messages.

She moved to the kitchen and grabbed one of the empty boxes stacked in the corner. All pots and pans went in it. She grabbed her cell from the kitchen counter. 7.40 p.m.! Nothing new, nothing missed!

'UGHHH! How long does it take to drink coffee?' Gayatri growled at her cellphone. 'I could use a glass of wine! BUT SOMEONE GOT RID OF IT ALL.' She shouted at the empty room. She dragged herself, got another empty box and packed it. She cussed, ranted, growled, even yelled, yet the phone continued to sit quieter than a statue. She turned it off and then waited for a whole minute, tapping her foot anxiously, before switching it back on. Still a statue!

At 9.00 pm the phone finally woke up from its comatose state. It rang! Gayatri jumped off the bed, scaled over the open suitcase in the doorway, avoided tripping over a packed box and managed to reach the phone without any broken bones.

Gayatri saw the number and was quick to answer it. 'How long does it take to have a cup of coffee?

Viraj, after a pause, said, 'Were you waiting for my call?'

'No! I was packing! I was busy!'

'Of course!' Viraj said, smiling.

Gayatri trying to be supercilious repeated, 'Of course!'

A long pause!

Viraj rolling his tongue against a cheek walked out on the balcony. 'So are you going to ask me?'

Gayatri walked back to her bed. 'If you don't want to tell me about it, that's fine!'

Viraj grinned down at his shoes. 'Are you jealous?'

'Are you mad?'

Viraj pulled the phone closer to his ear, liking how her voice sounded on the phone.

Resigned, Gayatri asked, 'So how was it?'

'Good!'

Gayatri perked up. 'Cool! Good like really good or very good?'

'What does that even mean?'

'Okay forget that. Give me some details?' Gayatri asked.

'Like you said, we had a lot in common and we talked a lot. She opened up today. Sana even felt comfortable enough to crack a joke or two. She is funny and very likeable!'

Suddenly, Gayatri scowled at the sheet. 'Great! Just great!'

'You don't sound happy! That was the plan, right? That Sana and I cosy up. Come close.'

'You can't come close in one night!'

'No, but I have known her for a while. So after today I feel this can really work. She and I can really work!'

Gayatri felt like breaking something. 'That is awful. Sorry, I meant awesome! Simply awesome!'

Viraj stayed quiet.

'You know what Vee, I'm tired. Let's catch up tomorrow. Good night!' Gayatri was quick to hang up.

Viraj looked at the phone, then the ocean, then phone again and then the sleeping sparrows. *What happened? What did I say?* And something hit him, something that made him smile. 'She called me Vee!'

In her apartment on her bed, Gayatri ran her hand down her cheeks, her expression tortured. 'Oh god! I called him Vee!'

I Am Dismissed

The following day, even though Gayatri stayed on his mind, Viraj stayed away from her side of the warehouse. *Don't know what ticked her off last night. I'll give her some time to cool down!* Viraj tried to tackle the design print on his table. They did not seem interesting enough, so he took out some more blue prints of various design components from the safe. After some time, Viraj sat back frustrated and unable to focus on any of them.

On her side, Gayatri viciously attacked the keyboard as she created an excel spreadsheet of overheads. *One coffee date and he has forgotten all about me. I'll be damned if I'll say hi to him. Like I give a flying fuck!*

The two passed most of the day avoiding eachother. It was only in the afternoon that they finally met.

A scientist had informed Gayatri that one of the vending machines was eating money but not dropping out candy bars. So after lunch she decided to take a look at it.

'Why aren't you giving any candy, you dumb machine?' Gayatri peeked inside the vents. They weren't blocked. She tapped the electronic panel. 'Obey me!' She tapped it harder.

'Obey me!' she threatened. Then she kicked the side of the machine hard. The machine shook but did nothing else. She kicked again. 'Do not be like that scientist and ignore me!' She lifted her foot ready to give it another kick.

'Which scientist is ignoring you?' Viraj's dulcet voice came from behind.

Damn it! Gayatri cringed, closed her eyes and then opened them. She slowly turned around. 'Huh?'

Viraj was leaning against the door jamb, his eyes twinkling, his chiseled face creased in a knowing smile. He wore a pale lavender T-shirt that sat snug over his well-toned chest and grey trousers with front pleats that hugged his muscular legs. His long hair was neatly combed and still fell on his shoulders. *God he is so handsome!*

'Do I pass?' Viraj smiled, his voice deepened.

You are the most handsome man I have seen! 'You are missing your glasses!' Gayatri sounded breathless even to herself. She felt tingly and her stomach knotted.

Viraj came inside the breakroom. Gayatri lowered her eyes and turned away to stop herself from staring at him. Viraj halted behind her. They both stared at the vending machine but all they felt was an unnerving awareness of each other's bodies.

'I ditched the glasses. They had no power anyway. They were just a part of the cover.' Viraj's breath tickled the top of her head. Gayatri felt hot all over. She moved to the side hoping to walk away, but Viraj put his arm out resting it on the vending machine, blocking her way. Lowering his face to her shoulder, Viraj said, 'The vending machine is not obeying the queen!' Now his hot breath grazed the bare skin of her shoulder that was exposed in her Queen Anne collar blouse. Gayatri closed her eyes and curled her nails into her palm to stop herself from falling back into him. She fidgeted around ready to move to the other side.

'Do you want me put my other arm out too?' Viraj's voice was heavy in her ear. His mouth grazed her ear fleetingly.

Gayatri felt singed and licked her dry lips. The entire atmosphere felt charged, like it were emitting sparks that were drawing them to each other as well as providing cover for them to do whatever they wanted.

The sound of the door opening forced them apart. Viraj moved aside freeing Gayatri.

'Everything okay?' It was Sana, her voice sounded timid as always.

Gayatri pasted a forced smile and pivoted. 'The vending machine is down. Dr Viraj is helping me fix it.'

Sana glanced at Viraj who had already walked over and was peering behind the machine. She walked over to him. 'Can I help?'

Gayatri blinked in surprise. *So they did open up yesterday. The earlier Sana would be quiet and nervous around Viraj but look at her now. Talking to him with such ease.* 'It happened in the afternoon—'

Sana cut her off, smiling shyly. 'We are looking at it. Give us a few minutes.'

Swallowing, Gayatri became quiet. *I have been dismissed!* Viraj was crouching behind the machine and Sana hovered over him. They were murmuring to each other. Gayatri felt like she was intruding. 'I'll be in my office if you need me!' She left them alone.

🍃

Viraj tugged the large plug out of the socket and the vending machine shut down. He waited for few seconds and then plugged it back in again. Some whizzing and beeping sounds later, the machine began dropping objects like a goat dropping you know what.

'It's working!' Viraj got up and came around. Gayatri wasn't there. 'Where did she go?' he asked Sana.

'She just left! She probably had something important to do,'

I hate vending machines! I was doing this for her. Viraj scowled. 'Fine then, let her know it's fixed!' He left the room in long strides. As he was passing by Gayatri's door, he paused. Viraj's hand went up to knock but then he paused.

Just then the door opened from inside. It was Gayatri. She stilled on seeing him outside her door, her expression boggled.

'The vending machine has been fixed!' Viraj's voice was terse as he brought his hand down.

'Thank you!' Gayatri kept her eyes fixed on his chin.

'Just got a call from Nikhil for a dinner party for the entire team! That's why I came to see you earlier,' Viraj said

'Do you have a minute?'

'For you I have more!' Viraj did not hesitate in replying.

Gayatri met Viraj's eyes. She opened the door and stepped to the side. As soon as he walked in, she shut the door behind him. Viraj stopped in the middle of the room and turned to her. Gayatri chose to remain near the door. 'We are doing this party to say thank you to the team and you, to celebrate our success and provide an opportunity to everyone here to have some fun and socialize.' She could not drum up any enthusiasm in her voice.

'Why are you being such a pain?'

Gayatri flinched. 'Excuse me?'

'You are bothered about something. Did I upset you? Are you upset about something else?' Viraj rubbed his forehead. 'I'm not good at reading minds!'

Gayatri exhaled heavily and leaned back on the door. 'It's all me! I'm sorry I have been acting weird. It's just that I have taken some hard decisions this past week or two. And I'm anxious and tired.' Gayatri's mouth twisted apologetically.

Viraj immediately came closer and clasped her face. Her skin was warm and softer than cream. 'Why didn't you say something? I can help you. Anything, just name it!' He stood close, towering over her.

Gayatri was thrilled at the way he held her face and the concern his eyes. His words penetrated the electric haze his closeness was swirling around her. *I can help you!* Gayatri brushed Viraj's hand away and put some distance between them. 'If I need any help, I will ask. But I really want to be independent. Do it all on my own. Like you all do!'

Viraj nodded. 'Whatever you want! But you don't have to prove anything to anybody.'

I do! Oh I do! Gayatri's smile was tepid. 'Thanks! Also one more request—you are going to be with Sana. So it's best we spend less time alone, you know. And we should keep a physical distance, at least a foot apart always.'

'Really?' Viraj crossed his arms and fixed her with a piercing stare.

Gayatri swallowed and her gaze flickered. 'Yes!' she replied hoarsely.

Viraj's features hardened. Without another word, he left her room.

Gayatri felt cheated when he did not slam the door behind him. She turned around gripped the chair and then kicked it. Her right foot cried silently. It was sore from the all kicking it had done today.

Shake It

Viraj went straight to his cubbyhole and slammed the door behind him. He felt angry and frustrated. 'Dammit!' He shoved some paper close to him. He rubbed his face. 'What is wrong with her? What is wrong with me?' He yelled at the empty room. *Why is Gayatri shutting me out? Did I touch her inappropriately? Did I make her uncomfortable?* A part of Viraj wanted to go and apologize to her while another part wanted to shake Gayatri and ki... *No, no, what am I thinking? Gayatri is right, I need to stay away from her.* Viraj sat down on the stool with a thump and stared blankly at the floor. He walked over to the safe. Unlocked it with unseeing eyes, he grabbed some confidential documents and splayed them on his desk.

Just then a loud rumbling broke out under his feet. The room swayed while things fell off his table. Viraj grabbed the side of the wall to steady himself. EARTHQUAKE! A strong one.

The ground kept shaking under his feet. Viraj ran out of his office. His team members were running towards the front door. He pushed open all the lab doors and left them wide open. 'Get everyone out! Get everyone out!'

Viraj rushed to the other side of the lab, to Gayatri's office. He thrust the door open. 'Gayatri! Gayatri!'

'In here, under the desk!'

Viraj ran to the other side of the desk and found her beneath it. He dropped to his knees and reached out to hold her but stopped, remembering her warning about touching. 'Are you scared? Are you stuck? Are you scared?'

Gayatri grabbed Viraj's wrist and pulled him closer. 'Get under the desk! Drop, cover and hold on.'

Viraj scuttled in under the desk next to her. 'What are you talking about?'

Gayatri gave him an are-you-kidding-me look. 'Basic earthquake safety rules—drop cover and hold on!'

The swaying stopped. Gayatri and Viraj looked at each other. 'Do you think it's over?'

Viraj nodded. 'Let's get out of the building. And for the record, you broke the one-foot rule.'

Gayatri rolled her eyes. 'Exigent circumstances. The rule is back in place!'

Snorting, Viraj came out from under the desk. One or two paintings on the wall had come loose and crashed on the floor.

'That's why I don't decorate!' Viraj quipped.

'You are so smart!' Gayatri prodded his back with her fingers. 'Let's get out of here!'

'You broke the one-foot rule again!' Viraj said, leading Gayatri out of the building.

Gayatri made an impatient sound.

Outside, the others were huddled in a group away

from the structure. Most of them were on their cellphones. Gayatri rushed towards them. 'Is everybody out? Is everybody accounted for?'

The employees gazed blankly at her.

'Okay let's remember who was working next to each other and see if we see them outside.' Gayatri turned to Viraj. 'Anything inside that can be damaged or leak and cause any kind of contamination or fire?'

'No, everything is 8.0 earthquake proof. This one felt moderate,' Viraj replied feeling a bout of pride in the manner in which Gayatri was taking charge.

'Julius and Sana are missing!' Someone called out.

'Shit!' Viraj hotfooted toward the entrance. Gayatri ran behind him. He stopped. 'You wait here, I will go and get them.'

'You can't bring two people by yourself! If you are going, I'm going!'

'I'll go in with Viraj sir!' Interrupted a voice.

'Yes, let's go Ashraf!' Viraj ordered. Chewing on her thumb Gayatri watched them head towards the glass door. Just then Julius came out supporting Sana who was leaning on him. Gayatri and Viraj ran to them. Gayatri took Sana and supported her.

'Are you okay, Sana? What happened, Julius?' Gayatri asked.

'During the earthquake I think she hit her head on the wall or something. I found her lying unconscious in the hallway outside the last lab.'

'Why don't you take Sana and sit her down under the shade. Some of us will go inside and get some bottles of water.' Viraj gestured a few from his team to come with him.

'Grab some change and get some food from the vending machines!'

Viraj's look at Gayatri was testy. 'You want me to use the vending machines?'

'Please!' Gayatri made the face she did not know Viraj could not resist.

Viraj gritted his teeth and went inside. *Of course she has to make the face I can't resist.*

Gayatri took Sana and helped her sit on the ground. She felt the girl's pulse; it was normal. 'Are you feeling dizzy?'

Mumbling, Sana rested her head against the tree behind her.

'Let me call up and cancel tonight's dinner.'

Sana squeezed her hand tightly. Gayatri winced. 'Please don't! I don't get to go out much and my parents allowed me this one time. So please!' she pleaded.

'Let me check with Sneha to make sure that they all are okay.' Gayatri extricated her hand from Sana's painful grip. She got up and glanced at the other side of the road. People were out loitering in front of their houses, shops and offices. But there were no fallen buildings or injured people. *Thank god!*

She made some calls to Sneha and Nikhil. They were fine. The earthquake's epicenter had been in the adjoining mountain range. Thus, except the moderate jolt, there had not been much damage to life or otherwise. Next, Gayatri went to each employee to inquire if their families were okay.

Viraj and his team came out carrying bottles and small packets of snacks. They distributed it amongst everyone.

Gayatri joined them. 'So I checked and everyone is okay!

And I spoke to Sneha. She said the dinner party is still on.'

'Where is Sana?' Viraj asked.

'I'm here!' Sana called out weakly.

'Glad everyone is okay. Now let's party!' Viraj went around talking to everyone, explaining the details of the party venue and handing out water and snacks. Gayatri noticed the surprised looks on everyone's faces. Normal Viraj was as normal as a Yeti sighting.

All of them said a jaunty 'yes' to the party. Gayatri saw Viraj walk over to Sana and take a seat next to her. Heads lowered, they talked with each other. Gayatri felt a sudden flicker of something in her insides—like somebody was dropping acid over a part of her body, several parts of her body. *Okkkayyy the earthquake shook my brains!*

Gayatri went and joined the other scientists. She couldn't help peeking at Sana and Viraj. They kept conversing. Sana played with a loose strand of her hair and then her dupatta. The acid dripped some more!

Bored with the conversation and company around her, Gayatri walked away from the group. Something stopped her, something made her look sideways. *If something scares you, don't run from it! Study it, observe it and then it is just another thing that's not scary because you understand it!* Gayatri remembered her therapist's words. Her therapist was a smart lady.

Taking a deep breath, Gayatri walked to the pavement—the pavement where she had been attacked. Sweat beaded her face and her gall bladder tingled. Gayatri forced her mind to remember the moment when she had all the attackers on the ground—not the fear but the feeling once she overpowered the fear. Gradually her heart returned to its normal beat and her bladder calmed down.

Someone cleared a throat behind her. Gayatri's face softened and she turned slowly.

Viraj stood there, his arms crossed, gazing at her watchfully. Gayatri waited for him to say something and he did. 'I'm letting everyone go home early today. You too!'

Gayatri opened her mouth but Viraj was already walking away from her. *That's it?* 'Thanks!' she murmured. Acid wasn't dripping any more, it was flowing!

Gayatri walked back to the warehouse.

'Hi Gayatri!' someone called out.

Gayatri stopped and glared. Thes she smiled and turned. 'Hi Sana!'

'Can you open this bottle?'

Sure Sana, whatever you say, Sana! 'Sure!' Gayatri went over and twisted the bottle cap.

'I think Viraj sir, I think Viraj likes me! He and I look nice together, don't we?' Sana extended her hand up and took the water bottle from Gayatri.

Gayatri gave a tight smile and walked back inside.

Welcome Back, Bitch!

Gayatri parked her car and made her way to the restaurant. She was drained. Physically and emotionally she was more twisted than jalebis on a platter. Her feelings for Viraj were pounding the hell out of her mental balance. *Being good, responsible and a person with integrity is effing hard!* She straightened her bracelet and grimaced. The worst part of all this was that the changes in her seemed irreversible. 'Dammit!' Gayatri frowned when she caught herself smiling at the antics of some three- or four-year-old girls in the park outside the restaurant. They did look adorable in their polka dot frocks and pink satin bows tied in their dark locks. 'Darth Dutta, come back!' she muttered and stepped into the restaurant. The party was on full swing. Nikhil was closest to the door. Gayatri hugged him. 'What took you so long?'

'Sorry, I had a previous appointment.' Gayatri glanced around. 'This is nice. Sneha and Nandini did a great job.'

'Nandini more. Sneha and I just arrived ourselves.' Nikhil adjusted his collar. 'The scientists are having fun.'

'Yes they are!' Sneha grinned. 'Oh god I never thought I'd see Kalra dance to It's the time to disco!' She waved at the older scientist who was grooving on the dance floor and resembled giant waving displays.

'By the way let me be the first to tell you that you have done an amazing job at the lab. The team has said wonderful things about you. Including the main scientist.' Nikhil pulled Gayatri's ear lobe like he had been doing since she had been in pigtails.

'Stop it!' Gayatri gave him a mock frown. 'And by the way you are not first to tell me that. Your wife was.'

Nikhil poked her in the side. 'My wife is smart. After all, look who she married.'

'Ouch!' Gayatri flinched. She pinched the skin at his wrist. Nikhil jerked. 'She had to be smart. What choice did she have? So she married you!'

'Oh so you have grown a mouth. Don't make me tackle you!'

'This is sweet! To see you two like that,' Sneha said, joining them.

'Barf!' Gayatri grinned and gave her a hug.

'Ditto!' Nikhil said and hugged them both together, squishing them.

'Stoppp Nik!' Gayatri wiggled. Sneha laughed.

'Family picture!' Nandini came armed with her cell.

Gayatri, Sneha and Nikhil obliged, all of them still tangled up in arms.

'Purrfect!' Nandini clicked a few. Nikhil let go of the two women he had his arms around.

'Gotta go and meet my brain bank!' Gayatri smiled wryly and made her way to the table full of her colleagues.

She flicked her gaze around the room. *I don't see him or*

Sana! 'If he can ignore me, then so can I and I can do even better!' Gayatri promised herself, curling her upper lip.

For the next ten minutes she mingled around and even did the Macarena with two enthusiasts on the dance floor. Yet her gaze kept wandering around. *Where the fuck is he? If I can't see him how will I ignore him?* Gayatri's expression was part fierce, like a warrior itching to run into battle, and part frustrated, like a passenger waiting for a train that was running 365 days late.

Gayatri felt someone come up from behind. Her stomach tightened and her heart thudded in anticipation. She was, after all, expecting the crazy mad scientist. On pivoting around, she felt sharp disappointment—it was double trouble.

'Oh my god, you missed it Gayatri?' Nandini said, puckering her mouth.

'You did miss it!' Sneha added, grinning.

'What did I miss?' Gayatri titled her neck.

'Viraj's reaction to a stunning Sana!' Nandini preened. 'I did her makeup! You missed it!'

Gayatri worked her mouth but could not utter a simple thanks.

'Why are you glaring at me? Did I do something wrong, Sneha?' Confused, Nandini slowly rotated her neck.

'She is not glaring, she is listening intently, Kuls!' Sneha clarified. 'Right?'

'Yes! Of course!' Gayatri swallowed. 'So they are here already?'

'Oh yeah! They have been here for a while. Viraj took Sana out to the garden at the back of the partyhall. I think they are "chatting"!' Sneha did the quote and unquote gesture with her fingers.

Nandini giggled. 'Yeah right! Just like you and I chat with Nik and Adi.'

Sneha raised her eyebrows. 'You look green! Are you ok, Guy?'

'I'm fine!' Gayatri nodded quickly.

'Let's take a peak, Sneha. We can see the garden from the window across the room,' Nandini suggested, her expression mischievous.

'Don't be silly! We should give them privacy,' Sneha wagged her finger.

'C'mon we are just taking a look. We aren't running them over with a bulldozer or anything,' Gayatri said, her voice sounded normal even though her eyes were hard as a rock. 'Which window, Nandini?'

Nandini's mirth wavered. 'Ughh!' She glanced at Sneha who nodded at her. 'That one! Last on the right!'

Gayatri walked right past them.

'Do you want us to come?' Nandini called.

'Sure!' Gayatri threw back.

Gayatri skirted around the crowd and went to the window Nandini had pointed at. She lifted the gauze curtain and sneaked her head behind it. It took her few seconds to adjust her vision to the darkness outside. She definitely saw a garden with different levels, a koi pond, a gazebo and then a bench—a bench with two figures. Viraj and Sana, sitting close! Sana was talking even as her lips creased in a wide smile. And Viraj was leaning and listening closely, his face turned sideways to look into her eyes.

Gayatri bit her lip. She covered her mouth but like a

sadist getting her fix from pain. She could not take her eyes off them. *I hate Nandini. She's made Sana look all soft and beautiful.* Ms I'm-so-timid's glasses were gone, her usually braided hair was loose and curled framing her thin face in the most becoming way. She seemed to be wearing a form-fitting pink tee and a black sequin skirt. And then Gayatri glanced at Viraj. She bit deeper into her lip.

Viraj was looking even more handsome than she thought possible for any man. His dark hair was combed back showing his chiseled cheekbones, his pronounced jawline, his brooding eyes fringed by long eyelashes. The lights in the garden seemed to add a shimmer to his eyes. His clothes were sharp—a black silk shirt teamed with formal gray trousers and black suede shoes. He was looking every bit a rake, actually something even more dangerous than a rake—a well-dressed, intelligent rake!

The beautiful and mysteriously lit garden with Viraj and Sana's stillness made them seem like couple some artist had painted across a canvas.

'You did a great job, Guy!' Sneha whispered from behind.

'Yikes!' Gayatri jumped from being startled. However, she kept her face angled away from Sneha as she needed some time to repair her mascara. She was positive it had messed up in the last few minutes. 'What do you mean?' She blinked her eyes and then ducked her head. 'Shit, he is looking this way.'

Sneha pressed back into the wall. She looked down at Gayatri cowering below the windowsill. Sneha chuckled, 'We are so brave!'

Gayatri slowly backed away. 'Yes we are!' She straightened once she was away from the window.

Sneha frowned, 'Hey, your mascara—'

Gayatri shrugged, 'I know! I'm just going to the bathroom to fix it.'

'Listen Guy! Don't be mad, but I kind of invited someone I'd like you to meet.'

Gayatri paused and searched Sneha's face. 'A blind date? For me?'

Sneha raised her hand appealingly. 'He's a hunk! Please don't be mad!'

Gayatri clicked her fingers and smiled. 'I'm not mad! Not at all! You had me at hunk!'

She went into the bathroom. 'Game face on, Sistah!' she said, winking at her reflection. Gayatri pulled her hair open and let it cascade over her shoulders and down her waist. She opened her clutch, took out some make-up and aligned it on the counter in front of her. In less than fifteen minutes she was done. 'Welcome back, bitch!' Gayatri winked at her reflection, tossed her things back in her clutch and sashayed out of the restroom.

The Man Has Made up His Mind

I'm wasting her time! Viraj watched Sana, his eyes hooded. She was telling him about her family—her father was a retired bank manager; her older brother had his own accountancy firm and her middle brother worked in the sales department of a car company. *She's pretty, but!* Viraj gave an odd nod or two, feigning he was listening. *How was I so wrong?* Viraj glanced at his shoes, which were different from his regular sneakers. *Who exactly am I trying to impress here?*

'Do you like me dressed like this? Am I less intimidating?' Viraj cut off Sana as she was talking about her nephew.

'No! I mean liked you fine as before,' Sana replied timidly. 'You are so knowledgeable. You are a genius. All of us at the lab look up to you. Even Dr Kalra.'

Viraj sat back crossing his arms. 'That old fusspot! He fights me tooth and nail on everything.'

Sana peeped at him from under her lashes. 'He's like that with everyone. So do you like how I look?' Her colour was high and her hands not the steadiest.

'Yes! Yes! You look very pretty. Very different from the girl we all are used to seeing.' Viraj narrowed his eyes at the window of the restaurant. He thought he saw movement at the window.

'Did you hear what I said?' Sana asked.

'No, I'm sorry! I thought...' Viraj pointed at the window. 'What were you saying?'

Sana gave him a shy smile and looked away. 'I did this makeover for...for...'

Viraj got uncomfortable as she hesitated. He chose to interrupt her. 'Maybe we should—'

'I did this makeover for you,' Sana blurted.

Viraj got to his feet and straightened his cuffs. *This makes perfect sense—she and I. Should I say something?*

Sana was blushing to the roots of her hair. Her hands tightly clasped in her lap were quivering.

Viraj opened his mouth. 'I...I...' *Dammit! Why can't I say it? It's my opening to ask her out! This is what I wanted.* Viraj swallowed, trying to will his mouth to say what he had planned. *This is what I want...but with Gayatri.* Viraj blinked and turned away from the girl gazing at him with hope. *Fuck!*

'It's her, isn't it? You hesitate because of her. Don't you?'

Viraj turned at that.

'Gayatri! You hesitate because of her.' Sana stood up, her eyes lowered. She sounded pained.

Viraj walked to the koi pond and watched the fishes. 'I'm sorry!' He exhaled.

'You wish she was here. Don't you?'

Heck yes! 'What? No! Actually we should go inside. The others must be wondering.' Viraj avoided the question.

'Why not?' Sana sighed and walked ahead of him.

Viraj followed her, knowing he had arrived at a decision.

It's like he knew exactly what he wanted to do with his life at this moment. He had an instantaneous clarity as to who he wanted...*for life!* Ms Manipulation, who could kick ass, all the while beaming like an angel! Gayatri Dutta.

Shit Is about to Hit the Ceiling

'What? I'm sorry the music is too loud.' Gayatri leaned in to hear better what her blind date, Manish Sood, was saying. She noticed him look down her blouse, not that she cared. With his tall, muscular frame, clean cut features and prep boy haircut, he was quite pleasant on the eyes. Only on the eyes!

The moment Gayatri leaned in to hear Manish, he sneaked an obvious glance down her blouse, again. Right then, Viraj and Sana entered the party hall. Gayatri turned and her eyes immediately met Viraj's. For a second that felt like an eternity neither of them looked away. Then Viraj's dark gaze ran over Gayatri. He took in her dark hair that was open today unlike the usual sleek ponytail, the flushed cheeks with some natural colour and some brushed on, eyes that were painted alluring with golden and red eye shadow and her lips were the colour of blood. Gayatri saw Viraj's eyes dip and take in her blouse that was unbuttoned dangerously low.

'Time to say hello to my boss!' Gayatri started to swagger down towards Viraj, leaving Manish hanging mid-sentence. Manish put a retraining hand on her arm.

Gayatri saw Viraj's face tighten at Manish's possessive touch. 'Darling, why the rush, we have all night,' she murmured throatily in his direction, knowing very well that Viraj was watching her. She saw the gleam in the hunk's eyes at what he thought she was suggesting. *Idiot!* Gayatri focused back on her target. She glided, in the direction of Viraj and Sana.

'Ohh!' Nandini elbowed Sneha. 'She looks unhinged!'

Sneha nodded discreetly. 'Yup! She does!' Double trouble had parked themselves in the corner of the hall to have a full view of the proceedings.

'Is Gayatri drunk?' Nandini asked.

'No! She's mad. Did you notice how she changed her appearance?'

'I thought that was for the mad scientist.'

'Oh it was for him, but not to please him. To make him mad. This is Guy going into battle. She's doing what she does best!' Sneha hid her mouth behind her glass.

'What might that be?'

'Making a bad situation worse!'

'Do you think we might have overstepped? Nandini gulped.

'Nandini!'

Nandini straightened. Sneha rarely called her by her name. That was meant for super serious situations. Serious situations with tragic ends.

'Yes Sneha?' Nandini whispered.

'Shit is about to hit the ceiling!'

'So we are not the bulls?' Nandini's voice was a whisper.

'Nope!'

Sneha grimaced. 'We are the red chaddis!'

'Damn!' Nandini squeaked. 'I always wanted to be the bull!'

Don't Let the Herd in

'Hey you two! Where did you disappear?' Gayatri asked, her look coy and suggestive.

Sana visibly shrank from her.

Gayatri put a hand on Sana's shoulder. 'Don't be scared of me. I don't bite!'

Viraj took her arm. 'Can I talk to you?' He did not wait for her to answer; he nearly dragged her to the corner off the room.'

'Hey! Your scientist girlfriend might get jealous.' Gayatri yanked her elbow out of Viraj's grip.

'Why are you looking like that? And who's that joker?' Viraj's eyes were stormy, his mouth a thin line in his face.

Gayatri's laugh was low and sarcastic. 'Look like what? Sexy? Confident? In control?'

'In control? You look nothing like yourself. You looks like some...some,' Viraj cast a derisive glance at her appearance, 'like some tart.' He was literally biting his words.

Gayatri blinked. A damn good poker player, and a proud one at that, she would never show the rip in her heart. 'Just because I spent a month or two with you, you think you know the real me?' Gayatri sneered. 'You don't know Jack about me! You only know what I want you to know about me!'

Viraj scowled. 'You are talking rubbish!'

'Hello!' Manish, the hunk, interrupted.

'Buzz off! She's busy.' Viraj retorted.

Before Manish could get in a word, Gayatri let a contrived laugh escape her throat. 'Sorry Manish. The boss is always right,' Gayatri paused and then she shook her finger. 'But not in this instance. In this instance I think the boss is incorrect, way incorrect, completely off the mark incorrect.' The laugh again!

Viraj took her elbow again. 'Have you been drinking?'

'Is that a crime? Have some fun, boss!' Gayatri took Manish's arm and dragged him. Manish was only too happy to oblige.

Viraj curled his hands. He wanted to hammer Manish six feet under, no six thousand feet under. *Gayatri has no business looking like this! Like she was Venus, the goddess of sex, love, beauty and fertility.* This Geek knew his Greek. *And being with some loser...*

'A penny for your thoughts!' Sneha interrupted.

'Hmm!' Viraj grunted.

'Okay you can drop the act now!' Sneha clucked her tongue.

Viraj, taken aback glanced sideways.

'You are normal. I know that. Gayatri told me!'

Viraj began to walk away. His mind was like an explosion of conflicted feelings. Each pulling him in different directions!

'I had my life planned after my divorce. It was my chance to do things my way or so I thought.' Viraj paused at Sneha's words. She moved closer to him. 'But then just when I thought

I was on the road to achieving them, Nik came into my life. All the plans I had made went for a toss. I got distracted, I lost sight of my plans.'

'Is this a warning?' Viraj asked, scuffing his shoe on the wooden floor.

'When people come into your life—'

'They crowd it, they complicate it.'

'Yes and yes!' Sneha flexed her shoulders. 'But they also make your life worth living, they make you feel alive. You make new plans with them and around them!' Sneha patted his arm. 'But please don't let the whole herd in, just one or two people.'

Make your life worth living! The phrase seemed to play in a loop in Viraj's head. He realized that it had been ages since he had any thoughts about Lunxemborg. Now he wanted to live till his last breath. And even if he did not have Gayatri, she had shown him that life always has a trump card up its sleeve. 'Gayatri!' Viraj uttered her name with reverence, with hope.

'Gayatri…!' Sneha moaned. 'Is about to take the mike! You'd better run!'

'No I'm staying, but probably in the back of the room!' Viraj walked away.

He Is a Con

'You play such bad music. Can you shut it off! I have to make an announcement!' Gayatri said to the DJ. The DJ, a thirty-year-old man covered in tats and several body piercings, gaped but then turned off the music and arrogantlywalked away . 'Do you ever get past airport security with all those rings?' Gayatri scoffed at his back. He showed her the finger. 'No sense of humor!'

Gayatri grabbed the wireless mike and walked to the edge of the dance floor. The employees were scattered. Some were near the food counter, some on the dance floor wondering why the music had stopped and some seated at the table.

Lowering her head, Gayatri spoke into the mike. 'Good evening, people and scientists!' Then she paused. 'You know what, I can't see you all and I need to see you all, so I'm going to do something. Please don't try this at home!' She dragged the nearest chair to the dance floor.

Gayatri tossed her shoes to the side and climbed on the chair, carefully holding the mike close to her. She straightened herself. 'Okay, much better. I can see you all.'

Someone whistled in the crowd. It was the hunk.

'Thank you, Manish,' Gayatri bowed just a bit, afraid she might fall off the chair. 'Okay! I'm gonna keep it short and maybe sweet!' That got some laughs.

'Everyone, thank you for coming here tonight. This is the company's way of saying thank you for all your hard work over the past months. Please enjoy the food and the music. And please don't come to my office to eat the leftovers.' The inside joke definitely got some laughs from the scientists.

'Why has Gayatri climbed on the chair?' Sana asked, coming up behind Viraj.

'Like she said, so she can see everyone,' Viraj replied, unable to look anywhere else but at Gayatri. *She is so damn beautiful. I have to talk to her, let her know how I feel. Will she shoot me or reciprocate?* Viraj's body warmed and hardened at the thought she might reciprocate and the definite direction he would take their mutual reciprocation in.

'Everybody is staring at her,' Sana was quick to point, censure in her voice.

'I know!' Viraj couldn't help a smile. 'I'm sure she is enjoying that.'

Sana giggled. Viraj glanced down at her and then realized that she has understood his last comment as something snarky against Gayatri. Smiling, he opened his mouth to deny it but then stopped. *How is that important?*

And at that very instant, Gayatri peeped in their direction. Viraj saw her eyes harden as she stared at him and then she whipped her head away and smiled.

She is going to skewer me!

Viraj was on the money.

Gayatri saw Viraj and Sana huddled close, smiling. Sana's glance gave Gayatri a feeling that they were discussing her. *THEY ARE LAUGHING AT ME! Hope they extend the same humour to themselves.* And then Gayatri smiled—the smile of a hitman about to pull the trigger.

Sneha and Nandini shared a worried glance at the smile. Nikhil and Aditya had joined their wives.

'So tonight we are out of the lab, having fun and getting to know each other and hopefully beginning to like, if not like, at least not hate those who we work with,' Gayatri announced.

Her audience chuckled. She only grew bolder.

'So in the spirit, of getting to know each other, let's get to know our quintessential boss, Dr Viraj.'

Everybody in the room grew quiet.

'Oh don't look like that. He is as normal as you and I. His weirdness is all an act. He is a CON!' Gayatri smiled even as her eyes met Viraj's challengingly.

There was a deathly silence in the room.

'There she does it again!' Nikhil muttered, his mouth constricted.

Sneha murmured under her breath. 'Bad situation just got worse!'

'Is she mad?' Aditya barked in lowered voice.

Nandini shook her head, disappointed. 'She's the bull!'

Everyone's eyes were trained on Viraj. They all awaited his reaction. Most people in the room were sure that they were about to see Gayatri fired live.

Gayatri brought the mike down and the confidence on her sultry face wavered.

Viraj studied her face. Reaching out to the nearest table he picked up an untouched glass of water and raised it. 'To the team and our Operations Manager whose sense of humour is not confined to her office or chair.'

Loud laughter and glances of surprise broke out amongst those in the party hall. Gayatri appeared put out, for she had been spoiling for a confrontation. Nikhil helped her off the chair. 'Today is your lucky day, Guy!'

Gayatri took his hand and jumped off. 'I scared you, didn't I?'

'You scared everyone here!' Sneha remarked dryly joining them.

Gayatri saw Viraj coming toward them, her stomach churned. *He can still fire me!*

'Oh, your cell is going off like crazy. Someone called Bawi keeps calling you.' Sneha handed Gayatri her cellphone which she had dropped while spying on Viraj and Sana.

'Shoot! I have to take this outside.' Gayatri was pleased at the timely interruption. Viraj had stopped to make polite conversation with those who accosted him. *Now everyone wants to talk to him.* Gayatri treaded to the door.

'I knew it! I knew it. I knew the scientist was bloody faking his weird behaviour. Thank you, Gayatri.' Aditya stopped her, his handsome face animated.

'You are welcome. Excuse me!' She hurried to main door.

A text message appeared on her cell. 'The money has been arranged. They have agreed to what you asked. But you have to come now.'

Gayatri grabbed Nandini who was passing her. 'Hey! Can you do me a favor? Will you please let the others know I have to leave now? It's super important.'

'Now? But you are the life of the party.' Nandini protested.

'I almost got myself fired.' Gayatri's expression was sheepish. 'I've gottta go. Please apologize to everyone on my behalf.'

'But at this hour? Should one of us come with you?'

'I'm good. I'll text Sneha or Nik! See you later. Bye!' Gayatri hurried out. At the door of the restaurant she paused and peeked over her shoulder. Her heart ached, for only she knew of the big change coming her way. 'I will miss you all.' She spoke of everyone but she looked only at Viraj, who was still surrounded by people. And then Gayatri was gone.

Nandini joined Sneha and their husbands. 'So Gayatri bailed on us. Something important came up.'

'What? She's gone? She livened this zombie ball,' Sneha said.

'Did she say why she was leaving?' Nikhil asked Nandini.

'Nope! She said it was something important,' Nandini replied.

'Oh Manish is gone too!' Aditya smirked. Manish was his golf buddy. 'Wonder if something is cooking there?' Nikhil glared at him. Aditya was quick to make amends. 'They have probably gone to get coffee or drinks, separately of course. I can vouch for Manish, he is stand-up guy.'

'Yes right Adi, we all saw the way Manish was looking at Gayatri,' Nandini teased.

Sneha put a hand on Nikhil's arm. 'She'll be fine. Don't worry.'

'I'll call her.' Nikhil dialed her number. After a minute or two he hung up. 'She isn't answering.'

'We'll try again. She's fine, don't worry. For now let's focus on our guests,' Sneha reminded.

They did not notice Viraj standing close by with a group of his team members. As the music was still off Viraj had clearly heard their conversation. Taking his cell out, Viraj texted Gayatri. 'What time should I come to help you with the move?'

Her reply came in a few minutes. 'You are off the hook. Manish is helping me (smiley and a winking face) You and Sana have fun. Take her out for a movie. She likes action, Avengers type.'

Viraj read the text a few times. He made his way to the food counter, specifically to the jug of water. He dropped his cell in it and then without saying a word to anyone left the party.

Number 34th

Monday Morning
Viraj's apartment

'GO AWAY!' Viraj hollered to the loud knocking on the door. Lying face down on his bed, his hair matted over his face, his body felt stiff. *Have I been in bed for years?* His lips were stuck to his pillow. The knocking continued!

'What the fuck!' Viraj lifted his head. His eyes ached and were crusty. His head weighed like someone had placed a fifty kilo rock on it. 'Dammit!' Cursing some more, he pushed himself out of the bed. The daylight stung his eyes. Shading his eyes, Viraj staggered to the door. He unlocked it. 'What the hell?' He shouted at the burly, six-foot-four man who had his fist raised, ready to pound the door.

'I work for Nikhil sir!'

'Well, he is not here!' Viraj leaned against the doorjamb for he had a hard time supporting himself. His mouth tasted like he had been eating from the trash. 'Get lost!' He turned to shut the door but the man put his hand on the door and held it open. 'I can break your arm dude!' Viraj threatened but then he spoilt the effect by belching.

The big man waved his hand over his face. 'You need to brush!'

Viraj closed his eyes and slumped against the door. 'And you need to go.'

The big man dialed a number on his cell and gave it to Viraj. 'It's Nikhil sir, please talk to him. Please!' The man turned away the phone. 'He will fire me if you don't!'

Grudgingly, Viraj took the cell. 'Hello!' He heard Nikhil for barely few seconds when he interrupted forcefully. 'That's bullshit. I'll be there ASAP!' Viraj tossed the phone back to the man. 'Can you drive me there?'

'Yes sir! I'll be in the car downstairs. The silver Mercedes!'

'Give me ten minutes.' Viraj staggered back inside and went to the bathroom. He went straight for the pot and threw up. Drinking straight for two days along with the allegations made by Nikhil made him sick to his gut. He flushed a few times and went to the sink where he unloaded half of the toothpaste tube on his brush and thrust it in his mouth.

Next followed a quick shower. He put on his clothes and ran to the door. *I don't care what Nikhil says. Gayatri would never sell me out.*

Viraj was a restless passenger. He kept egging the driver to drive faster.

The last two days had been a haze. After seeing Gayatri's message, Viraj had gone off in a drinking spree. The last he remembered was buying several bottles of whiskey and drinking himself until he passed out. It was all a haze. He remembered his mom and Keshav had come to check on him but he had feigned flu and waived them off. He knew he hadn't fooled them because his Mom was unlike other mothers in that she believed one has to work on his or her own demons. She had come and left him home-cooked food regularly but she had broken all the bottles loudly. After she had left, Viraj had just staggered out and bought some more booze.

'Dammit!' Viraj kept reaching out to pull his phone from his pocket and then he remembered that he had dunked his cell in a water jug. Scientists can be stupid too!

When they reached Nikhil's building, Viraj thrust some money in the driver's hand and ran in.

'This is not a taxi!' the driver called out.

Viraj pressed his finger on the doorbell till someone opened the door.

The maid was expecting him. She pointed him straight in the direction of the library. Viraj did not knock, he just walked in.

Nikhil wasn't alone. Sneha, Aditya, Nandini and a few other people—Viraj's investors were—there. Everybody wore matching expressions—grim. On the large television screen, Viraj saw a few more faces via video conference. More investors!

'What happened?' Viraj asked Nikhil.

'I'm sorry my stupid daughter sold us all out,' one of the faces on the screen spoke. Gayatri's father!

Viraj ignored him. 'What did our competitors get?'

'Initial designs. But the damage is done. They know what we are making. They know what you are making.' Nikhil thumped the table. Water bottles shook and some papers slid off the table. Sneha stepped forward. Nikhil waved her off. 'I'm fine!'

'And you all think Gayatri sold us out?' Viraj brushed

his wet hair back.

'Who else could it be? I know my daughter. She is stupid, selfish and greedy. I warned you, Nikhil, not to let her in and you did not listen. And look where we are. Gayatri only cares about money. She was going to marry Aditya just for his money. I'm sorry, gentleman. Feel free to file a police report against her. I will not stop you.'

'Have you spoken to Gayatri?' Viraj only addressed Nikhil or Sneha.

'I have been trying to call,' Sneha replied. 'Her phone keeps coming switched off. She is no longer at the hotel. We all knew she was moving this weekend. None of us have her new address. Do you?'

'No!' Viraj frowned, his expression thoughtful.

'And tell him how she came into sudden money. And how she used her access card on Saturday to enter the lab. A day when everyone was off. She's very clever. I told you son—'

'Will you stop calling me your fucking son!' Viraj finally had enough of Gayatri's father.

For a second everyone froze and then Dutta Senior started. 'Look here—'

Viraj put his hand out stopping the older man mid-sentence. He looked at Nikhil and Aditya and at then all the investors. 'I will make you a deal. In the next forty-eight hours I will prove Gayatri innocent. If I fail, I will give a million-dollar discount to each of you on what you will be paying me after Phase 3.'

'And if you succeed?' Aditya asked.

'If I succeed, I will buy his share out,' Viraj said, pointing at Gayatri's dad.

'You little upstart, how dare you?' Gayatri's father blustered. 'Who the hell do you think you are? I will crush you, I—'

'Deal!' Nikhil extended his hand out.

'I second that!' Aditya added.

'Let's take a vote,' Nikhil said to the table even as Gayatri's father kept making angry sounds but went ignored. Everyone voted in favour of Viraj's buy-out option.

'I'll see you all day after tomorrow.' Viraj turned to leave and then stopped. He turned back to face his investors. 'All my designs at every stage are patent-protected, on the design as well as utility. Sue the company that has my designs. Go make some more money because of me!' Viraj swung his head and met Senior Dutta's angry narrowed eyes. 'What? Did you think this was my first big invention? 34th!' And then Viraj left the room.

The door opened behind him. 'Viraj, wait!'

He stopped. Sneha came, followed soon after by Nandini.

'We want to help,' Sneha requested.

'What can we do?' Nandini added.

Viraj sighed. 'I'm going to find who did this, who leaked my designs and this will automatically prove Gayatri innocent. Meanwhile, you both can actually work on finding Gayatri.'

Nandini and Sneha exchanged blank glances.

'Ab kya?' Nandini asked.

'Like he said, find Gayatri. I just thought she was with him.' Sneha chewed her bottom lip. 'I just assumed that she had found her happy ending.'

'Happy Ending? Picture abhi baki hai mere dost!' Nandini

waved her hand. 'Shit, we should go to the police. Essentially, Gayatri has been missing since the last two days.'

The door to the library opened and the investors trooped out. Even though Viraj's declaration that his designs were patent-protected had exponentially brought stress levels down in the room, the after-effects of a stressful night and morning still showed on their faces. Their exit was hurried. Aditya came out of the library and signaled Sneha and Nandini to come in.

In the library, Sneha found Nikhil sitting on a chair with a blank look on his face.

Sneha walked to Nikhil and pressed her hand on his shoulder. 'We'll find Gayatri, Nik. I'm sure she is okay!'

'What kind of an asshole brother am I? I have no idea where she is!' Nikhil said, his mouth twisting bitterly.

'Let's not waste time talking. Nikhil and I will go to the police station. You and Nandini go to the hotel where she was staying and get some information.' Aditya made some quick decisions.

Nikhil nodded and seemed okay for once to give the charge to someone else. Nandini impulsively gave him a quick hug. 'We will find her, Nik!' She peeped at Sneha. 'Shall we?'

Sneha nodded. 'Let me just check on Vey, and tell Amla. Give me a sec.'

'I'll come with you!' Nikhil followed her.

Once Sneha and Nikhil had left the room, Aditya walked to Nandini and gathered her in his arms holding her close.

'I'm scared, Adi.'

Aditya rubbed her back. 'Don't be. This is Gayatri we are talking about. She's tough.'

Nandini tipped her head up. 'They why are you going to

the police station?'

Aditya dropped a peck on her lips and then hugged her close.

'If you don't feel up to it, don't go. I want you to be careful now, Nandini.'

Nandini smiled, her head resting on his chest. 'I'm pregnant, not disabled.'

Aditya hugged her tight.

'I love you, Nandini Sharma Sarin.

'And I love you, Aditya Sarin Sharma.'

Aditya rested his chin on her forehead. 'Have you told Sneha?'

'No, not yet! I don't want to give such epic news now. Let's find Gayatri first!' Nandini sighed. She could not get enough of touching her belly where a new life was growing. It was in early stages, first trimester. They had just found out last week. Even though it wasn't planned, Aditya and she were giddy beyond words.

'Sneha will be surprised!'

'Oh, she will be!' Nandini closed her eyes. *Crazy cow has news of her own!* Just that morning when she was trying to find Sneha, Nandini had located her inside the bathroom,throwing up. Sneha had assured her she was okay. Nandini's suspicions had been confirmed when she had spied Sneha constantly eat something sweet or the other. Just like the time she was pregnant with Advey. Nandini snuggled deeper in Aditya's embrace. 'Gayatri wherever you are please be okay!'

Sometime later, Sneha and Nandini drove to Gayatri's prior

hotel. The two friends didn't speak much.

'Kuls, you remember once we had gone to Gayatri's place she had told us about a Parsi Aunty, the one who made cupcakes for her.'

'Ya! Ya! Mrs Perez! She might know where Gayatri is.'

'We should talk to hotel staff too!' Sneha murmured. 'Where is she? She is not answering her cell. She has moved to a new address. No one has her old address.'

'Pretty darn irresponsible!' Nandini voiced.

'You are right. Pretty darn irresponsible of us. How can neither Nikhil nor I not know where she is going? Why didn't one of us find out? She is Nik's family, we should have been more involved.' Sneha's voice choked.

'I have never seen you cry before!' Nandini said with wonder.

'You are not going to see it today either, Kuls! Just not feeling myself,' Sneha retorted.

They stopped at a red light. Nandini reached out with one hand and touched Sneha's stomach and then with her other hand she touched hers. 'You and me! Sneh!'

'What?' Sneha studied Nandini's face and then her hands and their positions. She blinked. 'Shit...you are going to see me...cry!' Tears ran freely down Sneha's face. 'You too, kulta?'

Nandini was crying and laughing 'Me too!' The two friends who were closer than mothers and daughters, hugged each other tightly. Mumbai traffic wasn't emotional but definitely impatient. Horns blared at them!

Sneha and Nandini broke apart. 'Oh my god!' Sneha wiped her eyes and put the car in gear. 'Gayatri mil jaaye! Then you and me are going full toss into baby-planning, kuls!'

Nandini laughed. 'Full toss!'

The two friends reached the hotel where Gayatri used to live. Sneha dropped the car in valet. 'Walk carefully!' She advised Nandini.

'Don't you dare do an Adi on me. I will smack you!'

Sneha raised an eyebrow. 'Wow. I'm impressed. Your hormones are feisty. Definitely a girl!'

Sneha and Nandini entered the foyer and went straight to the concierge who gave them the room number of Mrs Perez. Fortunately she was home. She had more than an address for Gayatri. She had information. Sometime later, Nandini and Sneha were back in the car.

'So Gayatri lost her cell!'

'And because of the holidays the shops were closed, so she could not buy a new one,' Sneha said. 'That totally makes sense.'

'So this is the new address? It is not far from your place,' Nandini remarked.

'But it is borderline between industrial and residential. Why would she live in this area?'

'We shall find out.'

In some time, they reached a nondescript two-storey gray building.

'You are right, it is definitely industrial.' Nandini opened the door and got out. Sneha came around and joined her. 'Shall we?'

Nandini and Sneha walked to the large brown metal door and walked inside. Taking the few steps they entered the hallway. They walked into the first door. They stopped stumped. 'Gayatri is such a liar!'

Sneha nodded equally boggled. 'And a fraud!'

I'll Wait

Viraj's apartment

Evening

Viraj rubbed his eyes. He had watched the CCTV footage of the lab from the last two days countless times. Over and over! A loud knock on his front door interrupted him. 'Get out!' he called out his customary greeting. The knocking turned into a palm down slapping the front door. *Nikhil sent his crony again!*

Viraj walked to the front door and pulled it open. 'GO AWA—' He froze. It wasn't Nick's crony.

'I'm coming inside whether you like it or not!' Gayatri pushed Viraj forcefully aside. Viraj stumbled back and had to hold the door for support. Gayatri walked, her head held high. Her eyes shot sparks and her temper turned the tips of her cheeks red. Her magenta lips were puckered. Peaches and rosebud!

'Where the hell were you?' Viraj growled shutting the door behind them. Heartfelt relief burst in him seeing Gayatri intact. No one had seen her or heard from her for nearly two days. And just like that relief turned into anger! Anger because she had disappeared on everybody including him. Walking up to Gayatri, Viraj grabbed her elbow, his grip rough. 'I asked you, where the hell have you been?'

Gayatri struggled to free her elbow. 'You know I can hurt you!' She gritted her teeth. 'And believe me, right now I'm trying very hard not to.' Gayatri tried to kick his shin but Viraj pre-empted her move and blocked her leg.

Gayatri reacted instinctively. She reached with her hand to grab his wrist that gripped her elbow. Viraj reached there first. His other hand came up and grabbed Gayatri's wrist before she could twist his arm. Forcefully, Viraj yanked her hand above, tipping it behind her head and causing Gayatri to go off balance.

'Stop it!' Stumbling, Gayatri gripped his shoulder and tried to raise her knee to deliver a kick to his groin. Grunting, Viraj bent down causing Gayatri to misstep and her knee connected with his waist. With one swift sweep of his hand under her knees, Gayatri fell backwards as both her feet went off the floor.

'Ughh!' Going down, Gayatri grabbed Viraj's shoulders attempting to flip him on the floor. Viraj was anyway off balance.

Viraj and Gayatri both tumbled to the ground. She landed half on the floor and half on Viraj who fell back under her sudden weight. Her expression was quizzical as she looked down at him. 'You know how to fight?'

In a flicker, Viraj had Gayatri on her back and her arms were pinned above her head. He raised his eyebrow arrogantly. 'What you think, I only do pushups?' He smirked.

Watching Viraj loom over her, his hard body pressing

her down, Gayatri's anger deflated like a punctured balloon. Some other feelings exploded in her. Feelings that made her very aware of Viraj and his muscled body.

'Why are you smelling of cake?' Viraj lowered his head and sniffed her closely. His dark hair brushed Gayatri's jaw.

She shivered and closed her eyes. 'Please let me up!'

'Not till you give me some answers!' Despite saying that, Viraj's grip around her wrist loosened. Gayatri thought he was letting her go but Viraj had some other ideas. His fingers stroked the soft skin of her wrist.

'Viraj!' Gayatri gasped his name. A strange lethargy swept over her. She fought it. 'Sana...'

'Is not for me. She never was.' Viraj smiled down, his eyes seemed to penetrate right through her. 'I wasted so much time.'

Viraj lowered his head, and his mouth hovered centimeters away from Gayatri, his hot breath sizzling her already warm skin. Staring deep into her eyes, Gayatri felt held captive by his inky, hooded gaze. A very willing captive!

'You are so beautiful!' With a feather-like touch, Viraj brushed his lips across from hers, starting from one side of her mouth to the other end. 'So beautiful!' His soft lips kept brushing against Gayatri's softer ones. With every brush, his lips pressed some more into hers. 'I have wanted to do this for so long.' He murmured between kisses, his voice thick.

Shivers of anticipation ran down Gayatri's body, over her breasts, her stomach, her legs and ended at the tips of her toes. She couldn't help a quiet moan, for she wanted more.

Gayatri's fingers curled in her palms which Viraj still held above her head. Her muscles clenched and then went limp under Viraj's body half on her. The good half! Viraj continued to madden her as he brushed his lips over hers, slowly, very slowly. It was as if he was seeking her permission.

'Please!' Gayatri moaned arching her body. She wasn't encroaching on someone else's turf. Viraj wanted her.

Viraj slanted his mouth over her parted lips and sank his lips on Gayatri's. He was ravenous for a taste of her. Viraj groaned a sound that came deep from his heart. Gayatri's mouth was succulent, sweet and juicy, like a fruit for gods. And it was all his for devouring. Viraj deepened the kiss, moving his mouth repeatedly over her lips so he could taste every sweetened corner of her mouth. Gayatri tugged her hands free and thrust her fingers in Viraj's hair pulling him closer.

Viraj more than matched Gayatri in ardor. His tongue plundered Gayatri's mouth sucking her velvety tongue before he licked it, stroked it and sucked at it again. Viraj thought his body would burst in flames when Gayatri mimicked him with her tongue.

Her round and pert breasts dug into his chest. Their bodies slithered on the floor seeking and finding different angles to press into each other. Gayatri's hardened nipples rubbed in his torso. Viraj moaned in her mouth and intensified his sucking on her tongue. Desire that felt like brush fire, lit his whole body in seconds. His mouth, particularly his tongue, hungered to taste the soft swell of her mounds pressing into him.

Liquid heat coursed down Gayatri's body, pooling in an ache at the centre of her legs. Viraj's kisses were drugging her, her senses long gone. Restlessly, she moved her legs apart and Viraj's knee fell in between and connected with her centre.

Viraj was ruthless. Still kissing deeply, he rubbed his knee against her. Gayatri whimpered in pleasure and arched her body into him, pressing herself into his hard knee. Her fingers dug in Viraj's taut shoulder and her head fell back. Eyes closed in ecstasy, her lips were red and swollen from his kisses.

Like an addict to the taste of her skin, Viraj lay down a line of open mouthed kisses on her jaw and then swirled the tip of his tongue over the soft skin under her jaw. Her light floral scent drove him wild. His tongue and lips moved lower and sucked on the pulse beating at the base of her neck.

His one hand snaked under her soft plaint body and pressed her lower back, moving her closer into him. Gayatri's eagerness to follow him where he led only pushed him closer to losing all control. He rewarded her and himself by dropping his mouth and lightly biting her fleshy lower lip.

'Ohh!' Gayatri gasped in delight.

'I want you! All of you!' Viraj's fingers shook as he unbuttoned the pearl buttons of her blouse.

Gayatri closed her eyes in surrender. Viraj swept her open blouse to the side. She wore a lacy white bra underneath and her light brown nipples were hard and visible through the lace. Viraj's tongue moved restlessly and ravenous within his mouth. Gayatri saw the hunger in his eyes. Shyly she tried to cover herself.

Viraj held her hand down. 'You are beautiful and mine!' His voice was hoarse, his throat dry. Viraj hooked a finger in her bra strap and pulled it down over her left arm and did the same with the other strap constricting her arms. 'Feel what you are doing to me!' His hot, hard arousal dug into her lower belly. A wave pleasure pulsed through Gayatri.

'Please...' she whimpered softly.

Viraj lowered his head and pressed his lips to her sweet

skin behind her ear. 'Please what?' He licked her skin and nuzzled her nape with the overnight stubble on his jaw. Gayatri shivered. His plaid shirt rubbed her breasts. Her hands found their way under his shirt and touched the bare skin of his back. Viraj's back flexed under her touch and his eyes closed against Gayatri's neck as her hands stroked his back up and down.

Viraj moved his head lower and brought his mouth over her breasts. He kissed the swell and her fingers dug into his back. The sound of their quick breathing was the only sound in the room. Gayatri writhed under him even as Viraj's hot mouth feasted on the swell of her creamy breasts. Gayatri moaned. Her fingers now out of his shirt were in his hair, keeping him close.

Viraj smiled and he let her feel his smile against her skin. He dropped sweet kisses on her creamy mound as he laid a path of wet kisses leading to her hard nipple. He pulled her hardened nipple with a sweeping swirl of his hungry tongue. Gayatri made a keen sound and arched pushing her breast into his mouth.

Viraj lost all control. He sucked at her creamy breast hungrily even as his hand kneaded her other breast. Gayatri quivered and felt reduced to a tub of jelly as his tongue that felt like rough velvet stroking and devouring her one breast and then when she would die of desire, Viraj moved onto her other breast giving it the same attention. Viraj was a skilled lover. His hands were all over her, touching squeezing and moulding her skin, reducing her to throaty moans and whimpers.

'I want taste you down there!' Viraj's words in his thickened voice were a promise that drove Gayatri wild. His eager and seeking fingers left Gayatri in no doubt of where he wanted to taste her.

'Let move to the bed. I don't want our first time on the floor!' Viraj said kissing Gayatri deeply. Slowly he got to his feet and gently pulled Gayatri to hers. Gayatri marveled at his ability to stand straight as well as support her.

She rested her hot cheek against the bare skin of his chest. Her smile was cheeky as she realized that she had slipped his shirt off.

Putting a hand under her chin, Viraj raised his face to her. 'I don't want miss a single expression on your beautiful face.'

Gayatri sighed and offered him her lips. Viraj swooped down and they kissed long, slow and deep. His hands on her back moulded him to her and Gayatri wound her arm around his neck kissing him back.

'Don't ever disappear on me again!' Viraj said between kisses.

His word brought some clarity to Gayatri's mind that was still reeling with desire for the man who had his arms around her tighter than a wrapper around a piece of chocolate. She brought her arms down from his neck.

Viraj sensed Gayatri withdrawing. Her pulled her close and nuzzled her face with his. 'Stay in the moment!'

Gayatri's smile was wry. 'That was cheesy,' she said, cupping his cheek.

'Sorry, I'm not at my smartest right now.' Viraj turned his face and dropped a kiss in her palm. 'I'm just too horny!'

A startled laugh escaped Gayatri's lips. She firmly pulled Viraj's arms down from around her waist and stepped away. Her breathing wasn't steady, her colour ran high and her heart was racing.

'I already miss you!' Viraj exhaled giving her a crooked grin as he brushed his hair back.

Viraj's expression and smile tugged at her heart. 'Me too!' Gayatri replied shyly.

'Then come back here!' Viraj drawled captivated by her. He wanted to haul Gayatri back in his arms and kiss her senseless. Take them to a place where no one or nothing else mattered except them!

'We have to talk!' Gayatri moved a few paces and straighted her askew clothes and hair. She sat down carefully on the cane sofa.

'I guess the moment will have to wait!' Viraj came over and took a seat next to her. He left his shirt on the floor where Gayatri had taken it off. He took her hand and their fingers played with each other's, twining, clasping and simply touching.

'Please forgive him!'

'Forgive who?' Viraj cocked his head to the side, still holding her hand.

'My father. Forgive him and take him back in the investor group.'

Viraj dropped Gayatri's hand and got to his feet. His forehead was wrinkled. He walked around the room back and forth. A few times he opened his mouth to say something but then he shut it and walked around some more. He picked his shirt off the floor and buttoned it. Gayatri simply watched him, her eyes anxious, her lips swollen and her hair swept to one side.

Finally Viraj dropped on his haunches in front of Gayatri. 'My father abused with hands and yours does it with words.' He took her hands in his and gazed at her somberly. 'You know I care deeply for you and your opinion really matters to me. But about your father, I'm sorry, that is my final decision. If I prove you innocent, which I will, he's out.'

Gayatri pulled her hands free of his.

Viraj's face became austere. 'I'm actually helping here.'

'I did not ask for your help.' Gayatri averted her face. 'What my father is or isn't is not your business.' She moved her knees away from Viraj and positioned her body away from his.

Viraj rubbed his head and got to his feet. 'Did you know the things he called you? He was quickest to blame you in that room. He's a jerk. And I'm not having him around, whether you are guilty or not.' His jaw was pronounced, his mouth a firm line.

Abruptly, Viraj grabbed Gayatri by her arms and pulled her up, holding her close to him. Gayatri did not push him away and met his eyes as they searched her face.

'Did you do it? Did you steal my designs?' Viraj looked straight in her eyes.

Gayatri defiantly stared back at him, her chin pointing up. Her eyes sparkled. 'What do you think?'

Viraj's eyes softened. 'I got my answer, queen.'

His soft tone and endearment confused her.

'Viraj, please reconsider about my father.'

Viraj stepped away. 'NO!'

Gayatri stomped her foot. 'You know what I resign. Go stuff yourself.'

'Until the next forty-eight hours you still work for me. After that, I don't care what you do.' Viraj thrust his hands in his pockets.

'You just want to be the next man to tell me what to do!' Gayatri scorned, her expression bitter.

'No!' Viraj paused. 'Instead of telling you, I want to be the man who does something for you!' Viraj met her eyes briefly.

Gayatri studied his unyielding profile for a few seconds and then she grabbed her bag off the floor. Her face was flushed remembering how Viraj and she were entwined on the floor just a few minutes ago. He had seen more of her than any man she had ever known. 'Don't bother trying to prove me innocent.' She walked to the door.

'What about us? What about what just happened?' Viraj asked quietly.

'I did that hoping you would reconsider your position on my dad.' Gayatri wanted to hurt him. She succeeded.

Viraj's eyes narrowed to angry slits. 'What did you say?' He came at her.

Gayatri backed to the door. 'I have started my own business and I'm done working for you!' Gayatri pivoted away as tears swarmed her eyes. She was not going to show him her tears. Poker player and all!

'I'll wait!' He called out, sounding hurt and vulnerable for the first time.

Gayatri stopped and nearly bolted in Viraj's arms. But something made her walk again toward the door...away from him.

Viraj did not try to stop her. All he asked was, 'What business?'

Gayatri opened the door, tears flowing down her face, and replied in what she hoped was an emotionless voice. 'Cupcakes.'

Don't Believe Everything You See

Wednesday morning
Around 10.00 a.m.

Viraj entered the warehouse and walked from one lab to another lab, requesting his entire team to gather in the breakroom. Viraj's eyes were bloodshot, there was more than two days of stubble on his face and his clothes looked like he had slept in them.

In a few minutes, everybody had assembled.

Viraj took his position next to the vending machines. 'I'm sorry I have some bad news. We had to let go of Gayatri over the weekend. We are pretty sure she sold our designs to our competitors. But you all have nothing to worry about. Our design is patent-protected, so no one can use it. We still own it a 100 per cent and the board is legally going after the company that bought our designs. That's all I have to share right now. Back to work as usual.' Viraj scratched his cheek. 'Yeah! In case you have any HR-related questions, don't bug me. On the break-room bulletin board I have posted the HR head's number. He works for Nikhil's company who has loaned him to you all. Use him, not me...please! I'll be in my office. We will have the usual huddle after lunch.' Viraj turned around and walked to the door.

'Gayatri didn't seem bad. She was nice,' Professor Kalra remarked.

Some 'Hmms' and 'Yesses' followed his words.

'Don't believe everything you see,' Viraj retorted, leaving them.

Going into his office, Viraj fell on his stool and stared blankly at the desk in front of him. Gayatri had not reached out to him and neither had he tried to contact her. He closed his eyes and ran his fingers through his hair for the millionth time. Earlier, the dreams about Gayatri had been hard enough to forget but now he was in constant pain. Now Viraj actually knew how sweet she tasted, how perfectly her curvy body fit against his and how eagerly and wantonly she responded to his hands and mouth. Gayatri's floral scent mixed with the smell of sugary cake dough continued to haunt him. Disgusted with his lack of self-control, Viraj walked out of his cubbyhole and went straight in search of a specific someone.

Viraj found Sana working by herself at her station. 'Hey Sana, do you have some time? Can we talk?'

Sana nodded like a bobble head. 'Sure!' The she wrung her hands like she were twisting the neck of an imaginary chicken. 'I'm sorry about Gayatri. She did not seem the kind of person who would do this.' Her mouth was downcast. Today her hair was styled in loose curls. She wore mascara and her usual cotton salwar kameez had been replaced by jeans and a loose blouse.

'You look different!'

'Yes! Nandini, your other friend, taught me some basic

stuff,' Sana replied eagerly.

'Who's Nandini?' Viraj pondered, twisting his mouth. 'Oh yeah! The one whose husband I almost blew up! She is not my friend and her husband is a pain. Anyhow, do you have time for coffee? We will just go across the road. I could use some company today!' He sighed.

Sana slipped off the stool. 'Of course. Let me just log out of the machine. Safety first!'

'Good call!'

The Bottle Did It

Viraj held the door open for Sana as they entered the cafe. Only one table was occupied.

Sana stopped. 'What is my brother doing here?'

'Have a seat, Sana!' Nikhil got to his feet and offered her a chair.

'What is going on?' Sana looked at Viraj and then at her brother, and then at Nikhil, Aditya and two more people who sat at the table wearing suits.

'They know, Sana!' Her brother started crying. He put his head down on the table.

Sana spun around all set to walk away. Viraj blocked her way. 'Why did you do it, Sana? Of all the people who work in my lab, I never thought you would—'

'Why because I'm all quiet and sweet—' Sana yelled at Viraj.'You betrayed me! She betrayed me!'

Everyone at the table looked at Viraj whose face bunched like a sock out of the washing machine. He glared at Sana. 'What are you implying?' Viraj towered over her.

'You were supposed to be mine. Gayatri promised!' Sana cried and sat down in an empty chair. Her words, like a fired bullet, silenced everyone.

'She did what?' Nikhil leaned forward.

Sana's brother resumed his quiet sniveling.

'I heard Gayatri. And I heard you too!' Sana raised an accusing finger at Viraj. 'I heard her when she promised she would bring us together. That's why you let her work in the lab. I was there that night at the parking lot waiting for my brother to pick me up. I overheard the deal Gayatri and you made!'

The others just stared at her. Viraj, for once, was speechless as he worked his mouth but no words made their way out.

'What is she talking about?' Aditya asked.

'Yes please tell them!' Sana flung at Viraj. 'Tell them!'

'It does not excuse what you have done,' Viraj said to her and then he addressed the others at the table. 'Gayatri noticed that I had an interest in Sana but we would never talk because I…' He shrugged his face tinged red by now. 'Because we are the way we are, she and I!' Viraj glanced at Sana. 'Gayatri thought she could help me get close to Sana and in return I would let her have a job in the warehouse.'

'Then?' Nikhil prodded.

'Then instead of me and him, it became Gayatri and him!' Sana reached across and patted her brother's arm. 'It's okay, bhai! I will take the blame.'

'Why did you frame Gayatri? She was only trying to help,' Viraj demanded.

'She came in between us. If it wasn't for her, you and I had a chance.' Sana wiped her eyes.

'We had been working side by side for ten to twelve hours almost every day for the last eight or nine months. Nothing happened between us because nothing could, nothing would.' Viraj sat down, his expression like that of a man who had fought several wars.

No one spoke for a few seconds.

'How did you find out about me? And I know my brother did not give me up!' Sana asked, her eyes narrowed in defiance.

'You are right, he did not. You did!' Viraj scratched his cheek, his expression weary. 'Very few knew of the safe inside my office, actually only my team did. Gayatri never knew about it, that is assuming none of the scientists told her. However, what no one knew how I labeled and saved my work, under what name or version. The terms on the USB labels were complex terms, which only we would understand, Gayatri wouldn't. So the person who had taken it did have some familiarity with those terms. These two things took my suspicions away from Gayatri.'

Sana snorted under her breath. 'Still no proof against me, sir.' Her brother finally sat up, wiping his eyes,. His face was red and swollen from crying. Aditya passed him some napkins and a bottle of water.

Viraj picked up another bottle, still sealed, from the table. 'This bottle is what gave me the final piece of evidence in proving you the thief.'

His audience peeked at the bottle and then at Viraj, nearly everyone's eyes narrowed in confusion. Viraj pushed his chair back and got to his feet. 'Everyone assumed that the designs had been taken from the lab on the holiday weekend.'

'Because Gayatri used her access card to enter the lab on Saturday when it was a holiday,' Aditya replied.

Viraj and Nikhil swung their heads to him.

'Hey! I'm just saying what everyone already knows.' Aditya raised his hands. 'If you ask me I think it was some kind of mechanical malfunction.' Viraj and Nikhil moved back to observing Sana. Aditya flexed his shoulders and smoothed his shirt's front.

'Like I was saying, everyone assumed the designs were taken on Saturday. I assumed they were taken after I had checked them last, which was actually when the earthquake happened. The safe had been open at that time and when the building shook, I had left it like that and run out to—'

'You had run out to save her!' Sana's mouth twisted bitterly. 'We had coffee the day before that. We had talked, we had come closer but when the earthquake occurred and everybody was in danger, you just flung open the lab doors and shouted "get out" to us, but you rushed to save her. Not once did you look to see if I had gotten out. Only Ms Gayatri was good—'

'And that is when you stole the USB from the open safe. Julius did find you in the hallway outside the lab which is also outside my office.'

Sana jumped to her feet. 'I was hoping you would come for me. But you didn't, Julius did. If you had come for me, I would have never—' she broke off abruptly.

'So it is Gayatri and Viraj's fault that you stole?' Nikhil interrupted, his face seemed carved in stone and his voice was frosty.

Sana could not meet his eyes. She slowly sat down in the chair with her eyes lowered. 'I still see no proof!' Her voice was weak.

'But the bottle? You said the bottle...' Sana's brother trailed off seeing the looks everyone gave him. 'I just wanted to know.'

Viraj continued with his explanation. 'Apart from proving Gayatri innocent, I also wanted to make sure to prove the innocence of each of my team members. So I studied movements, family profiles, known associates, etc. of family and friends of those who worked in the lab. When it was your turn Sana, we, actually a very good hacker friend of mine,' Viraj sat down in the chair across from Sana, 'came upon your brother!' He glanced at the man with swollen eyes and inflamed cheeks. 'The freelancer CA who had several corporate clients and amongst one of those was the sister company which was owned by the firm which bought our stolen designs.'

'Still no bottle!' the accountant reminded.

'Control your excitement, Sherlock! He's getting to it,' Aditya muttered frowning at the accountant.

'So when we found that link, I decided to study Sana's movements during and after the earthquake.' Viraj gave Sana a disappointed glance. 'It was obvious you had been planning this for a while because you knew exactly where the blind spots were for all the cameras inside and outside the building. During the earthquake when everyone ran out you got the perfect opportunity, for you were alone in the lab and the safe was open. But what you did not know was that recently, after a certain attack on the outside pavement, I had installed more cameras for the parking lot and the approaching road to the lab. And that day, when Gayatri helped you to the tree after the earthquake, you sat directly in the line of vision of one of the cameras.'

Viraj grabbed a bottle from the table. 'Thus, coming back to the bottle. While you sat allegedly recovering from passing out during the earthquake, Gayatri handed you a bottle of water. You tried opening it but you couldn't open it, because in one hand under your dupatta you were holding the USB drive which is clearly visible when you took the bottle from Gayatri after she opened it for you.'

Nikhil, on cue, opened the file in front of him. He took out a couple of pictures and laid them on the table. There were several shots of Sana sitting down, Sana trying to open the water bottle, Sana handing the bottle to Gayatri. And then the final nail-in-the-coffin shot of Gayatri handing the bottle to Sana and the end of the USB drive clearly visible in Sana's palm showing the code P1D.

Viraj took out a USB drive from his pocket and laid it on the table with the label facing up and next to it, one with similar lettering P2D. 'I rest my case!' He glanced at Sana. 'Now do you want to tell them about the access card?' It was an order.

Sana's habitual timidity resurfaced. 'After the earthquake when Gayatri was helping me, I took her access card and then came to the office on Saturday and used it to show that she was here.'

This time the silence on the table was longer.

Nikhil narrowed his eyes and peered at Viraj. 'I have a question for you.'

'Go on!' Viraj bobbed his head.

'When every evidence was pointing against Gayatri—the sudden money she came into, her suspicious way of moving into a new address, not answering her phone, her using the access card on the day when no one was in the lab which we know now was Sana but we did not before today, and just after that our competitors get the designs—you didn't doubt Gayatri even for a second?'

Viraj stayed quiet studying the pictures on the table, specifically the ones which had Gayatri in them. No face had every appealed to him as hers did. 'Gayatri is reckless, has her own damn way of doing things for reasons she does not feel the need to share, discuss or justify. She does not give a damn whether others agree with her or not. But there is one person she would never betray come what may,' Viraj addressed Nikhil. 'You! You are her father and brother rolled into one. Gayatri would never do anything to harm you. And selling these designs would hurt you!'

'You love her!' Sana accused, her mouth twisted like she had sipped spoilt milk.

'It's is better than hating someone!' Nikhil voiced sharply.

Viraj pushed the chair back and got to his feet. 'Sana, we will not press charges against you or your brother.' He glanced at Aditya and Nikhil and the other two on the table. 'We will not! But you are on your own with the company you sold the designs to. Email me your resignation ASAP. And never put your work here on your resume. If anyone contacts me for reference, they will not hear good things about you.'

Babies and Breakup Milestones

2nd month
Nandini and Aditya's apartment

Chewing on some chocolate, Nandini focused on the pink and white book in her hand. The book was a month-by-month guide elaborating on the changes in the fetus and the pregnant woman. 'Sneh, it says pregnant women fart a lot!'

'So what has your excuse been for the last so many years,' Sneha retorted stretching her arms over her head and bending gently to the side. '*Yoga kar lo*. Tumhari first pregnancy hai, sali!'

'Eggjactly! That's why education first, exercise later,' Nandini retorted flipping a page.

Sneha picked up the small pillow under her knee and threw it at Nandini.

'Oww! Sneh, chocolate gir jati yaar! I hate wastage!'

'For you pregnant means eating for five because your whole life you have been eating for three.' Sneha wiped her brow. 'C'mon please, just a few stretches for the baby, please Kuls!'

Nandini shut the book. 'Fine!' She got up and joined her best friend on the mat already laid out for her. 'Any news of your Guy?'

'Yup! She's super swamped with her cupcake business. She got a big contract for a socialite's party. Plus, a bakery.'

'Who knew she had it in her? Good for her,' Nandini said lying down and taking position on the mat. 'Is she talking about Viraj?'

'Nope, she does not say a word about him. In fact, if Nik or I bring him up she changes the topic faster than the remote can change channels,' Sneha said looking thoughtful as she wiggled her toes.

'Hmm!'

Sneha looked sideways. 'Will you please get the heck up and stretch! Poke the koke, Kuls!'

Nandini chuckled. 'Don't make laugh please Sneh or else!'

Sneha stopped midway as she was about to stretch her calves. 'Or else?'

'Or else I'll fart! Chocolate wali!' Nandini threatened still lying down.

'You are disgusting with a capital D and a capital ING.'

'Whatevs! It's nap time!' Nandini pulled a cushion from behind Sneha's back and put it under her head.

A Baking Facility—Frosties

Navi Mumbai

'Didi, all orders for tomorrow are ready are in the fridge. The ovens have been cleaned. All bartans washed and wiped!'

Gayatri looked up from her cluttered desk at the petite, dark-skinned girl, Rinky Singh. Her month-old assistant cum manager cum head baker! 'Great! So I'll close here. You all go home.'

'No Didi, can't leave you by yourself here. This area gets very lonely after dark.'

'Don't worry, Rinky! I can take care of myself. But thank you. You all should go. Go to your babies! I will see you tomorrow,' Gayatri waved.

After ten minutes, Gayatri glanced at her cell. It was close to 7.00 p.m. She yawned and stretched her arms, popping her shoulders and knuckles. She had been up since 4 in the morning.

Since leaving her job at the lab, almost two months to date, life had changed drastically for Gayatri. Monday to Saturday, she opened the kitchen at 5 in the morning. Her first shift of one baker and two helpers came at 5.30. With them Gayatri baked and frosted cupcakes for the next five hours using several professional industrial size ovens and other paraphernalia. She would step out of the kitchen only when Rinky came in.

Then it was coordinating the delivery trucks to make sure her cup cakes reached the individual clients and several bakeries closer to her. Gayatri hated to step out of the bakery but sometimes she had to meet, greet and win some more accounts. And in all this madness, two things Gayatri never forgot—firstly, that she was happier than a junkie on mushrooms for having started her own little business, Frosties! Secondly, like a junkie craving a fix, she yearned for Viraj, his smile, his teasing, his deep kisses, his scent, his unkempt dark hair... *Oh my god! I'm thinking of him again!* Gayatri jumped out of her chair.

Gayatri went to the kitchen to make sure everything was turned off after the girls had left. She heard some conversation coming from the room where the women workers changed into their uniforms, hairnets and gloves. Gayatri walked to the door to say a final goodnight to Rinky and Angela, one of her bakers.

'I told the Didi! But she wants to stay.'

'All the fault of that video. Now all women think they are fighters. Especially these young single kinds like Didi!' Angela replied, her bangles clinking as she changed her clothes.

'Hmm I don't even think that video was real. Otherwise why did that woman not come forward?' Rinky said shutting the locker.

'That girl is a pakka jhooti!' Angela snorted.

Gayatri walked away tapping her chin.

In another part of town, around the same time, Viraj entered his apartment. Carelessly he took off his laptop and dropped it on the cane sofa. He did not bother switching on the lights. The light from streetlamps outside pouring in through the windows were enough for him.

From the fridge, Viraj grabbed a bottle of beer uncorked it and drank half of it in one swig. Then his shirt came off.

He walked to his ipod hooked to a pair of speakers and blasted his favourite song on it—November Rain. Getting down on the floor, he started his customary pushups. He couldn't go beyond five. He fell slowly on the floor. Viraj did not even have to close his eyes to imagine her there.

'Fuck it!' Frustrated, he got up and went into the bedroom.

Several thumbing sounds broke out! In minutes, Viraj dragged out a white board and collapsible table. He did the one thing that always got him through every personal crisis—WORK!

Babies and Breakup Milestones… Phase 2

4th month
Nandini and Sneha's office

'Aee Sneh! My breasts feel like they are on fire man!' Nandini said, squirming in her office chair.

'You should have said that to Bruce Springsteen several decades ago!' Sneha remarked, still concentrating on the drawing board in one side of the room.

'Why, Bruce Springsteen was an OBGYN then. If I was to tell someone like that about this,' Nandini pointed to her chest, 'I'd rather tell Hrithik Roshan!' Her look was coy.

Sneha snorted, 'Bruce Springsteen's very popular song that came out in '80s was I'm on fire. If you had told him breasts on fire,' Sneha waved her hand, 'forget it! If one has to explain a joke, then it's bad joke.'

'Talking of Bruce Springsteen, how is your firangi sis-in-law?'

Sneha gave a thumbs down sign. 'Last month was bad. Had some delivery snafus. She got no new accounts and actually lost the major one she had. Nikhil and I offered to help but she is adamant—'

'To do it on her own!' Nandini sighed. 'And the scientist?'

'He has gone back to his old mad ways. Always working. He rarely goes home, sleeps in the lab. Nikhil is thinking of installing a shower in the lab. The scientist hardly talks to anyone. But the breakroom is maintained perfectly.'

'Can I tell you something?' Nandini chewed her thumb, her expression glum.

'What?' Sneha asked, paying full attention.

'Yesterday morning I was in the area close to Gayatri's factory, so I thought I would drop in and say hi. I went there and saw her, her eyes were red. She had been crying, Sneh.'

'Shit! Did you talk to her?' Sneha came over and sat down in her chair.

Nandini shook her head. 'Not about it! She kept up the pretense and I didn't think it wise to...' Nandini shrugged. 'Why won't Viraj and she talk. Heartbreak itna lamba? Why yaar?'

'Didn't Adi and you stay apart for like four years?'

'Ya but I had my crazy family and a crazier friend around me. Gayatri is fighting on so many fronts. And alone!' Nandini put her face in her hands and started sobbing.

Sneha got up and patted Nandini's back. 'Sshhh! It's okay, Kuls. It's just pregnancy hormones making you emotional!'

'What do you mean, if I wasn't pregnant I'd be a cold heartless bitch?' Nandini accused between tears.

Sneha frowned and straightened. 'I'm freaking pregnant too, remember? Next time you bawl, I'm switching offices.'

Nandini controlled her tears and wiped her face. 'Fine! I'll stop. But I'm hungry now and so is my baby. And it's all your fault.'

'Not Hrithik Roshan's?'

6th Month
Sneha's apartment

'Oh my god Sneh, did you see that yesterday?' Nandini hollered at Sneha as she opened the door. 'She is a mastermind, your firangi sister-in-law.'

'Tell her in person! She's here!' Sneha moved to the side ushering Nandini into her apartment.

Nandini walked in and found Gayatri sitting in the living room. She smiled on seeing Nandini.

'Give me a hug!' Nandini demanded.

Gayatri got up and hugged her lightly. 'I don't want to hurt you.'

'I'm so proud of you. We all are!' Nandini stepped away and looked for somewhere to sit.

'Thank you! Wow, you are showing!' Gayatri pointed at Nandini's tummy.

'I know I am!' Nandini beamed. 'Seventh month is almost here baby!' Nandini touched her belly tenderly.

Nikhil came out of his office. 'It's done, Guy. Five big ass corporate events. Two five-star chains and coffee store franchise. I closed the deal with them. Their contracts options were the best!'

'Yay!' Gayatri shook her fists in jubilation. 'Thank you, Nik, for all your help with the contract negotiation.'

Sneha came and sat down next to her. 'Please, that's the

least we can do. You blew the whole country away.'

Nandini sat back. Nikhil pushed an ottoman near her legs. 'Thanks!' Nandini said, putting her feet up on them. 'So what made you go on TV and reveal you were the girl who kicked ass?'

Gayatri rubbed her nape. 'For women out there, in general, and my therapist and business.'

Nikhil sat down next to Nandini. 'Therapist? You are seeing a shrink?'

Gayatri nodded. 'After the incident, I suffered from post-trauma stress disorder. I started drinking heavily.' She saw the concern across the three faces listening to her. 'It's all good. It's a thing of the past. Someone,' Gayatri paused, 'someone nipped it in the bud.'

Sneha and Nandini exchanged a knowing glance.

'Is this therapist good? How did you find her?' Nikhil asked.

'Someone!' Gayatri exhaled and avoided looking at any of them. 'Viraj recommended her. She is good.'

'Hmm!' Nikhil sat back.

'As for business, last two months were bad, so I thought of something out of the box,' Gayatri blurted.

'Atta girl! One bird, three stones!' Nandini exclaimed. Sneha opened her mouth to correct. 'I know!' Nandini raised her hand just as her cellphone rang. 'Excuse me!'

Sneha added, 'Of course! It's probably easier for you to talk about it if you think you are getting something out of it too, right?'

Gayatri gazed at Sneha in surprise. 'That's exactly what my therapist said.'

'I saw a shrink after my divorce. I too had a problem with opening up.' Sneha leaned over and squeezed Gayatri's hand.

'I don't understand how can anyone have problem talking about their issues!' Nandini spoke with genuine amazement.

Nikhil patted her shoulder. 'Ignore these two. They are freaks!'

'So Guy, you will need more space, more bakers and more trucks,' Nikhil voiced.

Gayatri got to her feet. 'I already found a bigger place to work out of and a better equipped delivery service. I did that before I went on TV.'

'But what about extra bakers?' Sneha asked.

'I have a source.' Gayatri smiled taking out her cell. 'I have to get back to the bakery. I'll see you all later!'

'Come for dinner!' Sneha suggested.

'I'll confirm in the evening.'

'I'll walk you down!' Nikhil got to his feet.

After they left, Nandini raised an eyebrow at Sneha.

'She's very smart. Ladki aisi honi chahiye!'

'True!' Nandini smiled. 'So how are you feeling?'

Sneha did not hesitate even a moment. 'Tired and tharaki!'

'What a weird combo. I barely sleep with the number of times I have to get up to pee!' Nandini scratched her growing belly.

'Nikhil is the one making the ghise pite excuses! Headache, I'm tired, etc.!'

Nandini grinned. 'Payback, baby, payback! Switching gears, how do we get those two to meet?' Nandini asked.

'Gayatri sees through all my ploys to take her to the lab. And only Gayatri can handle Viraj. I'm not even going in that direction.'

'Something will have to happen to bring them together.' Nandini said placing her feet on the ottoman.

Viraj's cell rang. It was his mother. He answered the call with a bit of a surprise. She never called him at work. 'Veera, do you have a minute?'

'Sure!' Viraj rubbed his eyes. 'What day is it?'

'Still sleeping at your office? Not everything should be internalized! Why don't you talk—'

Viraj pursed his mouth. 'You called me for this?'

'No! I want to discuss something with you. Some girl called me and offered jobs to all the women of the shelter. The pay is very good but she said that she will pay their first salary after two months and then it will be on a monthly basis.'

'Sounds shady!' Viraj said, twirling a pencil in his hand. He was living on caffeine and carbs and immersed in work. 'I'll find out more about her or whatever company she is from. What is her name?'

'Hold on. I wrote it down somewhere!' His mom paused. 'Gayatri Dutta!'

Viraj dropped the pencil and jerked. 'Are you sure?'
'Yes!'

'Go for it, Maa!'

'You know her?'

'She's the girl, the one who is on TV nowadays. The one who fought back.'

'So I can trust her?'

'Yes, you can!' Viraj hung up. Getting off the stool, he

left his cubbyhole making sure to grab his wallet.

After some time, Christina Mendoza whispered to Dr Kalra, 'Dr Viraj has been in the breakroom for more than an hour now.'

'What is he doing?'

'Nothing, just sitting there drinking coffee, staring at the vending machines.'

Scotch, Tequila or Vodka

9th month

Holding the large Tupperware, dodging a few slow moving cars, Gayatri ran inside the hospital. Her cellphone rang. She retrieved it from the outside pocket of her purse. 'Haan Rinky. I've reached the hospital.'

Rinky mentioned a problem she was facing with delivery truck driver.

'Rinku, usko bol, I'm the one who can kick.' Gayatri laughed. 'No, I was kidding, I'll talk to Mistry sir. Gotta go. Sab bandh kar ke jana!' Gayatri stood on the side of the foyer and made a call to sort out the delivery truck problem and then walked towards the elevators.

'Here to meet Nikhil Chandel. 8th floor!' she said to the man sitting inside the elevator. *Gosh! Days fly! Sneha just got pregnant! And now she is here having the baby!* Gayatri slumped against the elevator walls. Nowadays, she was always tired. Business was booming but Gayatri never felt whole. She rarely remembered to eat, barely slept and was always working. Her therapist had warned her that she was hurtling towards an imminent nervous breakdown. One day her mind would just give up. *But I have no choice. If I stop even for second, Viraj's memories jump on me like an intruder behind the door and they hurt even more.*

Puckering her mouth, Gayatri happened to glance at her clothes. *Gosh! I'm even dressing like him.* She stared down at her skinny jeans, plaid shirt knotted at the waist and floral canvas shoes. Gradually using her work as a reason, she had started avoiding Sneha and Nikhil. Gayatri saw worry in their eyes when they saw her forced smiles, hollow laughs and her need to constantly chatter or do something. *I left him because I was a coward. But he? Not once did he fucking reach out to me! Not on—!*

'Madam, 8th floor!' the liftboy spoke.

Snapping her eyes open, sluggishly Gayatri pushed off the wall and got off. The private floor was eerily quiet unlike the hustle and bustle in the foyer. She didn't have to go far.

'Hi Guy!' Nikhil beckoned her.

'Hi!' Gayatri went over and her eyes popped out on seeing the other person in there. 'You too?'

Aditya nodded somberly and sat hunched low. The usually happy-go-lucky man's face was longer than unrolled tissue paper.

'Nikhil rubbed his neck. 'At around 4 p.m. Sneha went into labour and within an hour so did Nandini.

Gayatri nodded. 'How is it?'

'Not good!' Aditya rubbed his chest and grimaced like he was hurting.

Gayatri glanced at Nikhil. He just exhaled and cracked his knuckles.

Shit this is bad! 'Can I see them?' Gayatri asked biting

her lower lip.

'Sure! They are in there!' Nikhil pointed at the double doors in front of him.

Gayatri left her Tupperware on the seat and taking small steps went to the door. She pushed them open. The room looked and smelled like a hospital. Machines beeped silently and portable stands stood covered with medical equipment. The lights were bright and the floors spotless. There were two beds on either side of the room.

'Hi Guy!' Sneha waved at her.

'Finally, Gayatri! Did you get some cupcakes?' Nandini called out all chirpy.

Gayatri stood there, her expression confused. *There is a huge disconnect between the atmosphere outside and inside.*

'Hi!' Gayatri walked to Sneha. 'So are the babies out?' she asked.

'Babies out? Oh yeah! It was very simple.' Nandini's smile reminded Gayatri of the doctor who brought Frankenstein to life. 'We came here slightly uncomfortable like a splinter was sticking in our bums. Then the doctors gave us a lollipop, had us look the other way. A slight pull and the babies are out. Phataphat! Done! We are moms, you are an aunt.'

Gayatri just stared at her, open-mouthed.

'Kuls! Go easy on her yaar. Jab uska hoga then she will understand.'

'Hua toh mera bhi nahi hain, but still Sneh!' The usually sweeter-than-a-cupcake Nandini was spewing venom.

The doors opened and two nurses came in followed by a lady doctor. 'So we will check your dilation now,' the doctor said. One of the nurses pulled the curtain around Nadnini's bed, maintaining privacy.

Gayatri saw the other nurse with freakishly long, pink-painted nails reach under Sneha's sheet and Sneha obligingly raised her knees. Gayatri did not wait to see more, she turned and fled.

'How are they?' Aditya was quick get to his feet.

'It's good! They are fine. The nurse is checking Nandini, you should go in,' Gayatri said. Aditya began to walk past her. 'Oh you should ask her is if the baby is out…you know, show that you are eager to meet the baby.'

Aditya nodded. 'I am eager!'

Gayatri gave him thumbs-up sign. 'Awesome, show it!'

Aditya went inside the double doors. Gayatri took a seat next to Nikhil. 'The nurse is checking Sneha. Wait for ten minutes, then go in. They should have more info for you.'

Nikhil smiled at her, his face tight. Gayatri reached out and opened the Tupperware she had brought. She opened it and offered it to Nik. 'Care for some?'

'You want me to eat cupcakes, Guy?' Nikhil tilted his head to the side. 'Cupcakes? Now?'

'The filling is in three flavours—scotch, tequila and vodka!'

'I'll take the whole box!' Nikhil reached out eagerly.

'Cupcakes? Now?' Gayatri mimicked him. 'But go easy! I might have messed up the proportions.'

Nikhil picked up the cupcake and took a tentative bite. 'Umm, these are good!' He slipped the remaining in his mouth. 'You are the best sister ever.' Nikhil ate another. 'So how is business?'

'Hectic, growing and the best thing I could have done for myself.' She sat back, satisfied.

'You need a personal life too, Guy!' Nikhil said putting another cupcake in his mouth.

'Go easy, tiger!' Gayatri reminded. 'I'm okay!'

'Not lonely or sad?' Nikhil asked reaching out for another cup cake.

'Nope!' Gayatri lied, shutting the box cover.

The double door opened and Aditya came out and made his way to them. 'You can go in! The nurses are done checking them,' he said to Nikhil.

In seconds, Nikhil was gone.

Aditya sat down next to Gayatri. She craned her neck wondering what excuse to make, how to put some distance between Aditya and her.

'You set me up, didn't you?' Aditya asked.

Gayatri narrowed her eyes. 'What?'

'Is the baby out?' Aditya reminded.

Gayatri clamped her mouth.

'Nandini couldn't move. Thank god for the epidural, otherwise there might have been a third patient in there.'

Gayatri opened the cupcake box and offered it to him. 'Cupcakes with scotch, tequila and vodka filling.'

Aditya glanced at her and the cupcakes and then took two. 'Gosh, you are really nice.'

Gayatri nodded and moved to get up.

'No, please stay! Sit with me. We did know each other once.'

Gayatri sat back. 'It wasn't the best part of my life.'

The only sound between them was of Aditya eating.

'I sorry for that!' Aditya picked up another cupcake but had a change of heart and put it back. 'You know that when

I proposed to you, Gayatri, I actually meant to go through with it, until I met Nandini again.'

'What do you want me to say? I'm happy for you!' Gayatri sneered. The hurt from her past knocked on her mind.

'The time you drugged me and tried to break my marriage, the only reason I did not make a big scene was because I felt guilty.'

'Thank you!' Gayatri did not try to hide her sarcasm.

'Look at me, Gayatri!'

Grudgingly, Gayatri met Aditya's eyes, the man she once wanted to marry more than anything else in the world. *But not for love!* She blinked her eyes at the thought.

'Do you really feel that you and I would have been happy together? You think we were well suited?' Aditya asked not shying from meeting her eyes squarely.

Gayatri ran her eyes over Aditya's handsome face. She forced herself to feel something, anything for him. *Your hair isn't long enough!* Gayatri flinched and looked away.

'You okay?'

'No!' Gayatri's sigh was broken but long. She took out a cupcake and handed it to Aditya. 'Scotch! You did like scotch.'

'I did! I do!' Aditya took the cupcake. 'Thanks!'

Gayatri and Aditya sat back staring at the light blue double doors.

'You and I would have never worked. Divorce in three years!'

'I was thinking five!' Aditya took another cupcake. 'I want you to be happy. Very happy!'

'I am happy!' Gayatri sneered.

'No, you are not!' Aditya took off a big chunk of the

cupcake in one bite. 'We were friends once, remember?'

Gayatri smiled at him. 'We should have stayed friends!'

'We should have also had this conversation long back,' Aditya acknowledged.

'We were too busy avoiding each other,' Gayatri said and then grinned. 'And sorry for drugging you.'

Aditya snorted. 'You shouldn't have smiled. I would have believed you then.'

Gayatri chuckled. 'You went out like a girl!'

'Shit!' Aditya smiled. 'What the hell did the that witch of your girlfriend mix in my drinks?'

Gayatri shuddered. 'I was stupid and she was just plain bad news!'

Aditya sobered. 'You know, I'm very proud of you. We all are. How you have handled so many things. Nandini and Sneha can't stop praising you.'

'Thank you! They have actually been a big support to me. I never thought I would say this for Nandini but now I see what you saw in her.' Gayatri sighed.

'You wanna marry her?' Aditya ate another cupcake.

A surprised laugh escaped Gayatri throat. 'Nooo!'

Aditya got to his feet. 'Stand up!'

'Whaaat?' Gayatri put the cupcakes down and got to her feet. 'You are not going to kiss me or anything?' she teased.

'Worse!' Aditya wrapped his arms around her and pulled Gayatri close. 'Sorry for everything.'

'Stop apologizing, dodo!' Gayatri wrapped an arm around and with her other hand she patted his back. 'We are good! And quoting your wife's favourite movie's favourite dialogue, 'dosti mein no sorry no thank you!'

Aditya pulled away, his grin boyish. 'Another from the same movie, 'ladka ladki kabhi doston nahi ho sakte—'

Gayatri poked her tongue. 'Toh dushman toh ho sakte hain.'

Aditya cocked his head thinking of a retort.

'Am I interrupting something?' Nikhil asked from behind.

'Nope!' Aditya shrugged. 'How are the ladies doing?'

'They are fine. Dilation is slow. The doctor is saying, anywhere from five to six hours.'

'Okay!' Aditya moved to sit down. 'I'm going to do something for you Gayatri,' he stumbled.

Being nearest to him, Gayatri caught him and lowered him in the chair. 'Are you drunk, Aditya Sarin?'

Aditya sitting back waved his hand. 'Nope! I think I'm pregnant. I feel like throwing up and my head is spinning.'

Gayatri clamped her lips. Nikhil gave her a rare smile. 'How many cupcakes did he have?'

'Shit!' Gayatri picked up the box and counted. 'I got twenty four, ten are gone.'

'Twenty four, Guy?' Nikhil dragged her to another set of chairs.

'There were supposed to last the entire time and for the post-babies celebration,' Gayatri protested.

'He will probably sleep it off,' Nikhil said. 'Now let's talk about work. Share some updates and numbers with me.' They discussed Gayatri's work for some time, during which time seven more cupcakes disappeared from her box. Gayatri only had one. Her cellphone interrupted them.

'Gotta take this one, Nik. I'll be right back!' Gayatri got to her feet.

'I did it!' Aditya called out to her, his smile cryptic.

'He is slurring his words, Nik!' Gayatri said worried for Aditya.

'I'll babysit him. Also, after you are done with your calls, can you call home and check on Vey!' Nik called out

'I'll do that and get you guys coffee on my way back.' Gayatri walked to the other side of the hall, away from the noise and the doors.

An hour later someone tapped Gayatri on the shoulder. Urgently! 'It was the nurse.'

'The babies are coming!'

'Ohh!' Gayatri held the phone away from her. 'Are the dads inside?'

The nurse shook her head, her expression angry. 'They are missing, that is why I got you.'

What the? Gayatri ended the call and hurried back to the waiting area. 'You are sure they aren't inside?'

'I was inside. The madams are ten inches dilated, babies are about to come. We are about to ease the epidural. The pain is going to shoot up. Now is when they need someone around.'

'Should I look for them?' Gayatri asked, her heart thumping. She never heard more frightening stats.

'We'll look for them. You should go inside!'

Sweat formed on her forehead and Gayatri's steps became slower than a tortoise walking backward. Taking a deep breath she reached out to push open the double doors leading to Sneha and Nandini.

'Gayatri!'

It was the voice that haunted Gayatri day and night.

You Are My Yoda

Soundlessly, Gayatri pivoted. 'You!' Her eyes froze on Viraj's long lean form.

Within seconds, Viraj was there beside her. He stopped close, his eyes searched her face and then ran over her body. 'What happened?'

Gayatri just kept staring at his deep dark eyes. Her fingers itched to touch his long hair that gleamed under the lights. His face was sharper, more angled. His skin seemed to have been pulled over his imperious cheekbones.

'Gayatri!' Viraj's sharp exclamation jolted Gayatri to think and speak. At least one of those two!

'It hasn't happened…it's about to. The babies are about to be born. And…Nikhil and Aditya have gone missing,' Gayatri stuttered. 'But I'm…okay!'

'So the text "Gayatri is in hospital" literally meant Gayatri is in the hospital?' Viraj demanded still giving her a once over.

Gayatri ran tongue over her dry lips and glanced away. 'Who sent you the text?'

'Aditya Sarin!'

I did it! Gayatri remembered Aditya's mysterious words

from earlier. She swung back her eyes to Viraj and her breath closed her in throat. Now he was staring at her, actually looking at her. Viraj took a step closer, towering above her. He had Gayatri in his sights.

Gayatri felt a warm glow grow inside her under Viraj's penetrating gaze. Gayatri and Viraj stared at each other with enough intensity to burn the room. And they just kept staring.

'ADITYA! GET YOUR TUSH HERE!'

Nandini's shouts broke Viraj and Gayatri apart.

'C'mon! You like to help!' Gayatri grabbed Viraj's arm and took him in with her.

Nandini's bed was partitioned off. Gayatri could see a couple of feet moving in there under the curtain.

Sneha peeked over her shoulder. 'You and you?' She turned a bit more to look at Gayatri and Viraj better. 'Hey! Kuls, guess who's here?'

'I will wait outside.' Viraj tried to ease the deathly grip Gayatri had on his arm.

'Unless it is Aditya, the man who got me…owww!' Nandini screamed. 'Who the hell is it?' She sounded like a grizzly in pain.

'Gayatri, where are our husbands?' Sneha asked, getting up on her elbows. Her face was pale and her face and her hair was bathed in sweat. She appeared fatigued and in excruciating pain.

Gayatri was by Sneha's side in seconds. Grabbing the end of the sheet, she wiped her face. 'Let me get you ice chips!' Gayatri asked the nurses milling around. 'Does anybody have any ice chips or some apple juice?'

Someone handed Gayatri a glass of water. She brought it to Sneha's lips and helped her sip some.'

Sneha watched Gayatri rub her hands. 'You've done this before too.'

'My older sister! She has two kids and I was there every time!'

'Asking again!' Nandini grunted. 'WHO IS OUT THE—'

'It's Viraj!' Gayatri was quick to reply.

'It was Viraj!' Sneha flopped back on her pillow.

Not following Sneha, Gayatri peeked over her shoulder. Viraj was gone. MEN!

'So where are the husbands? You can tell me in whispers,' Sneha urged.

Gayatri spoke in lowered tones. 'Okay, so here is the thing, I got some cupcakes…' And Gayatri told Sneha all about the cupcakes with the dash of alcohol that might have actually turned out to be alcohol with a dash of cupcakes.

Sneha heard her out and then like the wise men and women who always see things for what they truly are and not what they seem, she simply yelled, 'Hi Kuls, Gayatri drugged both our husbands this time!'

Gayatri smacked her forehead. 'Just keeping them out of the way!'

'Okay then you get your tush here and hold my hand,' Nandini ordered.

'Do I have to, Sneha?' Gayatri whined.

'Sometimes I feel like I'm a mother to two girls and one boy!' Sneha said.

'Two boys! Who are you forgetting, Nik or Vey?' Gayatri muttered going over to Nandini's partitioned bed.

'I heard that!' Sneha said. 'Some more ice chips please, sister!'

Gayatri stuck her hand through the curtains.

'Why are sticking just your hand through and not your body?' Nandini yelled.

'Because I don't want to see your privates!' Gayatri's expression was like that of ten-year-old passive aggressively rebelling.

'My hands grow from my shoulder. So holding my hand does not automatically mean you will be seeing my vagina!'

'If I were a teenage boy I would be holding your neighbour's hand ten miles away and seeing your vagina.' Gayatri smirked, her hand still hanging in the air behind the curtain.

'If he was living ten miles away he wouldn't be my neighbour!'

'Why? Yyour neighbour doesn't drive?' Gayatri smirked outside the curtains.

'IDIOTS!' Sneha shouted. 'GAYATRI, GO INSIDE THE BLOODY CURTAIN! AND NANDINI, DON'T SHOW HER YOUR DAMN VAGINA!'

A nurse popped her head out from behind the curtain. 'You can hold her hand from this side!'

Rolling her eyes, Gayatri went behind the curtains. Nandini was heaving her legs in stirrups. Sweat and pain lined her face. Gayatri didn't take her hand, she grabbed it. 'I'm sorry for being an ass just now!'

Nandini grunted and then said in between taking big breaths, 'You want to make it up to me?' She spoke like she was trying to remember words.

'YES! Anything!'

Nandini tightened her grip on Gayatri's hand. 'Make up

with your scientist! Get your happy ending!' she pleaded.

Gayatri met Nandini's earnest eyes and then swallowed. The she fanned her eyes. 'It might not be happy!'

Nandini grunted. 'And,' she gritted her teeth as another contraction passed through her body. 'It might not be an ending.'

Gayatri did not seem convinced.

'Gayatri, can you please come and hold my hand!' Sneha called out.

'Guys, this is not about me. This is about you bo—'

'This what family and friends do!' Nandini interrupted. 'Go!'

Gayatri trooped back to Sneha. 'If you both stop telling me what to do, then I'll go and talk to him.'

Sneha appeared even paler. 'DEAL!'

Gayatri walked to the double doors and paused. 'So basically I would be doing what you both asked me to do.'

Sneha threw her hand in the air. 'Genius!'

Gayatri shook her head.

'Are you even sure he is waiting outside?' Sneha said.

Gayatri froze. In that instant, panic which was stronger than the voice of an angry Sunny Deol slammed her chest. Her eyes widened and she forgot to breathe.

'And you got your answer right there as to why you need to talk to him!' Sneha's smile was weak but kind.

'You are my Yoda!' Gayatri fled.

Coming Full Circle

There was no Viraj in the hallway. 'Shit! Shit! Shit!' Gayatri ran to the elevators. She didn't see him there either.

'Damn it!' Gayatri ran in the direction of the other rooms. She noticed something in her peripheral vision as she ran past a room. Gayatri paused and trotted back. Slack jawed, she stopped at the threshold. 'What happened?'

'They started the celebrations early! Found them asleep in here and on the same bed,' Viraj said helping Nikhil sit on a wheelchair of all things. A younger boy dressed in hospital uniform helped Aditya in another wheelchair. Both Aditya and Nikhil were groggy.

Viraj straightened and flexed his shoulders. 'Can you find some coffee for them?'

'Absolutely!' Gayatri started to turn around and then she halted. Trying to keep casual demeanor, she asked, 'You are staying, right?'

Viraj's mouth hitched up on the side yet his eyes remained serious. 'Let's get these would-be fathers to their wives first.'

'Of course!' Gayatri took the elevator to the cafeteria two floors below. She was back with steaming strong coffee in a few minutes. She found them all in the waiting area outside Sneha and Nandini's room.

Viraj relieved her of one cup. 'I'll help this one drink it.' He was pointing at Aditya.

Gayatri went over and held out the cup to Nikhil. She was a bit apprehensive of his reaction. 'Thanks!' He rubbed his eyes and stifled a yawn. 'I'm making these cupcakes mandatory at my board meetings and banning them at child birth.' He took a sip of the hot liquid.

'You didn't miss much. There is a still a lot of child birth left,' Gayatri informed, wringing her hands.

'Great!' Nikhil finished his coffee, handed the empty cup to Gayatri with a quick 'thanks' and then slapped his face a few times. 'Okay, game face on!' He got to his feet and then stumbled and fell back in his chair. 'Okay, can someone wheel me in?'

Viraj grabbed the handles and began rolling Nikhil's chair in the direction of the double doors. He briefly met Gayatri's eyes.

'You drugged me again!' Aditya tried to stem a yawn bigger than his face.

'You were supposed to eat one or two, not devour the whole shop!'

'Please don't scream!' Aditya begged, wincing.

Gayatri grinned. 'I'm actually not!' She signaled the attendant to take Aditya inside.

Left alone in the corridor, Gayatri stood still. Her nerves were dancing wildly. *I probably look like crap!* Gayatri hotfooted to the private room where Aditya and Nikhil had been sleeping. It was still open. She snuck inside and walked to the mirror on the wall. A quick brush of hair, retouching of the gloss on lips and a dab of perfume on her wrists, behind the ear and in the cleavage! *That's me being hopeful!* Gayatri blushed.

'So how have you been?' Gayatri measured her smile and expression in the mirror. 'Crap!' She inhaled and tried again. 'It's good to see you!' She clutched her stomach. 'Oh man, I think I'm going to barf!' After a few seconds of staring at the carpet, Gayatri raised her head, her expression resolute. Her colour ran high, her eyes sparkled brighter than headlamps of a car and her body felt hot like she were running a fever of 105 degree. She took a deep breath. 'Okay Gayatri, you can do better!'

'I agree!'

Pouting, Gayatri turned to the door. 'Why do you always do that?'

Viraj's smile was small but warm. 'Why do *you* always do that?' He teased bobbing his chin at her.

Gayatri's smile was tremulous and she broke the eye contact. 'How have you been?'

Viraj stayed at the door, leaning against its side. 'Busy! The design is in testing stage. It's almost done. How have you been?'

Gayatri sat tentatively on the edge of the unoccupied hospital bed. Her knees felt wobbly. 'Busy! Started my business! Appeared on TV. And back to business that is growing faster than kudzu.' Trying to look casual, she tried to twirl a lock of her hair but brought her hand down feeling stupid.

'Congrats! Kudzu?' Viraj crossed his arms but stayed at the threshold leaning back.

Gayatri smoothed jeans. 'It's a fast growing plant originated in China and can grow up to sixty feet in a single growing season.'

'Really?'

'Go figure!' Gayatri knew they both were buying time skirting around the elephant in the room.

'Long hours?' Viraj continued to skirt.

So did Gayatri. 'Very long but it's the best thing I could have done for myself.'

'Thank you for hiring all the women from my mother's shelter.' Viraj ran his fingers through his hair.

Don't ever stop doing that! 'I met your mother a few times. She is an amazing lady and very nice!'

Viraj's eyes stayed fixed on her and he stayed fixed at the door. 'She said the same about you!'

For few minutes, Gayatri and Viraj stared at each other. Every other sound simply stopped or faded.

Viraj was the first to speak. 'I'm taking a year-long sabbatical after this. Planning to go backpacking!'

Gayatri, slowly, got to her feet. 'A year?'

'Yes!' Viraj straightened. 'Congrats on becoming an aunt. I'll see you around.' He slowly backed away.

Gayatri felt a deluge of tears at the back of her eyes. She twisted her mouth fighting for control. She couldn't say a word, so she gave him a thumbs-up sign. Viraj turned around, his mouth twisted like hers.

'Viraj, wait!' Gayatri called out.

In a second, Viraj appeared back in the door. 'I have been waiting! How much longer?' His eyes weren't shining, they were dull like his expression.

'Not a second longer!' Gayatri smiled through the tears. 'But I can go backpacking only after a year,' she blurted.

And then Viraj dropped a bomb. 'Okay, but only as my girlfriend, fiancée or wife. Wife is better! No room for confusion!'

Gayatri's heart fluttered like a kite stuck to a tree. She tried not to cry and smile at the same time. 'Why not as friends?' She couldn't help a sniff.

'Because I don't have sex with my friends and I want to have lots of sex with you.'

Gayatri tried to laugh but it came out as a sob. Tears started rolling down her cheeks. 'Me too!'

'You want to have sex with you too!' Viraj teased.

Gayatri wiped her eyes. Through her tears Viraj was just a blur at the door. 'Why hell are you standing there?'

Viraj exhaled. 'Because I'm freaking chemically reacting to you for so many months and I want you more than oxygen and you are near a bed.' His voice wasn't steady and his eyes as vulnerable and as anguished as hers.

'That lock has a door.' Gayatri covered her eyes. 'That door has a lock.'

'You can't walk away from me again. I don't think I can survive a separation from you. It's been hell, Gayatri!' Viraj didn't move.

'I will never walk away from you. I can't live...' Viraj rushed to her and Gayatri flew to him. Looking back she couldn't remember who grabbed whom first but all that mattered was that she ended up being in his arms, pulled up against Viraj's muscled length and his mouth swooped down on hers. Gayatri and Viraj's mouths clung to each other, their bodies embraced like they would never come apart and their hearts beat like the flapping wings of a bird about to take flight. Wild and together!

Viraj's tongue slipped in Gayatri's mouth, hungry for a taste like a man starved for decades. Wanting his kisses eagerly, Gayatri opened her mouth and their tongues dueled and mated. She breathed in his musky scent, her hands climbed over Viraj's muscled chest bit by bit enjoying the feel of his muscles, her legs shifted allowing her body to feel more of him.

Viraj gave a smothered groan and sucked on her tongue with such intensity that Gayatri couldn't stand straight. She need not have bothered, for Viraj splayed his hand at her lower back and pulled her body on his. They final broke apart because of their lungs' need for oxygen. Viraj nudged Gayatri's head back and placed his hot open mouth on her soft skin and Gayatri closed her eyes and tipped her head back as his mouth relished her skin. Her hands ran through his hair and sighing, she tugged at it.

His mouth on her cleavage, Viraj propelled her back till she felt the bed against the back of her legs. 'Viraj, we are—' Viraj pressed quick hot kisses on her mouth. Gayatri held his face between her hands and deepened the kiss. Viraj's hand kneaded her soft breast and his other hand cupped her curvy bottom and squeezed it. 'I can't wait to peel these sexy jeans off you.' Viraj's voice was thick as he rubbed her nipple between his fingers

Moaning, Gayatri arched into his hand. 'We are in a hospital!' Her voice was husky. Her eyes slipped away from his for a second. 'And you left the door open. Shoot!' She pushed Viraj back and gave him a pointed glance.

Viraj only removed his mouth from her body, his arms stayed tight around her waist.

Gayatri reached out and cupped his jaw which had a sexy stubble.

Viraj leaned forward and plundered her mouth. Gayatri took a deep taste of him and then pulled back. 'Hey!' Viraj protested as his face nuzzled her forehead.

Gayatri's lips tingled because of his rough kissing. She wrapped her arms around his neck and arched his body against her.

'Oh, much better!' Viraj cupped her bottoms and pulled her against him and rubbed slowly and deliciously against his arousal.

'I can't say it like you, so I'm going to say it the only way I know!'

'What?' Viraj eased his hold on Gayatri.

'I love you!' Gayatri let her eyes say the rest.

Viraj dipped his head for a kiss.

'I have more to say!' Gayatri ducked out of his embrace. She sat on the bed, mostly because her legs weren't the steadiest.

Viraj's grin was boyish. 'It's all good, right?'

Gayatri put her hand out to him. Viraj took it and they sat close to each other.

'I want my shirt back!' Viraj said pointing to her shirt. 'Preferably now!' He moved his fingers as if to unbutton it.

'Listen to me!' Gayatri swatted his hands away. 'Do you know why I left that day?'

Viraj sobered. 'Because of my decision about your father!'

Gayatri shook her head and gripped his hand. 'No, I was scared.' Viraj's glance was confused. 'After days, months and years I finally got the courage to do something of my own and it wasn't easy finding that courage. At least not for me,' Gayatri paused. 'So I was scared that if I let you into my life, I might fall to my old ways and let the man in my life run my life.

'I would never—'

'You might not have. But I might have shifted focus from me to you and not even have realized it. I really had to do this on my own. Success or failure, it had to be mine.'

Viraj hunched forward, resting his elbow on his knees and his chin in his hands.

'I'm sorry!' Gayatri's voice was small.

'It makes sense now.' Viraj stroked his chin and straightened again at her level. 'So it wasn't your dad?'

'No, it wasn't. I totally get why you couldn't stand my father. I haven't spoken to him much either.'

Viraj put his hand on Gayatri's hair and caressed it. 'You are okay about that?'

Gayatri nodded. 'Yes! Mom has been coming for short visits. When she is here, she helps me in the office and brainstorms with me about new marketing and promotion ideas. I enjoy it and it is enough. Dad did call me a few times, even sent me congratulatory flowers but I'm not there yet with him. But there may be a time when I would want him to be more involved in my life as he wants to be.'

'And that would be okay. You have the right to decide on your relationships and as your husband I will totally support you.'

Gayatri swung her legs. 'You think I did not notice how you sneaked in the word husband.'

Viraj tugged hair back. 'I was hoping you did.'

'By the way, that was crappiest proposal.' Gayatri snuggled into him.

Growling, Viraj kissed her. 'I love you, woman!'

Gayatri said, breathless, 'I thought you didn't believe in love.'

'Guy!' Nikhil came rushing in the room. Conscious, Gayatri jumped to her feet. Nikhil did not even notice their proximity. He hugged her. 'I'm a father! It's a girl!' Gayatri squealed and hugged him back. 'I'm a father! She's so beautiful, she's taken after her mother.'

Viraj too got to his feet. He shook hands with Nikhil. 'Congratulations!'

'And Nandini?' Gayatri asked, excited.

'What do you know, Nandini had her baby two minutes after. A boy!' Nikhil beamed.

'And the moms? Are they okay?'

'Sneha hates me, but she will get over it.' Nikhil waved his hand.

'Let's go and see them,' Gayatri said, excited. She exchanged an intimate smile with Viraj. Nikhil let her lead the way.

'Do you have any news for me?' Nikhil asked, leaning toward Viraj.

'I asked her to marry me!' Viraj said, feeling somewhat awkward.

'Did she say yes?'

'No!' Gayatri called out from ahead.

'She will. Don't worry!' Nikhil assured Viraj. 'Just learn how to bake.'

As they stepped in the hallway, Gayatri stopped. A loud group of people came through the entrance. Two older women running in speed followed by an older man, his pace sedate. Behind him came a younger couple. The young lady was pregnant and showing.

Gayatri let Nikhil overtake her.

'That is Nandini's parents. Aditya's mom, brother and sister in law,' Gayatri said, pointing them out to Viraj.

Viraj slipped his hand in Gayatri's. 'Why is everyone pregnant?'

'Didn't Indian cricket team win the world series around nine months ago?' Gayatri smiled up at him.

'Yes!' Viraj nodded, staring in her eyes.

'We are surrounded by world-cup babies.' Gayatri giggled. She leaned over and kissed his cheek lovingly. 'By the way, Nik was right. She will say yes!'

Under Viraj's tender gaze Gayatri felt like a dark damp room suddenly flooded by warm and healing sunlight. Wrong means had led her to a right end—her crazy hot scientist.

Epilogue

Two years later
Gayatri and Viraj's House
Panjim Goa

'Mary, please take the drink and milk bottles out. And I will get the appetizers.' Gayatri tucked an errand strand of hair behind her ear.

Mary, her maid, took the large wooden tray outside in the direction from where came sounds of adults, laughing, talking and babies squealing. Gayatri balanced a plate of cupcakes in one hand and in the other she balanced a plate of salty appetizers. She followed her maid. And then stopped at the door leading to the backyard.

The sun was setting over the horizon ligting everything it touched in golden light. Lots of sounds were coming from the large infinity pool where three dads and five children swam and splashed. Nikhil with Advey and his two-year-old daughter! Aditya with his two-year-old son. And Gayatri's husband, Viraj Dheer, with their one-year-old twins, Pia and Sia!

Gayatri smiled. Viraj had been the best thing that could have happened to her. She was a mother, a wife, a businesswoman. Two years had flown by! Viraj and she had not had a long courtship. Five days! And for honeymoon they had gone backpacking for three months all over Nepal and Europe.

Her cupcake business had grown to a popular chain and Gayatri worked tirelessly to get it there. Viraj had been nothing but supportive.

And then nearly a year later, Gayatri and Viraj had become parents. They had given each other the best gifts that they could. Two perfect angels! Daddy's two princesses.

Hating the hustle bustle of city life, Viraj and Gayatri had moved to Goa soon after the twins were born. They could manage their work from here with occasional travel.

'Guy! Why are you standing there?' Sneha called out from the chaise she was leaning back on.

'You've got food right?' Nandini called out.

'Coming! Coming!' Gayatri said moving toward her sis-in-law and friend. She put the food down on the tables around the chaises. Mary had already placed the drinks.

'Can't thank you all enough for coming to the twin'ss first birthday.' Gayatri smiled down at the two women.

'Yaar humara toh banta hai. Don't know why they tagged along!' Sneha teased Nandini.

'I'm just here for the two angels and the cupcakes!' Nandini quipped.

'I'm just glad you all came before. So we can...' Gayatri smiled. 'Tomorrow everyone else comes,' she said, referring to Gayatri's parents and sister, Viraj's side of the family, Nikhil's mom and Aditya and Nandini's family. It was going to be a full house for Pia and Sia's first birthday.

'Grab your glass!' Nandini directed Gayatri.

Gayatri did so. The three women raised their glasses. Sneha said, 'To friends,'

Gayatri looked at the children splashing in the water. 'To family!'

Then the three glanced at the husbands—Aditya, Nikhil and Viraj.

'And to love!' Nandini clinked her glass with Sneha and Gayatri. 'Lots of it!'

Acknowledgments

'Alone we can do so little,
together we can do so much.'

HELEN KELLER

A big thank you to few others who are important to my work and me.

My parents—what would I be without all that they have done for me and continue to do. To my husband and daughter, for all the love and for being my strongest supporters. To my in-laws for their encouragement.

To my Snehas and Nandinis—Richa and Nidhi—this series would not be half of what it is without your opinions, advice and encouragement.

A heartfelt thank you to Ishita Bal for her immense and invaluable contribution as my editor. Thank you to the entire Rupa team for putting their best behind my work—Mr A. K. Singh, Vasundhara Raj Baigra, Purushotam Kumar Sharma, Neha Vats, Shorya Bhutani, and Saurav Kumar.

A very big shout out to the captain of the ship, Mr Kapish Mehra (M.D. Rupa publications) for his guidance and belief in my work. If he weren't my publisher, I might not be an author.

A big thank you to my publicist Navneet Kaur Sial for her dedication and hard work.

And the biggest thank you to all my readers. You all enrich and empower the writer in me.